800

Beside the h_____ _____ _____ in the darkness untouch___ _____ _____ the ghost of Jared St. Leg____ _____ ____ ____ m. *What the deuce is the matter with the blasted woman? The man looks a likely enough specimen and she is young enough and pretty enough to care about such things. What's making her behave as though she wished the personable Sir John would evaporate? If she keeps this up, I'll never be able to bring them together!*

Praise for the Novels of Christina Cordaire . . .

Turn to the back of this book for
a special sneak preview of

A Ghost of a Chance

the next Haunting Hearts romance!

SPRING ENCHANTMENT

CHRISTINA CORDAIRE

JOVE BOOKS, NEW YORK

To Dave,
a very dear friend
who was kind enough to lend
me his name for my castle

SPRING ENCHANTMENT

A Jove Book / published by arrangement with
the author

PRINTING HISTORY
Jove edition / June 1996

The Putnam Berkley World Wide Web site address is
http://www.berkley.com

ISBN: 0-515-11876-1

A JOVE BOOK®
Jove Books are published by The Berkley Publishing Group,
200 Madison Avenue, New York, New York 10016.
JOVE and the "J" design are trademarks
belonging to Jove Publications, Inc.

PRINTED IN THE UNITED STATES OF AMERICA

10 9 8 7 6 5 4 3 2 1

Prologue

"*Blasted wind,*" the man muttered. He looked over his shoulder at the solid bulk of the stone tower behind him, considering whether or not to allow himself to be driven inside. The stubborn set of his mouth indicated that he hated to be forced to any decision. Jared St. Legere, Fifth Earl of Mannerly, was not a man accustomed to bowing to any will but his own. That quality was one he had lived to regret. He regretted it even more bitterly now.

Then, as seagulls forced inland by the strength of the gale wheeled and cried just over his head, under the wind's invisible attack the man began to tatter. The edges first of his clothing, then of his very person began to appear less distinct, elongating and fraying, as if bits of him could be snatched away by the wind. He turned with an angry, impatient sound, his skirted brocade coat swinging away from his lithe figure, and stalked into the tower.

His tall, broad-shouldered form passed with ease through the solid stone wall.

Chapter
One

While her companion watched her, concern plain on her face, Lady Anne Kent, Marchioness of Kentwell, paced the handsome drawing room of her London town house. She felt like a caged animal in the city. She hated it. She hated London. She always had. She always would.

She'd been forced to go to school here in London. At Miss Haversham's she'd lived . . . no, she corrected herself . . . *existed* through two hellish years of being shunned by the rest of the girls there. Now she had the opposite problem. Now she was anything but shunned. She'd endured two annoying months during which her doorstep had been crowded with men who wanted to marry her . . . for her fortune.

Stopping a moment, she paused at the French door to the garden. Weak sunlight spilled in through the glass panes and painted rectangular patterns on the luxurious Oriental carpet and the unrelieved black of her widow's weeds. She rested one hand on the frame of the door. Her other hand went to her throat.

Looking out at the early spring flowers, she became aware of thoughts pressing at the edge of her mind . . . thoughts she'd forbidden for almost a decade. More early spring flowers, these in a huge cystal bowl on a nearby table, perfumed the air lightly. She inhaled their fragrance and let the bleak memories come.

She'd been married here in London, too. Straight out of the schoolroom in a hastily contrived service to a man who was half-drunk and all brute. She remembered that day well.

Her mother had wept through the ceremony. Her father had stood white-faced and with his fists clenched at his sides. He'd have interrupted the service if she hadn't kept her eyes on him. She'd had to keep her eyes on him. She'd locked her gaze on her father, drawing from him the strength to do what she must for his sake and the sake of her brothers. She remembered how she'd shaken her head, commanding his silence, when she'd seen his lips part to put an end to the marriage before it had even begun.

She'd wished a thousand times since that she had let him speak.

Her brothers had refused to come at all.

That night . . .

She kicked her black bombazine skirts out of her way as she turned from the window and the dark thoughts that haunted her. Hate it or not, she was again in London.

The trip had been necessary to settle her late husband's affairs, but that was done now. Montague Kent, Sixth Marquess of Kentwell, had been in his grave for almost two months, and Lady Anne Kent was finally free! Free of Montague and rich enough to do anything she pleased.

And she pleased to get out of the capital.

She was weary of the horde of fortune hunters cluttering her house daily. She was impatient to get away to where the air didn't smell of coal fires and too many people.

A need drove her to get busy doing something besides wearing black mourning clothes and pretending to grieve for a man she'd despised.

Turning to where Lois Carswell sat in a pale gray brocade-covered chair, she told her friend and companion, "I've decided to tear out walls!"

Lady Anne's companion wasn't startled. "So, dear, it has been as bad as all that."

Anne turned to look at the older woman, her expression wary. "What has been as bad as all that?"

Lois Carswell gave her friend a level look. "Your life as the wife of your late husband, of course." The last words were almost a whisper.

Anne thanked God that Lois hadn't said this before. Their tacit agreement that the subject never be discussed had enabled her to be strong. Sympathy would have been debilitating.

She lifted her chin and returned her companion's regard for a long moment. Then quietly she told her, "It's only fair to warn you that I plan to lie, Lois." Her eyes were shadowed. "From the moment I heard that Montague had been killed, I made up my mind that the world would never know what a monster he was. My sons are not going to grow up with that over their heads.

"Lying won't come easily." She smiled faintly. "Especially to someone who knows me as well as you do, Lois." Her smile took on a tinge of bitterness. "But then, there aren't any others who know me as well as you, are there?"

Lois cringed inside at the pain she knew Anne had suffered at the hands of society. She hated the fact that Anne had only one couple and herself for friends.

Anne sighed deeply. "For the sake of my twins' futures it's the only way. I detest lies, but I detest even more the truth of my marriage."

Lois took a deep breath and finally said, "Yes." It was agreement. It was all Anne asked.

Anne smiled tightly. "Thank you, my dear friend. I hope, frankly, that a polite silence on our part will be sufficient, but I had to tell you my decision." She came over to Lois and sat beside her on the rose brocade sofa. "Now," she said more cheerfully, "I have only to find a way to keep myself busy. And out of London." She laughed a little. "So I thought I'd undertake a few renovations at Castle Caldon." She smiled at her friend. "So you see, I didn't mean I wanted to tear down walls because of my marriage to Montague."

"Well, it wouldn't strike me as odd if you had, the way you've been all but kept prisoner at Kent Hall for the past nine years."

Anne noted the indignation in her friend's voice, and blessed her for her loyalty. For an instant, she remembered vividly just how awful it had been, but the tight smile never left her face.

She'd chosen her course. She'd submitted to marriage with the Sixth Marquess of Kentwell for the sake of her family. Until she'd become the Marchioness of Kent, society had shunned all of them as the descendants of a traitor. Her sacrifice had changed that.

She'd paid the price. It had been a heavier price than she could ever have imagined, but she'd paid it. Montague had sponsored her brothers into society.

"Well! I should think so!"

Anne wanted to catalog Montague's few virtues. She

was building a myth in support of her sons, a fabrication behind which she could hide. Playing devoted widow would keep potential suitors at bay. The revulsion she felt at the thought of any man ever touching her again made such a course mandatory. She told her friend, "My brothers' visits meant a great deal to me after having been away from them for most of the two years I spent at school. I was so lonely there . . . ignored as I was by everyone but you while I was at Miss Haversham's."

"Girls can be cruel, Anne. And it was very much their loss not to have made a friend of you. I know I enjoyed teaching you more than I can say." Fearing to be thought sentimental, she added quickly, "You have such a fine mind."

Anne smiled, seeing through her. "You were always my friend. From the very first day. I should have died of loneliness if it hadn't been for the friendship you offered me, Lois."

Hearing Lady Anne speak with such simple dignity almost undid Miss Carswell. She made her voice brisk. "Yes, and look how that tiny gesture of simple Christian charity has benefited me! Sometimes I feel guilty. You've done so much for me, Anne."

"Silly goose! I've done nothing for you." Anne smiled wryly. "In becoming my companion you've done wonders for me. I'd have been at Bedlam by now without you." She took both Lois's hands and gave her a little shake. "Life would have been truly horrible at Kent Hall without you. I tell you, I was already halfway around the bend by the time I learned you were without a post." Mischief lit her eyes. "Forgive me for saying so, but the closing of Miss Haversham's School for Young Ladies was a great blessing to me."

"For me, too." Lois chuckled. "What *were* you saying about the walls, then, Anne?"

"Didn't you hear me ask the solicitors about the castle?"

"Yes. Of course. And they told you that Castle Caldon had been left to someone else. It was the only property the twins didn't inherit. Montague left it to a distant cousin, if I remember correctly."

"Yes, some cousin Montague called 'Good old John' as if he detested him." Anne spoke with resentment.

"Oh, dear. Surely you don't begrudge the man the castle?"

"No. Certainly not. I have the use of it all the rest of my days, after all."

"Until you remarry."

"There's less than no chance of that, Lois." Anne's face closed. Her expression veiled her thoughts. "No. I don't begrudge the old gentleman his castle. Since I'm charged with its repairs, however, I shan't feel guilty about having it to do with as I please for my lifetime. No, the resentment I feel comes from finding that Montague had appointed some stranger—a man he'd mentioned only once, and that just to curse him—to be guardian of my sons without even telling me." Anger sharpened her voice. "He might at least have written to tell me of his intentions."

Lois patted her hand.

Anne rose and began pacing again.

"I don't care in the least that he left Sir John Kent the castle as a reward for serving in the capacity of guardian. It's hardly the man's fault that he's been pressed into service as guardian to my twins." She smiled and came back to Lois. "I'm certain the poor old gentleman will be no more interested in my boys as his wards than Montague was in them as his sons."

"That's probably true, more's the pity."

"Why do you say so?" Anne's tone sharpened.

"Boys need a man's influence in their lives." She saw Anne's lips tighten and amended, "A good man."

"Be that as it may," Anne closed the subject firmly. She didn't want a man, good or otherwise, to take an interest in her or her sons. She was well aware of Lois's hopes for her, though her friend had never voiced them. She'd no intention of permitting her to realize them, however. The subject of men and marriage was anathema to her.

It took an effort to lighten her mood. "There are repairs to be made at Castle Caldon, and by the terms of Montague's will, the estate must bear the expense of them. So"—she grinned at her dearest friend—"why should we not enjoy doing them?"

Lois held her peace. Her heart sank. She couldn't bring herself to approve of Anne running off to hide in a castle miles from anywhere. She wanted her friend to be allowed to find happiness despite the treason of Jared St. Legere.

Anne went on. "The castle and the plans I have for it will make a good project to keep me busy."

And safely away from society, Lois thought darkly.

"Surely the new owner will have no objection. He'll no doubt want to spend some time there in the future, and I do intend to make it infinitely more comfortable.

"And, since I have the right to the castle for the rest of my days, I think I'll want to live there now and again." She gave Lois a conspiratorial smile. "It lies such a *nice* distance from London. It's near enough that you and I may go to town when we want to, but far enough away so that no one can come for a visit unless they have an invitation to spend the night. I've checked, and there's no inn in the village."

Anne warmed to her topic. "We're to have Father's butler, Higgins. Mama and Papa say they won't need him as they'll be gone visiting my youngest brother and his wife . . . we're all waiting for the birth of Mariah's first child, as you know." She smiled at Lois. "I wonder what they would have done if there hadn't been that excuse to send Higgins to look after me?" She laughed and went on with her plans. "We'll certainly be well taken care of. He'll hire and bring with him a complete staff, so the food and service will be perfectly unexceptionable. I'll send down wagon loads of furniture, drapes enough to do all the major rooms we'll be using, and so many carpets you'll never know all the floors are stone." She waited for Lois's approval. When it was slow in coming she said, "Surely you're not worried the old gentleman—it was Sir John Kent, wasn't it?—will mind if we are in residence there sometimes as well as he. It's a very large castle, after all."

Lois wasn't thinking about Sir John. She was seeing her hopes dashed by the very person for whom she held them. It would serve Anne right, she thought almost spitefully, if Sir John Kent turned out to be young, dashing, and as handsome as a Greek god!

Across the broad expanse of the English Channel, Captain of Dragoons Sir John Kent, his dark curls brushing the canvas roof of his tent, stood staring at a letter and cursing.

His batman listened a while, appreciating his fluency, before asking mildly, "Bad news, sir?"

"Yes." Captain Sir John tossed the letter to him. "Kentwell has stuck his spoon in the wall and left me saddled with the supervising of his brats."

Danvers looked at him a long moment, choosing his words with care. "Perhaps it's for the best."

"Damn your eyes. Why do you say so?" He dared his longtime friend.

"You need time at home to recover, Sir John." He spoke quietly, a friend and equal.

The Captain's shoulders sagged. The memory of his last bout of fever rose to haunt him. Thank God it had waited to strike until he'd led his men safely out of that ambush! With a heavy spirit he admitted, "You're right, of course. A lot of good I was to the men once the fever took me." He shuddered to remember how it had reduced him to a shaking shadow of himself. He hadn't even been able to speak.

His men had brought him the rest of the way back to camp, two of them holding him on his horse. Out of loyalty and gratitude they'd taken him to his tent before the other officers could see him.

Danvers had nursed him through it, but they both lived in fear that it might strike again when he was leading troops in battle. It was a moral dilemma for Sir John. To lead men when he might collapse without warning was to endanger them. To go to his commanding officer and ask to be relieved of his duties because of a fever, recurring or not, debilitating or not, was to invite shame.

Danvers watched him, concerned. Moving forward, he put a hand against his captain's forehead.

It was struck pettishly away.

"Let be." John glared at his friend. Mollycoddling was the last thing he wanted.

Danvers noted that Sir John's eyes, under scowling brows, were bright with intelligence, not fever. His forehead had been cool. He waited a long minute before he said softly, "The fighting's almost over, Sir John. Surely the guardianship and training of a young peer of the realm is of sufficient importance to justify your absence for a while."

Sir John looked at his batman levelly. After a moment, he capitulated. He straightened his shoulders and acknowledged the wisdom of his old friend's urging. "Yes," he said slowly, "perhaps this is a timely call to another duty to the Crown." His voice grew bitter. "And perhaps it will save the lives of my men."

He picked up the letter again, his batman brushed down his uniform, and Sir John Kent, legendary Captain of Dragoons, went to ask his colonel if he could have a protracted leave of absence to go play nursemaid to the Seventh Marquess of Kentwell and his not quite eight-year-old twin.

It was only a short walk from his tent to that of his commanding officer, but it was as if he were crossing time.

His colonel, seeing the ravages of fever on the now gaunt frame of his favorite subordinate, was glad to grant his request.

"Good lad," he said, his voice oddly gentle. They both knew he didn't mean Sir John's zeal for his distant cousin's sons. "Good lad."

Then the colonel cleared his throat hard and said gruffly, "And get some rest while you're about it. Damned if you aren't starting to look like a blasted scarecrow the way that uniform hangs on you."

"Thank you, sir." Sir John's own voice grew husky. "I . . . I shall miss you all."

"Get out of here, you young hellhound!" His colonel snatched out a handkerchief and blew his nose noisily.

As Captain Sir John Kent saluted and marched smartly out of the tent, he heard his colonel add halfheartedly, "Get the hell out of here and leave some glory for the rest of us."

Anne was on her way out of London at last, God be praised. She looked across her traveling coach at Lois and congratulated herself that she'd successfully escaped. If she'd had to entertain one more gentleman fawning over her fortune, she knew she'd have committed mayhem.

Anne took one last look at Kentwell House and settled

back to endure the long ride to Castle Caldon. They were finally on their way to the castle on the coast, and she could relax and enjoy her new freedom at last.

Her companion frowned at the words she heard floating down from the box. "Finchley's still muttering over your insistence on leaving before the early morning traffic has thinned."

Anne closed the curtain on the window. "I want to reach the castle while it's still light." She smiled. "Besides, you know that if it wasn't the traffic, Finchley would find something else to grumble about."

Lois laughed a little in spite of herself. "Yes. What you say is true. The old curmudgeon never is cheerful, is he?"

There was no need of a reply, so Anne didn't make one. The whole family knew Finchley's dour ways. It was Lois's attitude that troubled Anne. The older woman was so adamant that Anne should remain in London and take the place in society that being the widowed Marchioness of Kentwell afforded her. Lois expected her to do it for the sake of her children.

Anne had refused, and didn't regret it. Lois might be full of disapproval that they were leaving London, but just as Finchley would cheer up once they were on the open road, Anne was certain Lois would come around when she saw how much happier they all were out of the noise and clatter of the capital.

The twins would have their ponies. Anne would have her horses. And they would all have air to breathe that wasn't full of coal dust and the stench of crowded city.

Suddenly, there was a string of particularly virulent curses from the box. The lead pair whinnied shrill fright.

Anne heard another driver's voice reply to Finchley with equal fluency. More horses neighed. The coach slewed, lurched, and slammed to a stop.

Anne clutched her sons to her as the vehicle swayed and sat bouncing on its springs. The moment she was certain they were safe, she swept aside the window curtain and looked out.

A splendid midnight-blue coach a little larger than her own was so near that she could have touched the rumps of its wheel pair. Her first glance told her that the two coaches had narrowly missed locking wheels.

Her second glance shot to the cursing driver. On the box of the strange coach, a tall, thin man with the face of an angry angel alternately coaxed his team to back carefully and cursed her own coachman for a ham-fisted fool. Thick, shoulder-length curls rioted on his broad shoulders. Eyes so crystal blue they looked as if they might shatter glared out of a face that could have been modeled after Lucifer's. Anne felt her breath catch in her throat.

Finchley gave as good as he got. "The dray caused me to swerve, you nodcock! If you'd been half awake you could have seen it and given me the inch I needed to come clear!"

"Damn your eyes! You might have lamed one of my horses!"

With the stranger's team so close to the side of her carriage, Anne couldn't open the door without risking adding to the confusion. She refused to huddle in her carriage and leave Finchley to take the younger man's abuse, however. "You there!" She raised her voice to be sure it carried to where the gaunt man sat on his box. "I'll thank you to refrain from verbally abusing my coachman. Finchley is one of the finest drivers in all England, and your disrespect is uncalled for. And kindly choose your words with more care for the ears of those who must hear them!" She glared fiercely at the other driver.

His cheeks, already marked by the hectic color of his anger at her coachman, flamed hotter. "My apologies, madam." His voice was deep, his accent surprisingly cultured. "And if you think your driver one of England's finest, my condolences!"

With that he extricated his team and sent them on with an expert flick of the whip.

"Well!" Lois fumed. "I never!"

Anne was torn between a scowl and a smile. While she was angry at the strange driver's words, she was distinctly amused by his cleverness. Also, he'd had the look of a soldier recently returned from the wars, and she had a soft spot in her heart for those poor creatures. Jobs were so hard for them to find. Angry as she knew she should be at his insolence, she also knew she'd do nothing to jeopardize his obviously hard-won position.

"It's all right, Lois." She settled back and hugged her twins to her again. "No harm was done."

In her mind, his image lingered.

A block away, the other coach turned into the first side street. Danvers, followed by the displaced coachman, pushed his way out of it the minute it rolled to a stop.

"Are you all right, Sir John?"

The man on the coach's box grinned down at him ruefully, flags of high color flying in his cheeks, his eyes alight with fever. "I think you might have been right, Danvers, old man. I think that I might not quite be up to driving in London just yet."

He collapsed then, and his coachman leapt forward to help Danvers get him down and safely into the coach.

Chapter
Two

"Stop! Stop the coach!" Anne had the latch off and was out the door before her startled coachman had managed to bring his team to a complete halt.

"Anne!" Lois's voice rose high with anxiety. "Have you taken leave of your senses?"

"Oh! No, dear." Anne pulled the hood of her light woolen cloak up over her hair and threw a smile back over her shoulder. "I just want to see the whole castle at once. We'll soon be too close under it, the way it looms over the road." Gathering her skirts, she ran back the way they'd come. An instant later, she was rushing up a steep path to an overlook she'd noticed as they'd passed by it.

Lois shook her head. She smiled a little to see her employer-friend so animated, and settled down to wait. Maybe Castle Caldon would be good for Anne.

"Where has Mama gone, please, Lois?" Brian, the

younger of the twins, was craning out the window. He was sitting on the land side of the coach, and he couldn't see anything.

Brandon, Seventh Marquess of Kent by virtue of having preceded his brother into the world by only a few minutes, hung precariously out the window on the sea side of their luxurious traveling coach. "Mama is running up the path to an overlook," he supplied helpfully.

Lois slipped over to the window to see what Anne was up to.

Lady Anne stood at the top of the steep path, her hand on the back of the bench that stood on the overlook. She breathed great lungfuls of the tangy sea air and looked at the castle that was to be their home for the summer. It was magnificent.

Bold and stark against the windswept blue sky, Castle Caldon rose high over the wave-battered cliff on which it had stood for centuries. With its four tall towers, it seemed a soaring extension of the living rock, huge and impregnable . . . and far from the welcoming place she intended to make it.

It was a grim fortress built by long-dead Englishmen— built to serve as a bastion to ensure the safety of these shores. A deep sense of history brushed the edges of her mind. She could almost feel the countless human dramas that had taken place within the huge gray pile. She'd come up to view it to plan for renovations. Instead, she merely stood, unable to tear her gaze from the immense granite bulk, giving herself over to its spell.

Suddenly, she became achingly aware of the sad cry of the wind around the massive walls. The awareness strengthened as something seemed to reach out to her from the castle. She struggled to repress a shiver that tingled along her spine.

Loneliness, vast and yearning, reached out and touched her. Never in all her life had she felt such depths of despair. Touched and torn by the intensity of feeling, she lifted trembling fingers to her lips and blinked away quick tears.

Then, as suddenly as it had come, the terrible sadness was gone. Again, the castle was simply a massive edifice that she had every intention of altering into a pleasant seaside retreat.

She spent another few minutes studying the exterior of the castle. Plans were forming at last. Finally satisfied, she turned and started back to the coach. On her way down the steep steps, she told herself that the feeling that something had reached out to her from the castle . . . the idea that there was something . . . eerie . . . about Castle Caldon was a product of her overstressed nerves, nothing more.

In the few additional steps it took her to reach the carriage, she'd convinced herself that she was simply tired. After all, there'd been so many things to take care of after her husband's elaborate funeral—so much to do before she could flee London, that she'd worn herself out to accomplish it all as quickly as possible.

That was it. She was just tired. Memories and her fatigue were playing tricks on her nerves.

Anne settled herself in the coach between her twin sons. The boys snuggled against her, one on either side, and Anne put an arm around each and pulled them even closer. She leaned her head back against the vehicle's gray velvet squabs.

"Are you all right, dear?" Lois's quiet voice came to her from across the coach.

Anne detected a note of concern. "I'm fine, thank you." She smiled at her companion. "I'm just a little tired."

"It's no wonder, what with all England chasing after you

the way they've been since Montague killed himself chasing a fox."

Anne don't answer. What was there to say?

Bitterness tinged her smile. Where had they all been when she'd been an eager green girl, hoping with all her heart that the young men of the *ton* would be kind enough to forgive *her* for her great-grandfather's treason? As far as society had been concerned, though, she'd been an outcast, marked forever by the stain of Jared St. Legere's treason to the Crown.

In the end, Anne had accepted Montague Kent, Sixth Marquess of Kentwell, for the good he could do her beloved brothers. In return for her acceptance of the immense, diamond-crowded sapphire that had been his family's engagement ring for centuries, the sometimes amiable gamester had established her brothers in society.

Anne closed her eyes and nervously smoothed the heavy black silk of her skirt over her knees. Still, evidently, she couldn't think dispassionately about what she'd endured as wife to Montague.

Mercifully, it had ended when she'd conceived the twins. Her conscience was guiltless as she acknowledged her relief at being free of the mercurial man whose only passion had been his gambling.

His gambling! She turned her head and looked out the window. Fortunately for those dependent on him, Montague's gaming, unlike that of so many Englishmen, had been successful more often than not. The fortune she'd inherited—by default, she having been carelessly left 'any remaining monies not already set aside for my heirs'—was fabulous. It was almost as vast as those left each of her twin sons.

Her husband had died in the middle of a run of luck that had left his coffers overflowing. As a result, she would never have to give up her independence, as so many widows were forced to do.

She smoothed the hair of one twin and then the other. She had her sons. When they were grown and gone, she'd have her grandsons. She needed no other man.

Her thoughts were cut short as the hooves of the lead pair struck the flagstones of the great carriage sweep in front of the castle. Excitement rose in her. Soon she'd see the interior of the massive fortress.

One of the footmen opened the door and let down the steps. "Thank you." She started toward the imposing front entrance of Castle Caldon and paused, anticipation stirring in her.

"Oh, dear!" Lois Carswell stopped dead as soon as she'd caught up to where Anne stood staring at the impressive pile.

The wind off the Channel skipped over the low wall along the sea side of the circular drive and tore across the flagstones of the carriageway. Lois grabbed the flying edges of her cloak and pulled them more closely around her spare frame. Her gaze traveled the long, tall facade of the castle. After a moment, she said in a voice full of awe, "Anne, I fear even your exceptional abilities at restoration and decoration will be sorely taxed here."

Far above them in the one tower that watched both the water and the land approach to the castle, Jared St. Legere's ghost stood gazing out to sea. Under his breath he cursed himself for letting his thoughts reach out to the woman who'd stood on the overlook. Even the brief contact he'd made with her mind had been enough to raise in him the awful, tearing loneliness he'd had to contend with all the days since his death, and he regretted it infinitely.

Who were these people down there on the carriage

sweep? Were they going to try to stay here in his castle? He'd make short work of that idea! He'd gotten rid of presumptuous people before.

But he was curiously drawn to the woman. He couldn't deny it. Perhaps he'd let them stay. For a little while at least.

He'd liked the quiet strength he'd sensed in the slender woman. She'd walked through her own private hell, and come out the other side whole. Her mind was clear and true.

She was beautiful, as well.

With a start, he realized that she might also be part—one half, at least—of the solution to his problem. Perhaps there was significance in her arrival. He studied the scene on the drive with a much more eager interest.

A beautiful wench, by God! And alone except for the other woman and the children. Could it be that she had no husband? Could this be the one? He firmed his decision to let then stay.

If a husband shows up later, then I'll chase them away!

In spite of his trying to quell it, hope soared in him.

Chapter
Three

Captain Sir John was feeling better than he'd felt in months. The days he'd spent waiting for a ship home and the easy voyage to England had worked wonders. The minor setback he'd had after his coaching incident was forgotten.

His batman, Danvers, had accompanied him home, nursed him through the end of his fever, and was now the valet who had him standing impatiently in front of this blasted mirror being dressed like some mindless fashion doll. He could see in the rosewood framed pier glass that he'd even gained back some of the weight that the rigors of war—and the blasted fever—had peeled off him.

Sir John flexed his broad shoulders, scowling. The bottle-green superfine drew tight across his shoulders without a wrinkle. "Blasted coat fits like it wants to be a second skin."

Danvers chuckled. "Get used to it, sir. There's no need for room in your clothes to swing a saber now."

"Is that any reason to squeeze a man to death?" Sir John tried crossing his arms over his chest. He was relieved to find he could at least accomplish that if he was careful. Still he grumbled, "Hell and damnation, Danvers."

"There's no point in complaining, Sir John. Fashion dictates to society, and you must choose. Follow its dictates and suffer, or"—he gave the Captain a wry smile—"suffer society's scorn."

Sir John gave his newly created valet a level look.

Danvers smiled. "Exactly. You'll invite duel after duel if they call you unfashionable. And dueling isn't the sport here that it's considered in the army. Here in London, it's forbidden, and that law is enforced." He peered at Sir John's reflection and tugged once at the hem of his employer's waistcoat. "Unless you want to live out your days in exile, you're going to have to choose to live them out in mild discomfort."

"Hell."

Danvers was pleased that the expletive had been uttered in a casual tone. "Yes," he agreed mildly.

Danvers admired his employer's reflection as he vigorously brushed nonexistent lint from Sir John's outfit. Rest and good food were already working their magic, and the Captain was again a fine figure of a man.

Danvers sighed. If he had to leave the army, and if he had to be a valet, he was damned glad it was to a man like his old friend, Sir John. The Captain's erect soldier's bearing and splendid athletic physique aroused envy in the men of the *ton*, and God alone knew what he aroused in the hearts of the ladies. Danvers supposed Sir John must be especially handsome. Lord knew the females thought so.

Everywhere Sir John went they turned their pretty little heads to gawk after him.

Which reminded him. "I understand from your secretary, Mr. Harley, that he has procured the staff for St. Legere House. They're all male, as you instructed. Not a female in the bunch."

"Good. Felicity can add the females after she's in residence." He frowned suddenly. "Hurry, Danvers, I haven't all day."

"Impatient to get to Lady Felicity, are we?"

Sir John grinned at his former batman. "I think I deserve a kiss for this day's work, don't you, my friend?"

Danvers smoothed Sir John's coat over his shoulders, and noted with satisfaction the way the doeskin riding breeches fit closely over his muscular thighs. "Aye." Danvers couldn't hold his tongue. "And for your expenditure. Why you had to purchase another town house is quite beyond me." Pointedly, he looked around the pleasant, blue brocade-hung room in which they stood.

"Yes." Sir John looked around, too. "This has always been a happy house. I intend to keep it, even though we remove to St. Legere House this very afternoon. It's been in my family too long to let it go."

Danvers smiled. He was glad that Sir John's pockets were so deep. He'd have hated to see the elegant little jewel of a house pass to strangers just because Lady Felicity wanted a larger, more impressive residence. "So all went well when you met the agent for St. Legere House?"

"Yes. Devilish funny business, though."

Danvers looked at him inquiringly. "How was that, sir? You certainly made quick work of it."

"That's what I mean. He accepted my first offer."

"Surely it was reasonable."

"Of course. But I expected to have to pay more, nevertheless. The house is in fine condition and it's a magnificent residence." His gaze met Danvers's. "Even so, the agent seemed almost relieved to sign it over to me. I'll be blessed if I've been able to figure out what ailed the man."

"Maybe it's haunted."

They both laughed at that. Then Sir John took one last look and turned from the mirror impatiently. "Damned if being a civilian don't cause one to spend too devilish much time in front of a blasted pier glass. Find a way to cut that time a bit, will you, Danvers? It's too damned bloody boring."

"Very well, Sir John." Danvers grinned and handed his employer his hat. With a knowing look in his eyes, he watched him leave the room.

As he packed Sir John's clothes for their immediate removal to St. Legere House, he smiled. Unless he missed his guess, Sir John was going to need something to do. Obviously, the life of a gentleman of the *ton* was already proving of insufficient interest.

Sir John's language had been the clue. It was always at its most colorful when he was irritated, and nothing irritated him so much as inaction. Danvers chuckled. It was evident that Sir John was finding England under the Regent a dead bore.

Sir John lost no time driving his new high perch phaeton out the London Road. It was only a few miles to the estate of the Earl of Whitherslea, father of his betrothed. He was eager to tell Felicity he'd purchased her just the house she wanted.

His tiger jumped down to tend the horses when Sir John drew them up. "Shall I walk 'em, Sir John?"

"Take them down to the stable, please. I'll be a few hours."

He cleared the steps to the imposing front entrance of the Hall two at a time. Felicity had sent a note round late last evening saying she had something of the utmost importance to tell him, and he was eager to hear her news.

The butler opened the door, and Sir John handed him his hat and gloves as he stepped forward onto the black and white marble squares of the foyer. "Kindly tell Lady Felicity that Sir John Kent is here."

"Very good, sir." The butler placed his hat and gloves on an elaborately carved and gilded table near the door and said, "If you would be so kind as to follow me, sir."

Before they reached the charming morning room that Felicity preferred, Sir John saw her come out of it. He let his eyes roam from the top of her head to the tips of her slippers. Her blond curls were in charming disarray; her India muslin gown, cut lower than fashion dictated to expose a bit more than the usual amount of creamy bosom, was filmy to the point of being almost transparent. Liking what he saw, he grinned.

Flattered by her obvious intention to display herself to him, he said, "Felicity." He heard the husky note in his voice and laughed. "You'll catch cold. It's barely spring, you widgeon."

Felicity turned to the butler. "Please bring tea for us in one hour."

When the butler had gone, Sir John raised an eyebrow. "An hour?"

"Yes. I've something to show you out in the belvedere first." She snatched up a colorful silken shawl from the back of a gold brocade-covered wing back chair and held out her hand to him. He clasped it, and they slipped out the French door to the terrace like two children bent on mischief.

"What was it you had to tell me?"

"Later. I'll tell you later." Tugging him along, Felicity led him to the vine-covered belvedere on the edge of her father's vast ornamental lake.

Laughing, John demanded, "What are you up to, Felicity? You're acting like a naughty child!"

She stopped on the marble steps of the round summerhouse and turned to face him. With her on the step above him, they were almost the same height. She looked him straight in the eye, reached for and cupped his face in her hands. "Good! That is a very good beginning, for I hope to get *you* to feel like a very naughty adult in just a moment." With that, she kissed him thoroughly, her mouth open and greedy, then turned and led him into the dimness caused by the heavy growth of the vines.

John saw the pillows that belonged on the benches arranged at his feet like some Oriental potentate's bed. Beside them on the white marble floor was a silver tray on which stood two wineglasses and a frosted wine cooler containing a bottle of champagne.

Felicity didn't even give him time to think. "I've waited for you for so long, John," she whispered against his lips, her pliant young body pressing against him. "I don't want to wait any longer."

His pulse quickened. Any inclination he might have had to be shocked went flying. He needed no second invitation. Hell. They were to be married in two weeks, and it had been a long time since he'd had a woman.

She helped him out of his coat, vest, and shirt. Then she drew back and surveyed him. "You have a new scar." She touched the long white mark along one of his ribs.

"It's nothing." He smiled to think she remembered his body from the only time she'd seen it—the time they'd gone swimming, half-clad, in the moonlight the night before he'd left to join his regiment. "Merely a saber thrust that missed."

She laughed, the sound a low excitement. "Not entirely." Then she ran a finger along the scar. "Hmmmm." Bending, she ran her tongue along it. "Delicious."

He shuddered once as desire for her took him, then he reached for and kissed her again and again as he removed her clothes. She met him kiss for kiss in a storm of passion as fierce as his own.

As her slip fell in a silken puddle at her feet, he lifted her in his arms, knelt and deposited her on the bed she'd made for them earlier in the day.

"Oh, John, I've wanted this for so long." Instantly, she spread herself for him. The simple gesture drove him over the edge. With a groan, he claimed her.

Their passion mounted swiftly. The hunger of his long abstinence spurred him, and Felicity met him with panting eagerness and wild abandon.

There was hardly time for more than kisses, and they were climaxing, spinning out of control on the edge of delirium. He caught the cries of her pleasure in his kisses, then fell against her, completely spent.

"John, darling?"

"Hmmmm?"

"Will you promise to do this when I am married?"

He could feel a frown gathering on his brow. Weary from his lovemaking, he lifted his head. "Of course I'll do this after we're married, widgeon. What the devil's addled you?"

"Do you remember the note that brought you here today?"

"Actually," he said, rising and beginning to dress, "it wasn't you note entirely. I came mainly to tell you that I'd gotten St. Legere House for you as you wished."

"Oh, dear."

"Don't tell me you don't want the blasted place. I've already sent my things over there. Don't tell me you've changed your mind!"

"Well, not about the house, John." She scooted away from him and slipped her dress back on. "It's about our betrothal." Her eyes slid away from his. "I've decided not to marry you."

John fought his way out through the neck of his shirt. The minutes his head was free, he shouted, "You've what!"

"Oh, do be quiet! One of the gardeners might hear you."

"Felicity! You love me, damn you!"

"Of course I do, John," she said matter-of-factly, "but so many other things have changed. You see, being your betrothed quite brought me into fashion when you were always popping up in the dispatches for some heroic action or other. That caused the Duke of Ashroth to notice me and, well, one thing led to another, and . . ." She shot him an impatient glance. "Well, surely you can understand that I'd rather be a duchess?"

He could only stare.

Felicity moved forward and placed his mother's ring in his hand. She closed his fingers around it. "I do hope you and I can still meet like this. You're a wonderful lover, you know."

John's head felt as if it were going to split with the effort he had to make not to wring her pretty little neck! He thrust his mother's ring into the safety of his watch pocket and stood trying to look casual as he tied his cravat.

"Please don't look so cold, John. Please say you forgive me." She smiled at him winningly. "Please tell me we can be lovers."

Anger rose in him until he was afraid to speak. A thousand remarks crowded his mind. None of them were fit to utter, however. They all contained the words "bitch" and "whore," and worst of all to his mind, "faithless."

Picking up his coat, he looked at her scathingly. She made a lovely picture standing there in her pale gown and blond beauty against the background of deep green vines that hung down between the marble pillars behind her. He waited for a sense of loss to touch him, but all he felt was anger . . . perhaps a little disgust at having found she wasn't a virgin, and a flaming fury at having been deceived and used and then told he was welcome to come back for more!

Finally, he could speak without betraying to her the riot of emotions that assaulted him. Looking at her coolly, he said simply, "I think not, Felicity."

He ignored her little moué of dissatisfaction. Anger flashed hotter that there was no more than a faint disappointment in her face. Obviously she had other candidates in mind for the post he'd just refused. Vaguely he wondered if there would have been lovers after she had married him. Instantly, he knew that there would have been.

He turned on his heel and headed straight for the stables. To hell with his hat and gloves! His only thought right now was to put as much distance between himself and his beautiful former fiancée as it was humanly possible to do.

Chapter
Four

Anne made a notation on one of the sheaf of papers she carried. "I think a long row of windows would be nice here, don't you, Lois?"

Lois looked around her. She knew it was bright morning outside, but the hall in which they stood was dark and dreary by lantern light. "I certainly agree that it needs something."

Anne gestured with her pencil. "From there to here, I think. Of course there will have to be heavy bracing between them to bear the weight of the wall above." She fished in the pocket of the apron she wore and brought out a thick piece of chalk. Going to the wall, she drew a heavy vertical line and walked to the other end of her proposed row of windows, dragging the chalk along the stones. "This ought to do it for the daytime hours. I'll have wall sconces put up, too, for evenings. Something with a medieval look.

We can have them lit at dusk, just as we do those in the part of the castle we live in. That way we can roam freely."

"Maybe you can roam freely, but I intend to stay very much in the area you've chosen for us to dwell in. Roaming around this gloomy old pile is the last thing I want do do." Lois snuggled deeper into her shawl and whispered to her friend, "It's cold again."

Jared St. Legere dropped back several yards. *Damn and blast! How the deuce am I to get to know the wench if every time I come near her, her companion takes a chill?*

Anne tried to lift Lois's spirits. "It'll be so much nicer when we can see where we're going without having to carry lanterns around with us."

Lois glanced uneasily behind her. "I'm just grateful for the lanterns, myself."

Anne laughed. "Come. See what I plan to do."

They walked down the long, wide corridor, Anne making notes and sketching new plans. She walked briskly, eager to see what waited around the next bend in the passageway.

Lois followed her. She kept glancing back over her shoulder.

Jared St. Legere loitered along behind them.

Lois grumbled, "I don't know how you find your way around in this place."

Anne smiled at her. "It's not difficult. The castle is built roughly in a 'U' that is made a square by the wall that joins the two towers on its back side."

"The wall at the foot of the garden."

"Hmmm. The great hall lies roughly west of center. The west wing has the armory, library, and study . . . and of course the guard rooms, but we won't change them yet."

"I'm glad to hear that you intend to leave something alone!" Jared clasped his hands behind his back and walked along twenty paces to the rear of the women.

"I've chosen the east wing to make into our residence. Being a rectangle with a center hall between the two ranks of bedchambers—or rather rooms I mean to make into bed-chambers—makes it easier to turn into a home. The west wing is too strung out. Besides, the kitchen is too far from the west wing." She laughed. "We'd have nothing but worn-out servants and cold food."

They walked on a moment. "Besides," Anne added, "I love the eastern side of the castle because of the wonderful views we'll have of the sea."

"Yes. And I suppose you'll be intruding into my tower next." Jared drifted closer. *"I warn you. Leave the south-east tower alone, or I'll drive the whole pack of you out, curse or no curse. A man has to have someplace he can call his own. Bad enough you've put your blasted morning room almost under my feet!"*

Anne frowned and looked around her. "I wish I could find out where that cold draft originates." She rubbed her arms and hugged herself. "Perhaps when the engineer gets here from London he can discover the source and put an end to it."

"Not bloody likely!" Jared roared at the top of his lungs.

Anne stopped in her tracks. "Did you hear something, Lois?"

"No."

With a puzzled frown, Anne surveyed the shadows be-hind them. "I thought . . . Oh, never mind."

Jared was intrigued. Could it be that she'd heard him? Not what he said, of course. No one had heard what he'd said for a century, give or take a year or two, but this slen-der young woman seemed to be aware of him on some level at least.

Interesting.

"Anne." Lois had had enough of her hair trying to stand

on end. She was running out of courage fast. "I'm getting a little tired. Do you think we could go have a cup of tea?"

Anne turned to her quickly. "I'm sorry, dear. Of course. I always forget myself when I'm planning things, forgive me."

"She's not tired. She's got the wind up! Send her back to take tea by herself. I want to see . . ."

"Come, we'll go ring for Higgins."

"Drat all women!" Jared stood his ground as the pair linked arms comfortably, turned . . . and walked right through him.

In the cozy little morning room Anne had created out of one of the few small—if she could call thirty by thirty small—rooms she'd found, they waited for their tea. Anne went to her desk and brought out a large sheet of paper. Spreading it out on the table, she invited Lois to look.

Lois stared down at the rough plan of the castle Anne had sketched. Seeing it made understanding the layout of the castle much simpler for her. "Thank you, Anne. This makes it all much clearer. The fact that there's a corridor and a cross corridor here in the center of the east wing had me confused."

"I doubt that it would have if the passageways didn't wind so. Do you think they did that so that invaders might be confused? I've often wondered."

Anne traced the distance from the great hall along the passageway to the drawing room, past it to the formal dining room and into the alcove where the steps came up from the kitchen. The wide alcove's depth made the room behind much smaller than those others on the south wall of the castle. The reduction made it just the right size for the family dining room Anne intended it to be.

Anne had indicated the circular stairway that led to the southeast tower with a graceful curl of pencil lines. Lois saw one of them at each corner of the sketched plan. "What are you going to do with the towers, dear?"

"I plan to turn them into comfortable places to read or to pursue whatever hobbies we might take up."

"No! Not my tower! Leave my tower alone or you'll be sorry." Damn and blast. The wench was turning into more aggravation than he'd bargained for. Why the blazes couldn't the man he awaited get here so that he could push them together and be rid of them all!

"What a nice idea." Lois pored over the paper. "Funny, it doesn't look so far from my bedchamber to the drawing room here on your plan."

Anne laughed. "I know."

Lois asked, "Why didn't you put us nearer?"

"I had to have that corner for my rooms. It's drafty and dark now, but it will be wonderful once the windows are in. I love the sound of the sea. It lulls me to sleep. And you know how I love my garden at Kent Hall. In that room I have both the sea and the flowers."

Lois smiled at her. "Convenient that the Knight who built the castle found such a sea-bound promontory."

"Yes, isn't it?"

"Convenient, too, that the walls of the castle are not half so thick there. I'd hate to have a windowsill ten or twenty feet wide."

"Hmmm, so would I. Still that corner is fine. The north-east corner troubles me a little. It appears to have been built much later."

"I wonder why?"

Jared snorted in disgust. *"It's a castle, ladies."* His voice was full of sarcasm. *"Castles get laid siege to. Parts of them get destroyed now and again."*

"Perhaps it got destroyed in a siege, and this is the repair we're seeing now." Anne looked pensive. "I'll wager that's what happened. The workmanship is not nearly so good as the stonework in the rest of the castle."

Jared brightened. *Had the wench come to that conclusion herself, or was she picking up on my spoken comments?*

Lois was cautioning her friend. "Then have a care when you go making changes."

"Yes, Lois."

They both laughed. Anne had mimicked her sons perfectly in the singsong boredom with which they pretended to respond to their governess when she got repetitive.

The door opened, and Higgins came into the room with their tea. He was smiling to hear their laughter.

With an effort, Jared refrained from chilling the tall butler.

Chapter
Five

"Gor Blimey, Sir John!" His tiger's voice rose to a scream. "Bad enough yer driving inta town 'thout no hat nor gloves, sir. Ya can't take 'em in at this pace!" The tiger hung on for dear life.

Sir John continued to drive like a madman, the phaeton threatening to overturn on every curve.

"Sir John!"

The tiger's anguished howl got through to him at last. It broke the cold fury that drove him. Sir John pulled the team in. Their sides heaving, their satiny coats lathered, the matched pair of blood bays dropped to a sedate trot.

After a long moment, in which he could feel the beginnings of a return of the blasted fever curling through him, Sir John said, "Thank you, McGee. You're quite right."

The little Irishman puffed up with pride. 'Tweren't often a swell praised his tiger that way. He couldn't wait to get back to the mews behind Sir John's town house to tell the tiger next door.

When Sir John drew rein in front of his town house, however, it was to find the knocker removed from the door. "Damn and blast! The place will be in holland covers. They've moved me to St. Legere House already."

McGee hoped there would be a tiger near the new house.

Cursing quietly at seeing how his hands shook, Sir John turned his weary team in the direction of the imposing edifice he'd purchased just this morning for his faithless fiancée.

As Sir John got down and started for his new front door, McGee took the ribbons to lead the team around the house to the stables. He let out a long whistle at the sight of the mansion. "Gor Blimey. The master's outdone himself this time."

Sir John, his blood running hot through his body, and his vision beginning to blur, staggered up the steps and pounded on the door.

Danvers swung it open. Startled, he blurted, "What are you doing out in town without your hat?" Then he saw his friend reach for the doorjamb with a shaking hand. "Oh, God. The fever's got him!"

Supporting Sir John, he half-dragged him across the dark green and white marble squares of the foyer toward the magnificent white marble staircase that curved away to the upper floors. "Collins!" he shouted.

Sir John was shaking uncontrollably now. Danvers needed help getting him up to his bed. There was no way he'd risk a fall for Sir John on those damned sharp-edged marble steps.

The footman he'd called came running, and the two of them got their employer to the master's suite. Stripping him expertly, they lay him in the huge, heavily carved four-poster and piled him high with blankets. From across the room at the fireplace they could hear his teeth chatter.

Hurriedly they piled additional logs on the small fire the servants had set early that morning to take any damp out of the room. When it began to blaze higher, Danvers left Collins to tend it and went back to the man in the bed.

"Poor lad. What the deuce have you done to bring the bloody fever on again?" He smoothed Sir John's hair back off his parchment-dry, fire-hot forehead and stood looking down at him with worried eyes.

Days and doctors later, it was safe to leave the new master of St. Legere House alone. The sumptuous room was silent behind heavy, carefully drawn drapes. Their shades of deep to darkest blue effectively turned the room's interior to twilight. Outside, thanks to the addition of tanbark to the street in front of the mansion, hooves and wheels passed almost silently.

Sir John was at last resting quietly, when he sensed something. Was that a faint illumination? Out of the corner of his eye, he saw a golden glow gathering at the door of his dressing room. It grew and sparkled with little flecks of light.

Sir John stirred, becoming vaguely aware of a presence. Fighting off drowsiness, he turned his head toward the door of the dressing room. He knew there was another dressing room on the other side of his, then the suite that had belonged to the lady of the house . . . the suite that would have been Felicity's. He frowned at the thought, and at the fact that he was still incapable of seeing clearly.

Finally, he made out a shape. It appeared, vague at first, then tentatively evolved into the form of a beautiful young woman. He had the oddest feeling that the faults in the outline of the figure were not entirely due to his temporarily impaired vision.

Slowly, hesitatingly, the lovely drifted toward the bed.

"Who are you?" Sir John tried to raise his head to see her more clearly, but fell back, fainting. "Ohhhh. Oh, damn . . ."

Bethany went over to the bed and peered down at the man lying there. *Poor dear.* His gaunt cheeks were flushed with fever, his lips cracked and dry. She wished with all her heart that there was something she could do to help him.

Unthinkingly, she murmured aloud, *"It was probably the shock of your fiancée running off with that dreadful Duke of Ashroth that brought on this attack of fever. What a jolt it must have been to find Lady Felicity so far from faithful!"*

"Felicity . . ." Sir John tossed his head fitfully against his pillow.

Bethany gasped, and her eyes lit with joy. Trembling with fear that she might have misunderstood . . . that it might be mere coincidence, she bent over him eagerly. *"Yes! I say your Felicity was a truly tiresome wench to engage herself to another gentleman when she should have honored her vows to you."*

The man twisted restlessly on his bed, entangling the sheets in his long, well-muscled legs. He made no answer, however.

Bethany tried again. *"You bought this house just for her, didn't you?"*

Still he was silent, but he frowned hard, and she was much encouraged.

"This house. St. Legere House. You bought it for your fiancée, Lady Felicity Blount, didn't you?"

Sir John's eyes opened, but even the dim light of the room must have seemed too bright. He squinted up at her.

She found him devastatingly handsome in spite of the

stubble on his face. How nice it was to think she no longer had to suppress such thoughts.

"Who the devil are you?" His voice was a croak, forced through fever-parched lips with an effort. Bethany thought him very brave.

She clasped her hands tightly together to keep from clapping them in her excitement. *"You can hear me! Oh, God be praised, you can hear me."*

"Yes . . ." He struggled to rise a bit, but was unequal to the task. Finally he gave it up and lay still, weak and shaking, against the crisp white linen. "Was my hearing affected this time?" His voice was that of a man braced to hear the worst.

Bethany's heart went out to him.

As if he hoped to ward off bad news, he added, "The fever never took my hearing before."

Bethany saw how anxious he was and hastened to reassure him. *"No. No, there has been nothing wrong with your hearing. Nothing at all. It is just that usually no one can . . ."* She halted in pretty confusion, brought up short by the knowledge that she shouldn't tell him why she was so glad he could hear her. Not yet, at least.

"No one can what?" His helplessness made him peevish.

Bethany plucked at the fullness of rich lace at the elbow of her old-fashioned gown with nervous fingers as she framed her reply. At last she said, *"No one can predict what these high fevers will do."*

She decided she'd better distract him before he asked her for a glass of water or to straighten his pillows. It was clearly evident that he badly needed both. She chose a statement she knew would take his mind off any physical discomfort he might be experiencing. *"I am so sorry that your Lady Felicity has jilted you for that Duke, for I am certain that it is a blow to your masculine pride."* Her voice became a little husky in her obvious sincerity. *"But you are far better off without her, you know."*

A grin tugged at the side of his mouth. "Oh, I am, am I? Why do you say so?"

"Because if she can *be taken from you, then 'tis best 'twere done speedily."*

"You think so, do you?" There was an edge to his voice now.

Suddenly, a strong surge of wistfulness overwhelmed Bethany. Wistfulness and a wave of deep longing for her absent husband. Her beloved had often had just such a tone to his voice when he was displeased. Poignant yearning filled her. Oh, how desperately she missed him! How fervently she prayed that they'd soon be reunited.

Valiantly she pushed her emotions aside to tell Sir John, *"Oh, indeed I do think so."* She leaned toward him earnestly, her dark brown eyes grave. *"What you want is a* Forever Love. *You must never settle for anything less."*

"A Forever Love?" He almost chuckled, but lacked the strength to pull it off. Something about her lovely, serious face made him glad he hadn't laughed. Instead he asked, "And just what is a . . ." He paused to draw a shaky breath. ". . . a Forever Love?"

Bethany was quiet a moment, watching his pale face and the fans his long lashes made on his cheeks as he rested his fever-bright eyes and waited for her reply. He was such a handsome man, and she knew that he was as rich as Croesus; the servants all said so. She was at a complete loss to understand how the perfidious Felicity could have jilted him. Obviously the wench sought naught but to place herself most advantageously, and just as obviously the title "Duchess" had done the trick.

To Bethany, Lady Felicity's reasons for having jilted Sir John simply didn't matter. She'd done it, the servants said, and Bethany was glad that she had. Sir John Kent was destined for a far greater love than Felicity Blount would have been capable of giving him. She knew it.

After another long moment, not even certain that he was still awake, the poor darling, Bethany told Sir John in a voice that was hushed to a whisper, *"A Forever Love is the most wonderful thing that can happen to a mortal."* Her voice strengthened. *"It is a love that transcends death and time, and reaches out across vast spaces."* She saw by the way his hands relaxed that he was indeed asleep. Nevertheless, she went on with her explanation. She found she took great comfort from hearing it herself. *"It is a love that goes on and on through centuries without the slightest diminishing . . ."* Her words trailed away, tears filled her eyes, and she pressed her hands to her lips to still their trembling. For a moment, she couldn't speak. Her words were choked off by the strength of the emotions that flooded her. *"Oh, Jared!"* her heart cried out across the miles to her husband.

After a long moment, she whispered, *"Ah, poor dear Sir John, it's just as well. You're exhausted, and I should let you sleep."* She leaned over his bed and studied him carefully. *"Yes, you must rest. Perhaps there will be another time that we might talk."* The very thought that they might brought her great happiness, and she smiled through her tears. *"I'll return soon,"* she promised him.

She reached out as if she would stroke back the hair that lay on his heated forehead, but withdrew her hand before it touched him. Instead she leaned even closer and told him in the barest whisper, *"You are so very like my own true Forever Love, Sir John. Surely, it must have some meaning that you have come into my dreadful loneliness, don't you think?"*

She turned away to leave him to his rest. She moved soundlessly, her face full of grave speculation. For just a moment she seemed to glow as she made her way to door of the dressing room.

Lightly she put her hand on the doorknob, stopped, and turned back to look at the man in the bed one last time. She smiled a little to see that Sir John seemed to be sleeping peacefully now.

Then she passed gracefully through the paneled door into the room that had once been her own . . . without opening it.

It was hours later when Sir John opened his eyes. He'd been given water and had his sheets straightened by his man, Danvers, but had no recollection of it. He only knew that he felt more himself and that the terrible thirst that had plagued him as he'd tossed and turned earlier was gone.

Something nagged at the edges of his mind, but in his fever-ridden state he was powerless to recall it. He frowned and closed his eyes in an effort to regain what it was that he wanted to remember.

When he opened them again, she was there. "You!" It was the lovely girl he'd been striving to recall. He felt as if his striving had brought her back to him.

Bethany looked a little apprehensive.

"You've come again."

"Yes!"

"How did you get in here?"

"Are you feeling better?"

"Yes." He added, "Thank you," as if impatient to get the formality out of the way. "Who are you?"

A friend." She said it rather shyly, feeling just a little nervous. It had been such a very long time since she'd spoken to anyone. Anyone who could hear her at least. She'd been silent for almost a century now. Sir John was the first living being ever *really* to hear her. She was almost afraid it was a delusion.

He repeated, "Who are you?"

She could tell by the firm insistence in his tone that she had no choice but to answer him this time. She sighed and told him, *"I am Lady Bethany St. Legere, wife of the Fifth Earl of Mannerly."*

"Mannerly?" He looked puzzled a moment, then his brow cleared. "I say. Mannerly is the Ninth Earl. I know Herbert well."

"Herbert." She sighed. *"I have never much cared for the name Herbert."* She brightened. *"Do they call him Bertie?"*

"I doubt he would like that any more than you seem to like Herbert. We call him Mannerly."

"Oh."

"That still doesn't explain who *you* are." John was certain now that he was still a little delirious, and that the conversation he was holding with the delightful lovely at the foot of his bed didn't really count, somehow. "How is it you can be Mannerly's Countess?"

"Oh, no. Indeed, I am not. Not your Mannerly's Countess." She really hated it when she fluttered, but it really wouldn't do to have her new friend think that she was saying that she was the wife of the present Earl. No, indeed! She hastened to make the matter plain. *"I told you I was the Fifth Earl's Countess."*

Sir John frowned, concentrating hard. In a flash he recalled something. When he was thoroughly drunk, Mannerly always mentioned his ancestor, the Fifth Earl, in a toast.

What the devil was it he said? His mind was still a little hazy from the fever, and he was having difficulty recalling Mannerly's toast.

Then it came to him like a bolt of lightning. Of course! The toast was always one that cursed the long-dead Fifth Earl because the Earl's treason was the goad that spurred the present Mannerly to take such foolhardy chances on the battlefield! Mannerly claimed he'd behave in a far more safe and sane fashion if he wasn't constantly obliged to atone for his ancestor's treachery to the Crown.

Dear God! Was this lovely thing trying to tell him she was the widow of the . . . No! That was impossible! She'd be over a hundred years old!

Bethany waited quietly at the foot of the bed, watching him work it out. *"The Fifth Earl,"* she coaxed gently.

"Jared St. Legere! The traitor!"

She winced at his words, and he was glad for the first time in his life that he lacked his full strength. At least he had only whispered it at her. "I'm sorry," he hastened to tell her. "That was thoughtless of me. Unkind. Please forgive me."

"Of course I forgive you. There's no way you could know."

He looked at her, longing to ask what it was that he could not know, but afraid to put his foot in it any worse than he already had.

She did it for him. *"There is no way you could have known that my dear husband was innocent."*

He tried hard not to look skeptical. She was the man's wife. What could he expect her to believe but that Jared St. Legere was innocent? She loved him, after all. In spite of it all, evidently. He felt a sharp pang of envy.

"You're skeptical. I understand. The conspiracy against my husband was one of respected men of great power." She sighed. *"We had one hope, however. A single hope. One of the conspirators had kept a letter. A threat written to him to keep him silent. In that letter there was proof of*

*the conspiracy against the King . . . and absolute proof of
my dear husband's innocence."*

Tears filled her lovely eyes, and the strength of her emotions seemed to steal away some of the strength she needed to remain solid-seeming. She reached out a hand to steady herself against a bedpost, and as she gently wept, she faded slightly.

Faintly, Sir John could see the blue of his draperies through her misty figure, the wood of the bedpost through her dainty hand. He remained utterly silent, startled to have his wildest suspicion confirmed. She was a ghost!

He focused intently on hearing her story. As much as he wanted to hear what she had to say, he realized deep in the center of his being that the ghostly lady needed even more to tell him.

"Jared pledged his eternal love to me and rode away to the castle of the man who possessed the letter. He knew that if he could obtain it, he could clear his family name of the taint of treason. Jared is a man of great honor." She looked at him, begging him with her eyes to understand, to believe. *"He had to go!"*

"Of course." His words were murmured with complete understanding, for he was a man of honor, too.

He was fascinated to hear her speak of her husband in the present tense. Could it be that she was telling him there was yet another ghost?

Suddenly, he was certain that this was all just the fever playing nasty tricks again. The thought of a second ghost pushed this out of the realm of possibility. She had to be just a figment of his fever-clouded imagination. Anything else was simply too preposterous!

His eagerness to hear her story evaporated, and he fell back against his pillows. Now he was merely waiting to see what further tricks the fever would play . . . how the dream would go on.

Bethany sensed the change in him, and her voice took on a desperate note. *"There was a letter! Truly there was!"* She leaned toward him, her hands outstretched, entreating him. She couldn't bear it if he refused to believe her. Not him, the first living human by whom she could be heard. He was the first person to whom she had been able to talk in almost a century! He *had* to listen! He had to *believe!*

Please, God, she prayed before she told him, *"Jared rode to the coast."* She was twisting her hands now, painfully remembering that awful time, those hours that seemed eons in length. *"He rode alone. Nothing I could say would induce him to take a friend. Nothing! He said he was no longer certain who his friends were. He was desperate!"* Her tears were falling fast.

Sir John could see them, and Lady Bethany, as clearly as he could see anything else in the room. His heart went out to her, and he almost believed again.

God help him, he was actually trying to believe in a ghost!

Lady Bethany struggled on. *"And it was a trap."* She sobbed aloud, *"A trap."*

John felt her pain as sharply as if it were his own. Betrayal. Loss. Poor little lady.

"They set an ambush in the great hall of the castle and left the door unlocked and unattended. They overwhelmed him there. Jared St. Legere, the most brilliant swordsman in all England." Her face twisted in agony to think of it, her eyes filled with tortured grief. With a mighty effort she regained her calm and said simply, *"They murdered him."*

Then she wept. Hard, silent sobs shook her slender frame.

John couldn't bear her distress, even if he was only imagining it. "Sweet lady. Bethany. Do not weep so."

She went on as if she hadn't heard him. *"Jared ranted when the Angels came. . . . Oh, yes, the Angels came for my Jared, for Jared St. Legere was an honorable man, and even the Angels cried out at the injustice done him.*

"But Jared refused to leave this earth while there was a stain upon his name. In pride and anger he refused to go to his rest."

Sir John felt the hair on the back of his neck rise as faint admiration for Jared St. Legere stirred in him. What sort of man would stand up to an Angel of God?

Bethany continued her story. *"And so he remains, bound by his pride and arrogance to the castle where he was so foully murdered by those despicable men. He is doomed to walk there until he has found the letter that will prove him guiltless of treason."*

Her story of her beloved concluded, Bethany began to fade again.

"And you, gentle lady?" As strongly as he had ceased to believe her real, he believed again. He didn't want to let her go. "What of you, Countess?"

"I?" She looked faintly startled. Then she smiled and the joy of it lit her whole being until she seemed to glow with an inner light. Slowly she became solid-seeming again as if she took strength from her words. *"I am here because of the great love we share, Jared and I. Long ago, when he rode away to go find the letter, I promised I would wait for him forever."* Her smile took on a touch of bravery. *"And so I do. Here I wait for him, just where he left me to go to his death. Here, where we shared a love that is transcending time.*

"Because of his arrogance, and because of my presumptuous promise to wait for him . . . which no mortal can re-

ally do, you know . . . the Angels set Jared a task for our penance." She sighed. *"I am here until Jared can bring two people together who will share a love as great as ours."* She sighed as if she believed that an impossibility. *"Here I wait. Forever."*

Silence hung in the room. For long moments, Bethany and Sir John regarded each other solemnly.

Finally, John heard himself breathe, "A Forever Love."

Even as he said it, a vague memory of her having used those very words to him stirred in his mind. After it came a vague, aching hunger to find such a love for his own.

But exhaustion was rushing over him, crushing his ability to resist it. Quickly he called out, "Bethany. Please, come back again."

He heard laughter that he thought was altogether charming. Then she said, *"But, John. You're not even certain that I exist."*

"I know, but you . . . are so . . . pleasant to talk to."

"Thank you very much, but I'd rather you believed in my existence than that you gave me pretty compliments, Sir John."

Sleepiness slurred his speech. "Don' believe in ghosts."

"Then we shall have to have proof." She put two fingers to her lips and thought a moment. *"I have it!"* She leaned forward eagerly. *"You do know what I look like, don't you?"*

He frowned. "Course!"

"Well, then, I shall tell you where to find my locket! I hid it when they were destroying all the portraits of Jared, the nasty little men. It has a miniature of me opposite the one of him. Then you will know that I really existed and am truly your ghostly friend."

"Sounds . . . as if that might . . . do the trick."

She frowned at him. Obviously, he was about to fall

asleep, and didn't really believe her anyway. In a half-despairing tone she told him, *"Look in the library. Beside the fireplace on the right-hand side, just under the mantel, there's a loose brick. My locket is there. When you see my picture, you will know that I am real."*

"Ver' well. An' I shall put it back the minute I have looked at it," he promised.

"No," she told him musingly. *"I think I want you to keep it. I think it will please me best if you give it to your Forever Love when you find her."*

"I shall give it to my . . . Forever Love, sweet Bethany. I promise." It was almost all he could manage before sleep claimed him, "Put it back if don' fin' her. Word on it." His strength was gone.

Just as his fever-weighted eyelids closed, he saw her smile.

"Sir John," Danvers spoke softly from the doorway to the hall. "Are you awake, sir?"

"Yes." Sir John looked around vaguely. "I think I am now."

"Good. It's time for your medicine." Danvers crossed the room briskly and began moving things around on the little table by the bed, measuring out various dosages.

"Danvers." Sir John spoke carefully, a frown marring his broad forehead. "Do I employ any maidservants? *Pretty* maidservants?"

Danvers almost dropped the glass he was mixing the medicines in. "Do you mean *females*, sir?" His startled voice sounded as if he were inquiring if Sir John meant fire-breathing dragons.

"Of course, females. Pretty girls don't come any other way, you know."

"Yes, sir. I know that, sir." Danvers eyed him uneasily.

"Well?" It lacked the force of his military bark, but the tone was still there.

Danvers snapped to attention. "Females! No, sir. The Captain was most specific, sir. No maidservants, you said, sir. Not even a woman cook." He relaxed enough to give his friend and captain an anxious look. "So there are no females in St. Legere House, Sir John."

"Strange."

"What is strange, Sir John?"

"I thought . . ." He shook his head slightly. "Never mind. What's for supper? I could eat an ox."

Danvers beamed. "You're on the mend then. Jolly good! This bout was of shorter duration than your last. Do you suppose we can hope we are getting over this blasted fever, sir?"

"I hope so, Danvers."

His batman turned valet looked at him sharply. It wasn't like Sir John to neglect making some wry joke about "we" getting over "our" fever when clearly the fever was his and his alone.

Danvers wondered what had occurred to distract his employer to the point that he'd neglected to do so this time. He frowned mightily. And just what the deuce did it have to do with pretty maidservants?

Chapter
Six

"Lois! He's coming *here*. Sir John Kent is coming here. I don't believe it!" She turned away, then whirled right back. "Oh, Lois. How very annoying. I don't want him."

She threw out her hands and confessed, "I didn't even want to invite Becky and Athelstain and their two boys, and you *know* how much I love Becky! I put *them* off for a month. Now, look at this." Anne thrust the heavy vellum sheet at her companion and started pacing the room. "I was so happy with just you and the twins. I was . . ."—she spread her hands helplessly—"putting the pieces back together."

"Hmmmm." Lois scanned the letter and spoke in noncommittal tones. "It seems the old gentleman has decided to come to see the twins." She shot a measuring glance at Lady Anne. "That's very commendable, dear. After all, he *is* their guardian. You're just upset by the thought of this unknown coming into your life before you've gotten it back . . . together, dearest. These last few months haven't been easy for you, you know."

"I should be more gracious and understanding . . . a little more hospitable. The castle *is* his, after all."

Lois made a soothing noise and waited for the rest. It was high time Anne admitted to more than the placid nature she'd shown the world for the past nine years or so. "You just need a little time, dear."

Anne snorted disgustedly. Lois's eyebrows rose. "Time is exactly what I just ran out of. Sir John Kent is coming!"

"So what, my dear?" Lois soothed. "The old gentleman is merely coming to pay a duty call and to have a look at the twins. Their high spirits will no doubt both convince him they are in perfect health and raise in him a wild desire to return to the peace and quiet of his own home."

Anne smiled a little at that. "Yes, I suppose that's true."

"Yes," Lois commented drily.

Anne sprang up and grinned at her companion like a naughty boy. Her spirits were revived by the assurance that "Good *old* John," as Montague had called his distant cousin, would run from her boisterous twins in short order, and she would have her peace again. She laughed. "Come. Let's go decide where we shall put the old gentleman. It can only be so bad, having a nice old body to shepherd around for only a little while. Surely I shall be able to do that creditably."

Lois laughed. "I think I begin to worry just a bit about the old gentleman."

Anne laughed back. "You needn't. I shall be all that is gracious to dear old Sir John for the brief time he is here."

They spent a happy half hour choosing a room to prepare for him. They put him near Lois's and her own rooms so that the old gentleman wouldn't have too far to walk to the dining room. Both of them were satisfied that they had done their best by Sir John by the time they went to change for dinner.

Later, tired from her explorations of the castle, Anne was content to retire. As the night wind whistled around the tall towers and high walls to cool the huge stone pile that was Castle Caldon, she slipped between the fine, fresh-pressed linen of her monogrammed sheets with a little sigh of satisfaction. She snuggled down in her bed and plumped her pillow until she had it just right. She smoothed her hands out to the sides of the bed, caressing the sheet. Taking a deep breath, she reminded herself that she was free. Free of him and his conjugal demands. And she was going to remain free. Never again would she be the victim of any man.

She'd always been of an independent spirit. She'd submitted to her husband only because she'd pledged to do so in her marriage vows. She'd never do that again. Never again would there be a man in her life. She sighed in relief and satisfaction.

Closing her eyes, she said a brief prayer of thanks. Then she ran quickly through her list of those she prayed for, her twins, her parents, her brothers and their families, Lois, old Hepplesworthy and his rheumatism . . . She yawned and gave it up, promising to do a better job in the morning when she was outside riding in the fresh air where she felt so much nearer to . . . She sat up abruptly! Every vestige of sleepiness gone. "Marie?"

There was no answer.

"Marie?" She waited a minute, straining to hear whatever sound had brought her jolting upright. "Lois?" She called her friend's name in an uncertain voice, knowing that if Lois had found a reason to come into her room, she would have knocked lightly and come in calling to her softly.

The noise she thought she'd heard had been slight. Perhaps it hadn't been a noise at all. Perhaps it had been more a touch to her senses than an actual sound.

If one of the twins had come, he'd have leapt into the bed with her like a shot. She'd be cuddling him now, not sitting here with her scalp prickling.

Unwilling to admit that her nerves were playing tricks on her, she reached for the flint and lit her bedside candle. In its warm golden glow, she could clearly see the pale blue and white brocade of her bed hangings, but not much beyond them. The tiny flame of the candle didn't help much beyond reassuring her. She couldn't see anyone. Still she felt a presence there. Someone, or something, was very near her in the room.

Clenching her teeth she forced herself to swing her feet over the edge of the bed, candle holder clutched tightly in her hand. Sliding off the bed, she began systematically searching her room, the Oriental carpet cool under her bare feet.

Jared St. Legere smiled. *"So, Lady Anne, you are disquieted by my little visit."* He hovered nearer her. *"And you have courage. You didn't ring for a servant to look for me while you cowered in your bed. You search for me yourself."*

He grew in form, changing from a nebulous, dark shadow until he was as solid as it was in his power to become. Deliberately, he stepped in front of the cautiously advancing woman. *"Here I am, my beauty."*

And he smiled. A twisted, bitter smile.

Anne walked right through him.

"Damn and blast!" Jared shouted his frustration at the top of his lungs. *"What's the matter with you, wench? If you can sense my presence enough to get out of your warm*

bed to search for me, why the bloody hell can't you see me, devil take you?"

Anne stopped as if she had run into a stone wall. Eyes wide with the fear she was fighting down, she whirled around to face back the way she'd come. There was nothing there!

She'd been so certain there was someone just behind her!

Shielding her candle with her hand, she moved swiftly to her door. Yanking it open, she stepped quickly into the hall and thrust her candle high. Her hair lashed her shoulders as she whipped her head first right and then left. No one! There was no one in the hall in either direction.

Still wary, she stepped back into her room and reached for and turned the key just under the ornate doorknob. Her hand was shaking!

"Coward!" Her voice was not as accusing as she had meant it to be, not as scornful. Nor, she admitted, was it as bracing as she'd meant it to be.

She turned as if she had to do it in only the tiniest of spaces instead of in the luxurious vastness of her well-appointed bedchamber. Through the thin lawn of her night-rail, her shoulder scraped the ancient oak of her door as she turned, and she pushed her back against the nail-studded surface so that nothing could get behind her.

One more careful circuit of her bedchamber, tiptoeing past all the familiar furniture she'd ordered brought from Kent Hall for her comfort, and she gave up. With a haste that ill-became her station, but that was held carefully enough in check to keep her candle from going out, she returned to her bed.

Replacing the candle holder on the table beside it, she stacked her pillows behind her, pulled the covers up to her chin, and prepared for a vigil that would last through the night.

"How courageous you are. I'd be doubly blessed if you were the one to break the curse that keeps my beloved Bethany from me." He sighed. *"Through all the long years I've waited for two people I could help find a great love, your brave heart is the first to give me hope."* His brows drew down in a fierce scowl, his legendary temper getting the best of him. *"How the bloody blazes they can ask me to join you to an old man such as this Sir John you are expecting is beyond even my selfish purpose!"* His laugh was bitter, his voice scathing. *"But I'll try, damn me. I'll try because more than anything I long to end the curse and bring my Bethany to me!"*

He flexed his knees and soared toward the high ceiling. His nebulous shape passed easily through the decorated plaster between the carved stone vaulting. He was gone.

In the great bed, Anne could feel the tension drain from her body. Whatever had caused her fear had gone. "How strange," she mused aloud. "I don't feel it anymore, whatever it was." She sat a moment longer, sending her senses out to probe the huge room, listening with her whole body for the slightest indication that there was anything to cause the fright she'd felt so palpably only a few moments before.

Nothing. She sensed nothing. Her bedchamber was merely her bedchamber again, as quiet and mundane as her room back at Kent Hall.

Frowning, puzzled, wanting to believe it was merely her nerves but denying the thought as unworthy of her, she slid down into her bed. Rearranging her pillows, she squirmed just a little to get comfortable, pulled up her white satin comforter, and, still wondering, drifted off to sleep.

"Are you certain you're up to this journey, Sir John?"

Sir John leveled a glare at his batman-valet. "Don't coddle me to death, Danvers. My estates have been neglected long enough, thanks to that bloody Corsican, and it's high time I had a look at my wards. It's been fully three weeks since I recovered from the fever. That's the longest I've been free of it since I caught the damn thing."

"That's true, sir." He added sotto voce, "God be praised."

"I think we can safely assume that I'm getting over it, just as the doctor claimed I would." He frowned. "Can't say I like them telling me that strong emotions and intense physical activity combine to bring the damn malady on."

He'd certainly been physical enough and angry enough with Felicity, though he'd never tell Danvers that. "Makes it sound like they want me to behave like an invalid."

"I'm just glad they think you're getting over it, sir." Danvers looked out the window of the well-sprung coach. "When you've visited your estates and we finally arrive at Castle Caldon the sea air should do you the rest of the cure, I'd think."

"God grant that you're right, Danvers. The last thing I need is to come down with the shakes at the home of the Marchioness. The poor woman must be a frightened little thing not to have left Montague after the first night. No lady of spirit would have suffered that brute long enough to have conceived twins."

Danvers was quiet for almost a quarter mile. Finally he could bear it no longer. "Just what do you have in mind for those twins, Sir John?"

"I beg your pardon?"

"Well, they are twins, which means double trouble, and they are boys, which means the worst kind of mischief. In addition, you've a no doubt doting mother hanging on to them for all she's worth. Take my word for it, this won't be easy." He cleared his throat before adding, "And we're not exactly experienced with children, are we, sir?"

A smile tugged at the corner of Sir John's mouth. There was that "we" again. Wryly he answered, "I haven't any idea of the extent of your experience with eight-year-olds, Danvers, but if it's no more extensive than my own, then it's indeed lamentably true that *we* are not exactly experienced with children."

Danvers gave up all pretense of subtlety. "Then how the devil are we to manage?"

"That, old friend, is a very good question. Perhaps *you* should give it some thought."

As they lapsed into companionable silence, John let his mind wander to another very good question. Just who the devil was the lovely apparition that had appeared to him while he was burning with fever? He vaguely remembered having more than one conversation with her, and he was almost certain that she'd entered his room the last time without bothering to open the door first.

The idea that he'd been conversing with a specter was less disturbing to him than the thought that he might have been carrying on some very satisfying discussions with a figment of his fever-excited imagination. She had, after all, had a name. And it was one that couldn't have come from the recesses of *his* mind because he had never heard it before—Bethany. Odd, quaint name. Lovely as its sad-eyed possessor, he thought.

He pulled her locket—the proof she'd given him of her earthly existence—out of his watch pocket and opened it to look at her again, smiling.

She'd been a wonderful experience, even if she were one he could never share the knowledge of, even with his closest friend Danvers. Admitting that he'd miss her until he returned home and saw her again, he chuckled aloud at the thought of a grown, sane man looking forward to again meeting the gentle spirit who haunted his house. Absurd.

Danvers raised his chin from his chest and opened one eye. "Did you speak, sir?"

"No, Danvers. Go back to sleep."

Looking at the miniatures once again he closed the locket and replaced it in his watch pocket. Wouldn't it be interesting if at Castle Caldon he was to meet the stern-visaged man on the other side of the locket.

Smiling slightly at the thought, he put his own head back against the maroon velvet squabs of his coach and let the motion of the well-sprung vehicle lull him to sleep, as well.

Chapter
Seven

"Good morning, Lois." Anne swept into the gloomy space she'd designated as the breakfast room. They'd also use it for dining when there was just family.

She'd chosen this modest room after carefully studying the outside castle wall to locate just the point at which she intended to break through it. There was a large rectangle chalked on the wall exactly where the window was to go. It was going to be a lovely bow window to give light and a wonderful view of the Channel to the awful place. The wall would have to be tapered in on either side of the window, as the castle walls were five feet thick at this point, and she didn't want the sill of the bow window to be more than three feet wide.

The silver tea service or the crystal punch bowl and its cups would look well residing there. She hadn't decided which yet. She'd make up her mind when the window was in and she could see how the sun hit the windowsill.

If there was a lot of sun, then the crystal would capture the sunlight and glow and sparkle with a life of its own and be lovely there. If she'd mistaken her angles, and there was less sunlight than she anticipated, she would have Higgins put a silver tea service on the windowsill to reflect instead.

She knew that the installation of the window would be a major task, but the results were going to be worth it. Until this renovation could be accomplished, however, the room would continue to be candlelit.

Just as now it was alight with dozens of candles.

Anne put a hand on the back of each of her sons' chairs. Bending into the space between them, she kissed first one twin and then the other. "Good morning, my darlings."

"Good morning, Mama," they chorused cheerfully.

Lois asked, "Lady Anne, when do you expect Sir John?"

Anne smiled. Lois always addressed her formally in front of the twins to give them a good example. "I believe we may look for him sometime today."

"Look for who, Mama?" Brian wanted to know.

"Whom. Look for whom," Lois corrected.

"Yes, Miss Carswell."

Brandon squirmed. Who cared what new adult was coming? "Could we be excused, please?" He asked permission for them both.

Anne nodded, and they left the room in a noisy dash.

"They're growing so fast. They'll be all grown up before we know it." Anne sighed.

"So they shall. That's the pattern life takes, Anne. The hardest thing a mother has to do is to let it happen." She added very softly, "And to let them go."

"Yes. That will be hardest of all." She turned a winsome smile on her companion. "When the time comes, Lois, I shall need all the help you can give me, for I plan to hang on to them like a limpet!"

Lois placed her crumpled napkin beside her plate and told Anne firmly, "We shall cross that bridge when we come to it. Sufficient to the day is the evil thereof. Just now, I want you to tell me why you look so wan this morning, Anne."

Anne's smile disappeared. For a moment, she looked acutely uncomfortable. With a little frown, she told Lois, "You will only think me extremely silly."

"I've never done so before."

Anne sighed and looked uneasily around the room as if she expected to find someone . . . or something . . . lurking in the shadows. She forced a laugh. "You'll scold me for being fanciful. Last night I imagined there was someone in my bedchamber." She laughed at herself. "There wasn't, of course, but faint stirrings and a coolness as if a window had opened kept me alert and awake through far too much of the night." She smiled at Lois. "It's merely that I'm not yet accustomed to the castle."

She gestured dismissively as if to rid them of the subject. "You know how a strange place takes getting used to."

Lois looked at her and wondered whether she should share her own misgivings . . . misgivings about shadows that formed where none had any reason to be, misgivings about cool eddies that stirred where there was no possibility of a draft.

After serious consideration, she decided that it would serve no useful purpose to do so at the moment. She'd wait until she'd formed a firmer opinion of just what, if anything, she was worried about before she shared it with her friend.

Shadows and changes in the temperature of the air never hurt anyone, after all.

Lois knew she'd be glad, though, when the workmen finally got around to putting in the windows Anne planned. A little more light would do wonders for their gloomy new home!

"Come," Anne invited. "Let's go for our walk."

Ascending the long road leading to Castle Caldon, Sir John's luxurious dark blue traveling coach wound its way around the last tight bend and stopped at the entrance. One of his footmen jumped down and ran up the broad stone steps to ply the knocker on the massive door.

"Impressive pile, isn't it, sir?"

"Aye. That it is, Danvers. A formidable fortress. God only knows how many invaders this castle has repelled."

"It's yours now, isn't it?"

"Yes," Sir John answered with a sight hesitation. "Montague left me the guardianship of his twin sons and this, Castle Caldon. His Marchioness is to have full use of it for as long as she lives." He turned away from admiring the castle's defenses and smiled at his valet. "I can't say I envy her the possession of it."

Danvers compared the grim castle to the comfortable homes on the three estates Sir John already owned, not to mention the two London town houses, and smiled. "I rather understand that, sir. Will we be staying long?"

"Not if I can help it." He jumped down out of the coach and threw back over his shoulder, "Especially not if you haven't discovered what it is one does to get along with eight-year-old boys."

His footman returned to meet him. "Sorry, sir, but no one answers."

"Thank you, Collins." He rubbed his fingers over his chin and mused aloud, "Hmmmm. In my letter, I distinctly informed them that I'd arrive today. Surely there must be someone about. Where's the bloody butler?"

Striding to the door, he twisted the handle and thrust it open. A blast of frigid air from the great hall met him. He backed up a step involuntarily.

Stepping resolutely forward into the slate-flagged great hall, he called, "Hallo! Anybody home?" His voice reverberated in the vastness of the immense, vaulted, two-storied room. When only echo answered he became irritated. "Hallo!" he shouted at the top of his lungs.

Having rallied men to him over the roar of cannon, he was certain that, had there been one, the butler would have come in answer to his call. What the hell did this mean? "Danvers! Where the devil are you?"

"Here at your left elbow, Sir John," Danvers answered in dulcet tones.

Spinning around, Sir John told his valet, "There's no butler. What the hell can the woman be thinking of, bringing *my* wards to a monstrous pile like this without a butler to manage the servants. For that matter, where *are* her bloody servants? I yelled loud enough to wake the dead, let alone slothful servants!"

He stood glaring into the dim interior of the castle, looking as if he were about to burst into flames. "I have changed my mind, Danvers." His voice was steady with determination. "We are going to stay here for a protracted length of time. It is obvious I must look into the welfare of my wards."

"As you wish, Captain. Shall I have the baggage brought inside?"

"Yes." His tone boded no good for whomever was in charge here.

Danvers turned to see to the luggage, but his mind wasn't fully on his orders. His mind was half-engaged with trying to discover why, with fires roaring in all four of the great fireplaces in this lofty hall, the air felt like that in the Pyrenees in the dead of winter.

High above Sir John, in the tower that overlooked both the drive and the Channel, his wards were wending their way up the circular stairs to the isolated room at the top. Their footsteps echoed eerily on the worn stone treads of the stairs.

"Was it up here that you saw him?"

"Yes." Brandon answered Brian's breathless question in a whisper. "It was when we were getting out of the coach. I looked up"—his voice became awed—"and *he* was looking down at us."

"What did he look like? Did you see him for long? And why did you wait so long to tell me?"

"No." Brandon's eyes grew even more round. "I didn't see him for long." He ignored his brother's last question. "When he saw me looking up, he . . . disappeared." The last word was barely a choked whisper.

Brian stopped dead on the very next step. He peered hard at his brother. "What do you mean, 'he disappeared'?" He held very still, waiting wide-eyed for the answer.

Brandon took a ragged breath, suddenly reluctant to say any more.

Brian finally blinked. "Look, Bran, it's time to tell me

what you saw. If you don't, I'm going to go straight back downstairs." He hated hearing his voice shake, but he couldn't help it.

"He *disappeared*. One minute he was there, and then he was . . . sort of . . . going dim?" Brandon's voice rose at the end of his statement of its own accord, making it sound as if he were asking a question. He bit his lip, humiliated.

"You mean he *faded* away? Like mist? Or fog, maybe?"

"Yes! Yes! Exactly like mist," Brandon agreed eagerly. "Getting thinner and thinner, don't you know. So you can see through it and then it's all gone." He was so relieved that Bri understood he could have hugged him. He started to smile.

"Like a ghost?"

"Yes! Just like a ghost." How much better he felt to have his twin share the burden of his awesome discovery!

Brian made an impatient noise and scowled fiercely. "Oh, quite! That's more than the outside of enough, Bran." He slammed his fists onto his hips. "Do you really think I'll let you trick me like this? I know exactly what you are about." He glared and talked louder, ignoring Brandon's hushing motions. "You want to see if you can cause me to get the wind up and then you'll shout 'boo' to see me jump, and you'll laugh all the way back downstairs to tell Mama."

Brandon glared at his twin. "No. That's not it at all." Brandon's temper was slipping. His own voice rose. "But if you think it is, then just go on back to Mama. I shall go find him myself!"

"All right, I will!" Brian turned and stomped down a few steps.

Above him on the stairs, Brandon clenched his fists and

marched manfully upward. His footsteps echoed on the cold, worn stone of the ancient steps.

Brian hesitated, turned, watched his twin for a moment, and called out, "Wait!"

Brandon stopped to stare haughtily down at him. "Why?"

"I'm coming, too."

"Well, come on, then!" Brandon was almost limp with relief.

Together the boys cautiously ascended the winding circular staircase to the room at the top of the tower. They didn't care if anybody saw them holding hands.

Chapter Eight

"That was lovely!" Anne led the way back across the terrace, relaxed and happy from their long walk in the garden. "The weather has turned nicely warm. It promises to be a lovely spring, don't you think?"

Lois smiled at Anne, glad to see the high color exercise always brought to her cheeks, the sparkle in her blue-violet eyes. "Yes, it *is* a nice day. And I think the sea air makes one feel especially healthy, don't you?"

"Hmmmm, indeed I do." Anne pulled the lavender ribbon from her hair and let the breeze coming from the doorway through which they were about to reenter the castle ruffle her curls. She didn't notice her butler's sudden reaction.

Higgins took a deep calming breath at seeing his mistress's hair blowing. Of late, he'd become more than a little edgy about currents of air where there shouldn't be any. He knew very well he'd ordered no windows left open in the castle, the weather, with the exception of today, was still too brisk. So, with no windows open, what was the source of this strong draft that blew his Lady Anne's hair? He steeled himself and went on guard.

Unaware of Higgins's distress, Lois tussled with her own. "Anne!" she scolded. "Must you permit your hair to fly about like that? You will look a perfect hoyden!"

"What does it matter?" Anne laughed gaily. "There are only you and Higgins to see, and Higgins has disapproved of me all my life."

Higgins used the excuse of turning to close the heavy outer door behind them to hide his indulgent smile. The breeze ceased as the door shut. Relieved, Higgins permitted himself to say, "Quite so, milady," with pretended disapproval.

Anne knew him too well. She only laughed again as she skipped past him into the always-frigid great hall, intent on thoroughly shocking him.

To her horror, she was successful beyond her wildest dreams! Except it wasn't her father's borrowed butler that she shocked.

Standing in the shaft of light spilling through the immense front doorway was the handsomest man Anne had ever seen. He was tall and straight, with shoulders any one of her brothers would have killed for, and strong clean limbs that bespoke the accomplished athlete. Dusky curls as dark as her own crowned a regal head, and wonderful blue eyes glared as he frowned at her.

She could have died on the spot! It took all the strength she possessed to keep her hands from flying up to smooth her wind-tousled hair. She could only hope her skirts hadn't gone above her ankles when she'd skipped—oh, dear Lord, had she actually skipped?—into the hall.

There was an eternity of long, censorious silence. Then, in icy tones and insultingly measured syllables, the glorious man in the doorway spoke. "The Marchioness of Kentwell, I presume?"

Feeling as if she were consenting to a trip to the guillotine, Anne could only close her eyes and nod.

With her eyes closed, she found herself thinking absurdly that this man reminded her strongly of the soldier from the near carriage accident in London.

The same breeze that had swept through the castle entry and whipped out the door to the garden to tousle their mother's curls fingered those of Anne's precious twins. It sang in through the narrow arrow slits and whined around them as they stood holding hands in the middle of the room at the top of the tower.

"I don't see anybody." Brian's voice shook just a little. "He must be somewhere else." He turned wide, hopeful eyes to his brother. "It's cold up here. That scary cold. Like the great hall. Let's come back another time."

"No!" Brandon scowled at his twin. "We're here now, and I'm going to find him. You're just scared."

"I am not!"

Brandon ignored his brother's heated reply. "Maybe he's outside on the parapet."

"All right." Brian made his voice firm with purpose. "Let's go out and see."

They turned their attention to the heavy, nail-patterned door standing firmly in the arch it had occupied for centuries. It didn't look as if it had been opened for many, many years. Rust streaked down the oak of the door from its hinges and seemed to weld fast its bolt.

"Do you think we can get the door open?"

"Why the devil should you want to unless you're stone-

masons. The damned parapets are all loose." The voice was a bored drawl, expecting no answer.

The twins whirled to face the speaker. Terrified, they clung tightly to each other.

There, in one dim corner of the room, leaning indolently in the embrasure of an arrow slit, was a tall man in the clothes of a bygone era—clothes they'd seen only in portraits of their long-dead ancestors. That wasn't what had them clinging to one another with their eyes about to start out of their heads, however. The thing that was making the hair rise on the backs of their slender necks was that they could see the stones of the wall against which he leaned quite clearly . . . right through him.

"Wh . . . whooo are you?" Brandon finally managed.

"Well, I'll be damned." The apparition straightened and darkened like a storm cloud rolling in. Slowly, in the midst of the cloud, he became more and more solid in appearance until all the cloud had returned into him, and he seemed as solid as either of the twins.

Lord Jared's thoughts of the handsome young devil who'd just stormed into the great hall and his possibilities as the second half of the couple he was expected to bring together went flying. *"Don't tell me that you two can actually see me!"*

Brian quavered, "Well, we will say we can't if you'd rather, but it wouldn't be the truth, for we most certainly *can* see you."

That put them all at a standstill. The man stood, smiling slightly, careful to do nothing to frighten the children further. He was puzzled to find that they could both see and hear him. The knowledge elated him.

After all the long years of silence, here were two humans who could actually hear what he said. He kept his elation damped down with a mighty effort and wondered instead at the significance of this.

The twins stood waiting, their eyes popping out of their heads. They were temporarily incapable of thought or movement.

Finally, with a shake of his head that set his curls bouncing, Brandon roused himself and offered, "I am Kentwell. And this is my brother, Brian Kentwell."

"Ah. Kentwell. That is your title, is it not, bantling? Have you a first name like your twin?"

"My name is Brandon Alistair Kent."

The stranger merely looked at the boys with interest. *"You can see and hear me. Extraordinary."*

"Your name, sir?"

"Oh." The tall man seemed jolted out of deep thought. *"Of course."* He bowed and made an elegant leg, the full skirts of his rich, scarlet brocade coat almost touching the floor of the tower room.

Brandon's eyes were already beginning to start from his head as he registered the fact that the man had left no marks of his presence in the dust on the tower room floor when the tall figure said, *"I am Jared St. Legere, Fifth Earl of Mannerly."* He smiled pleasantly. *"Or, rather..."* he paused and hoped it wouldn't startle the boys too much to hear him say, *"his ghost."*

The twins never knew how they got to their rooms. They only knew they were there, panting for breath and leaning hard against the door as if they thought the apparition from the tower room would thrust it open instead of merely passing through it.

Of one mind, they dashed across the room to the damask-hung bed. A soaring leap took them to its center, and they rooted into the covers like two trembling little pigs.

Curled into tight, self-protective balls, forehead to forehead, they were silent for a full minute. Then Brandon let out the breath he'd been holding in a whoosh. He sat up, throwing off the sunny gold and white damask comforter. Brian emerged from their cocoon of covers an instant later.

Solemnly they stared at each other.

"That was a ghost." Brandon's eyes were shining.

"Yes, it was. *He* was," Brian corrected himself.

"Bri, we've seen a ghost."

"Yes! Wait till the Athelstains get here and we tell George and Luther."

"Jolly good!"

"Should we tell Mother and Lois?"

Brandon gave the matter sober thought. "If we did, we might frighten them."

"And we wouldn't want to do that."

"No," Brandon stated staunchly. "Gentlemen do not frighten ladies."

"Especially their mamas."

"Right! We must take care of Mama and Lois."

"But we could tell Higgins."

"Yessss." Brandon was reluctant. "Then Higgins would tell Grandpapa. And they might make him go away."

They sat quietly in the rumpled bed, giving the matter serious thought.

Finally Brandon said, "I think he was here first."

Brian was silent.

"If we tell, they won't let us see him again."

Brian agreed. "Yes. That's probably true."

"They might even make us go back to Kent Hall."

"Without Mama?" Brian was clearly upset.

"No, they'd make Mama go, too. You know how careful Grandpapa and Higgins are of her."

"She wouldn't like that."

"No, she wouldn't. She has her heart set on reno . . . ren-oh . . . reno-something this gloomy old castle."

"It wouldn't be nice to stop her from doing that. Besides, when I think back on it, that ghost didn't seem to be mean."

"And he didn't really do anything to make us run away."

Brian made a face, finding his own next sentence distasteful. "No. I think we just got to the end of our courage."

Brandon scowled fiercely. "Well," he said aggressively, "it was our very first ghost, after all."

"True." Brian backed his twin, seeing the direction his logic was taking.

"So. We mustn't tell anyone because we don't wish to change Mama's plans . . ."

"Nor to frighten her and Lois," Bri supplied helpfully.

"And so we'll just keep the secret, agreed?"

"Agreed!"

They clasped hands firmly, shook vigorously, and slipped down off the high four-poster bed.

Brandon grinned at his brother. "When do you think we ought to try to go to see him again?" he asked breathlessly.

"Soon," was his twin's satisfactory answer.

Standing unseen in the deep shadow beside the huge fireplace, the ghost of Jared St. Legere smiled.

Chapter
Nine

"Oh, Lois. How can I possibly face him?" Anne struggled not to dissolve in laughter again at the thought of having to face Sir John after the spectacle she'd made of herself skipping past Higgins into the great hall. "Oh, dear Heaven. Skipping!

"Last night, it was God's mercy that his man had ordered dinner for Sir John in his room. If I'd have had to play hostess to him at table, I'd have disgraced us all." She threw back her head and laughed. " 'Good *old* John.' Montague must have been demented!"

Lois smiled. "Sir John certainly didn't look as if he were old to me, either! Evidently Montague grossly misled us about his cousin."

Anne laughed again. "Hmmmm!"

Lois addressed her next comment to Lady Anne's maid.

"That curl on the left is escaping, Marie. Another pin, I think."

Anne sat still as a statue until her hair was tamed enough to look well with her severely cut blue riding habit. From somewhere, the picture of the man who'd ranted at her coachman as they left London came to her mind. She decided that it must have been her own unruly dark curls that had recalled his to mind.

Marie placed her top hat precisely and fluffed its long veil down the back of her jacket. Then Anne rose and picked up her train, draping it over her left arm. Marie handed her her gloves and riding crop.

"At least I'll be free of Sir John while I have my morning ride." She smiled impishly at Lois. "I'll be back in time for breakfast with you and the boys." She hesitated and turned to tease her friend. "You don't think Sir John would appreciate my sending him a tray, do you?"

Lois flapped a hand at her, struggling with her own laughter. "No. I most emphatically do not. Vigorous young men do *not* take kindly to being sent their breakfasts on a tray."

Anne laughed again. "I was afraid you'd say that. I shall just have to stare down his disapproval over my morning chocolate."

She was full of mischief as she checked her appearance one last time in the pier glass. "Sir John isn't exactly elderly, is he?" Her eyes were full of laughter. Without waiting for an answer, she started on her trek to the stables.

Lois looked after her thoughtfully. So Anne had noticed that the handsome Sir John was not exactly at his last prayers. Well, she'd have to have been blind not to.

She watched Marie bustling about the room looking after her mistress's wardrobe and made a mental note to remind Anne to order some new gowns. Something a little more . . . how would she phrase it? . . . pleasing to the masculine eye?

And while she was thinking of the masculine eye, maybe an effort on her part to talk to Sir John's man wouldn't be amiss. If Sir John had a wife somewhere, Lois wanted to know it. For, if that were the case, the rather interested look she'd just seen on Anne's face could only mean trouble.

Her course chosen, she left Anne's suite and turned in the direction of the wing that housed the kitchens. She hoped to find Sir John's man there looking for breakfast. He'd looked a military sort to her; she'd wager he was an early riser. She set off briskly on her own long walk to the kitchens.

Elsewhere in the castle, Sir John was saying, "Thank you, Danvers," and stomping his feet more firmly down into the boots his valet had just helped him into. "I hope to hell the Marchioness will have something in her stables I can ride."

"I'm certain she must, Sir John," Danvers said soothingly.

Sir John shot him a glance. "After yesterday's sad display, I'm afraid to count on any of the usual amenities. Not even a footman at the door. No butler. What sort of a house does the woman keep? And will her stables be any better?" He put all the irritation he felt at Felicity's jilting him into his assessment of the Marchioness of Kentwell.

Danvers watched him for a moment with a faint gleam of amusement in his eyes. His face was straight, however, when he said, "You can always ride one of the coach horses."

When Sir John looked up to answer him, he saw the humor in the situation. "I hope it won't come to that." He smiled widely. "Egad. Skipping into the great hall like a six-year-old. Carrying her hair ribbon in her hand with her hair blowing every which way. She showed us her ankles, by God."

"And very pretty ankles they were, too."

Sir John burst out laughing. "That they were, Danvers, that they were. And looking over the rest of the woman wasn't exactly like getting punched in the eye, either." He took his curly brimmed beaver and his riding whip from his friend. "Go get yourself some breakfast, I'll chance not being deliberately poisoned by my hostess when I finish my ride."

Danvers grinned at him. "Very good, sir."

"Can I help you, sir?"

Sir John spun around to face the possessor of the cheery voice. "I should very much appreciate having a ride before I break my fast. Is there a horse I might have the use of?"

The open-faced stable man led the way to the stall of a big black stallion with a wicked look about him. "Do you like a stallion, sir?"

"Well enough. They're a challenging ride."

The groom led the horse out of the stall and had him tacked up in almost no time.

Sir John tossed the man a half crown, swung up, and aimed the big black at the door. Only his superior skill held the stallion to a trot until they had cleared the barn aisle. Out in the open, the horse bucked once and took off at a gallop, shrilly trumpeting a challenge to every other horse in the area.

Sir John let him have his head and settled in to enjoy the ride.

Five minutes later, the horse dropped to a sedate canter, and his rider took control and began to look around. The day was clear, and the Channel sparkled and glittered in the sunlight off to his right, calm in the absence of wind. Gulls wheeled and turned overhead in mewing flocks, resting on the air with wings outstretched.

He decided to get closer to the silver cloud of birds. He'd suddenly realized that it had been years since he had taken the time to just sit and watch anything for the simple enjoyment such a pastime could bring.

He smiled tightly. Any observing he'd done lately had been on his belly, well-hidden, as he studied the movements of enemy troops.

Enjoying watching the gulls glide first in one direction then in another, he could feel the magic of their lofty freedom calm and release some of the tensions in him. Until they began dropping away, he'd had no idea he'd carried them for years.

The stallion seemed to relax as his rider became less tense, and Sir John smiled. "Good boy." He stroked the animal's neck. The day was starting out well, and he felt his smile widen.

As he rounded a low cliff he drew rein and cursed. His hostess was there ahead of him on the edge of the cliff.

Before he could prevent it, his horse called to hers, and he was trapped. With faint annoyance, he admitted there was nothing he could do but ride forward and greet his hostess.

Lady Anne saw him coming with a flash of irritation. Her morning ride was hers alone, and she welcomed no intrusions. It had always been the time she was completely her own, and she guarded it jealously. Out away from everyone else on her mare, she could be herself, think her own thoughts, care only for what *she* wanted to do, and she heartily resented this man's invasion of that time.

She'd never enjoyed talking with her husband's male guests. She'd no reason to believe that his cousin would be any better. As etiquette demanded, however, she was the first to speak. "Good morning, Sir John."

"Good morning." Sir John tipped his tall-crowned beaver, his eyes keen. "I trust you don't object to my riding your hunter, Lady Anne?"

Seeing the easy way he managed the fractious stallion, Anne smiled. Horses had always been the one subject on which she'd talk to anybody. "Not at all. I can see you ride well."

"And if I did not?" He was pleased to find she was outspoken. He couldn't resist prodding her just a bit to see how far she'd take it.

Instantly she was reticent. The subject had changed from horses to the skill of the man watching her. It wasn't a change with which she was comfortable, but he'd asked, so she'd tell him. "Why, then I suppose I should be sorry to see you on Seigfried. He was my husband's mount."

Her wide violet-blue eyes regarded him seriously, and suddenly there was something odd lurking in their depths. As he wondered about it, she went on.

"He's a very fine horse, just a bit spoiled. He hasn't been handled properly."

Sir John filed that bit of information away without comment. Obviously, Lady Anne had not admired her husband's horsemanship.

He'd been quick to note that his hostess was more comfortable speaking of horses, so he turned the conversation back to them. "That's a fine mare you're riding."

"Yes. She's Seigfried's sister, actually." Anne frowned. There was something so familiar about him.

"Does she have gaits like his?"

"I believe so from observing his way of going, but I haven't tried him to see yet."

"Is there a long meadow or a ride hereabout?" How

would she react if he tried to get her to spend a little time with him? "We could take them there and compare them by riding side by side."

Lady Anne looked both startled and . . . what? Damned if he could tell. Something in the back of her eyes—a guarded expression, perhaps?—puzzled him.

His hostess ignored his invitation. She wasn't accustomed to doing things with men, and she had no desire to change. "I was about to start back for my breakfast. Lois and the boys will be waiting for me."

He realized then that his presence was unwelcome. Damn the wench! He'd done nothing to cause her any discomfort. Well, perhaps he'd been a little judgmental on his arrival, but she was the ninny who'd skipped into the great hall, not he! What the deuce was the matter with the woman?

He bowed gracefully from the saddle, both stung at her obvious wish to avoid his company and eaten up with curiosity as to why she should want to. It certainly wasn't behavior he was accustomed to from women! His voice was cool as he said politely, "Perhaps some other time."

"Yes," Anne made her own voice vague as she picked up her reins. Her mare moved off with long, easy strides, leaving him sitting there. She looked back at him over her shoulder. "I hope you enjoy your ride." It was clearly an afterthought.

Sir John's pride was piqued; he'd never had an attractive woman seek to rid herself of his company so hastily. He didn't like it.

He didn't consider himself a ladies' man by any means, nor did he aspire to be one, but he'd be damned if any of them had shown such a clear aversion to his presence before! Hoping to pay her back by making her uncomfortable, he told her perversely, "Indeed, I already have. I was about to start back to the castle when I came upon you." His eyes challenged her. "Shall we ride back together?"

"With pleasure," she answered him with a stiffness that belied her words. She was clearly irritated.

The words she spoke might have agreed to suffer his existence, but the ride back to Castle Caldon was accomplished without the first bit of polite conversation. During it, Sir John put aside his own irritation at having been found distinctly *de trop*, and determined to find out just what ailed the blasted woman!

Chapter Ten

Breakfast began peacefully enough.

Lady Anne, who'd remained aloof as they dismounted and turned their horses over to the groom, had broken her silence only once. "I intend to take breakfast in my habit," she'd told Sir John. "Please feel free to come just as you are."

Since he hadn't ridden hard enough to feel in need of a change of clothes, he'd accepted her invitation. Now, under the watchful eye of the butler, Higgins, he was about to meet his wards for the first time.

First the Marchioness introduced the attractive older woman he'd seen behind her when she'd skipped into the great hall. "This is Miss Lois Carswell, the boys' governess and my very dear friend." Then she turned toward two bright-eyed blond boys who were impossible to tell apart. "These are my sons." Lady Anne's voice was full of pride.

"Brandon." One of the boys popped up out of his chair and bowed formally.

Sir John half rose from his own chair and did the same.

"And Brian."

The second boy bobbed his bow with less grace but greater enthusiasm, and Sir John returned it solemnly before sitting down again.

Lois exchanged a meaningful look with Higgins. They wanted to approve of Sir John since he was the twins' guardian.

"I saw your ponies while I was down in the barn," Sir John said casually to the twins.

The boys looked at him expectantly; Sir John had hit on a subject dear to their hearts.

"They look like fine animals."

The twins beamed.

Sir John looked at Anne. "Did you select them?"

"I bred them." She wondered what he'd make of that. Ladies didn't go around telling men that they participated in the breeding of animals. She watched to see his reaction.

"You have an eye for a fine animal, Lady Anne." After a moment, Sir John said to the twins, "Perhaps we can ride together sometime."

Anne caught her breath. Suddenly Sir John wasn't here just to take a look at the twins. Obviously he intended to spend time with them. She tried to quell her anxiety. In the sensible part of her mind, she admitted that it was perfectly natural for him to want to do something with his wards. Having seen how splendid a horseman he was, it didn't surprise her that he wanted to take them for a ride.

She took a deep breath. She could always ride with them to assure her sons' safety. Glancing at Lois, she saw her friend was watching her carefully. Lois always knew exactly what she was thinking when it came to the twins.

Lois stepped in where Anne refused to tread. "Both boys love their ponies, Sir John. I know they'll enjoy riding with you."

"We won't have to ride on lead lines, will we, Mama?" Brandon was so anxious to have a good ride with this tall stranger that he risked humiliation to ensure it. His mama was a little unreasonable about lead lines when they weren't in the rolling pastures back at Kent Hall.

Sir John answered before Anne could do so. "Of course not." He spoke to the boy, but his eyes were on the mother. There was a hint of censure in his voice. "You are far too old to be riding on lead lines."

"Yes!" Brian almost leapt out of his chair in his excitement. "That is just what we tell Mama, but she's worried we'll ride off a cliff or something."

Sir John smiled.

It was the first genuine smile Anne had seen on his face, and she was startled at how it transformed him. For the first time, she saw him as a person instead of a handsome annoyance. She wasn't especially pleased to find herself doing so.

Sir John said, "Mothers are often like that, Brian. Mine would have kept me in a glass case if my father had permitted it."

"I say!" Brandon's voice was full of delight. "But she didn't, did she?"

Sir John laughed.

Anne couldn't help it, she liked the sound of it.

Her younger twin applied to Sir John for assistance. "Then maybe you can get our mama to let us have a bit more freedom, Sir John." Brian's tone was hopeful.

Anne's head turned quickly to look at her second son. Seeing the shock in her eyes, John took pity on her. "Perhaps we can get her to share a few adventures with us?" He directed his words to Anne.

She looked away. Determined only a moment ago to accompany them, now she wasn't quite certain she wanted to go adventuring about the countryside with the handsome, perplexing Sir John.

Lois and Higgins exchanged worried glances. Behind his back, Higgins crossed his fingers.

Beside the huge door that opened into the room, in the darkness untouched by the light of the many candles Anne ordered lit every time the room was used, the ghost of Jared St. Legere frowned at the scene before him. *What the deuce is the matter with the blasted woman?* The man looked a likely enough specimen to him, and she was young enough to care about such things.

By God, she ought to be jumping up and down with sheer joy that he is young, too. She could have been stuck with a doddering old wreck. Would have been if Sir John had been what she'd expected him to be—I'm going to see her marry this man or destroy the whole damned castle in my efforts to do so!

What's making her behave as though she wished the personable Sir John would evaporate? Damn it! If she keeps this up, I'll never be able to bring them together!

After enough years alone in the castle to drive any self-respecting specter quite mad, Jared didn't intend to permit his first real chance to win eternity for Bethany and himself to be lost by either of these two. Whatever was needed to unite Lady Anne and the dashing Captain must be discovered and put in motion.

First, he had to get the woman to spend time with the man.

Blast it! This wench and the Dragoon Captain are the people I'm to bring together in love, aren't they? What sort of chance do I have to do it if Lady Anne continues in this manner?

Concentrating fiercely, he willed Lady Anne to accept the blasted invitation to go for a ride. *"Go!"* When she finally did so, saying, "Thank you, I should love to go," he left the room.

Out of sheer perversity, he was careful to pass close enough to one of the footmen to cause the man to shiver. If he had to go around giving off a blasted frigid draft, he was bloody well going to get some fun out of it.

Chapter Eleven

Jared St. Legere decided to go up to the battlements to clear his head. After years of loneliness except for the sporadic presence of a few dull-witted servants, the sparkling intelligence of the crowd now inhabiting the castle was overwhelming his senses. Sometimes he was almost sorry he'd driven off everyone who'd tried to live in the castle since his murder. *"Their own faults,"* he grumbled. *"They persisted in showing up here already married, in love or not, blast 'em!"*

He ascended rapidly, his "body" passing through the ancient stone of floor, ceiling, and wall with the ease of wind through stagnant air. Well, hell. This was his big chance. His first chance. And he was going to make it his only chance, because he wasn't going to miss with this one!

He finally had the two unmarried people he needed. He had a surprising advantage in that he could talk to the twins. Perhaps they could even help him. He was happier than he'd been since he'd been killed.

He even had a bonus in the person of the lovely Lady Anne. There was the possibility that she just might turn up the letter he sought while she was doing her renovations!

He attained his favorite hideaway in minutes. From this, the highest tower, he could see the vast extent of the estate from the shore on which the castle stood to where it joined the next property a mile or so away to the west.

The day was bright, the air full of the healthy salty tang of the sea, and the wind gentle as it came in off the Channel. It wasn't too warm in spite of the bright sunshine, nor too cold, thanks to the abatement of the wind from the sea. It was a perfect day for a ride, and he found himself wishing for one.

Memory brought a rush of sharp longing to feel again the flowing rhythm of a good horse under him. What wouldn't he give to sit astride a prime bit of horseflesh and gallop cross-country just once more!

He'd tried long ago. At his approach the horse had rolled its eyes and gone half mad in its frenzy to escape his presence. He'd decided then that the only way he'd ever get to ride again would be if the Angels arranged it as a favor.

Jared St. Legere had nothing to give in return for such a favor. He had nothing but his pride, and he still had too great . . . too desperate . . . a use for that. For it was his arrogant pride that still spurred him on in his search for the long-lost letter that would prove him innocent of treason. He meant to find it. Nothing could turn him from that purpose.

Jared thought, *Not even death.*

He smiled, and his lips twisted bitterly.

If only his stubborn, foolish pride hadn't condemned his Bethany as well. She was doomed to wait for him, alone, until he could break the curse that kept them apart—until he could bring a couple together to love as he and Bethany loved. She'd done nothing to deserve so dire a fate. Nothing but to love him. His heart twisted in his breast. Her name was forced from him. *"Bethany!*

"Bethany!" He cried out her name, sending the sound of it skyward with all his might. Sending it out toward London, to her. *"Bethany,"* he whispered, and the pain of it nearly tore him apart.

Just the thought of her, the faint utterance of her name, conjured up a vision of his cherished wife. In his mind's eye he saw her, her luminous brown eyes full of tears as she promised she would wait for him forever . . . and his handsome face twisted with the agony of missing her. *"Ahhh, Bethany, my dearest love! I'd give my very soul to free you from sharing with me this hell of longing."*

The words brought no cessation of the pain, no relief from the torture of being without her. His shoulders bowed under the burden of the guilt he felt. He was the cause of her lingering, a lonely spirit, drifting unseen through the elegant town house in which they'd lived and loved.

This was what he'd won. This personal hell of heart-wrenching yearning.

Until now there had been no way that he could reunite them. He threw back his head and laughed, the sound a searing mockery of the joy he felt at being given this first chance. Overhead, the gulls fled back to the safety of the waves, for birds and animals could hear him where no human could . . . until the twins.

That thought hit him like a dash of icy water. Why could they hear him when no others could? There had to be something significant in that. There had to be a reason he could speak to these boys and be heard. He fought down heady waves of elation, and a still, sure knowing steadied him. Something important was about to happen, he knew it.

He took a deep breath and let it out in an explosive sigh. The twins. Jared St. Legere suddenly had much more than merely a kindly interest in the two brave little boys. He must contrive how they could best assist him. Something was most definitely in the wind!

So Jared looked down at the countryside spread out before him like a giant's quilt, and concentrated fiercely on the here and now.

Far below the specter in the tower, out on the landscape he overlooked, Anne was riding. She wished she were riding alone, for she needed time to marshal her thoughts and make decisions about her life and those of her sons . . . but she wasn't alone.

She rode with the twins and the Captain.

The day was pleasant, and she was greatly reassured to see that her sons could manage their well-trained ponies easily. Before she knew it she was enjoying herself.

"Mama!" Brian threw up a pointing finger. "Look at the gulls."

Anne laughed and swayed lightly in the saddle as her mare jumped sideways away from the sudden gesture right under her nose. "Yes, dear. They are all going out to ride the waves, aren't they?"

She watched the cloud of gulls, enjoying the flash of their white wings against the blue of the sky. She was glad she'd come.

Brandon halted his pony and squinted up at the distant castle. Peering hard at the tallest tower, he thought he saw a vague figure. The ghost! The ghost of Jared St. Legere had scared those sea gulls, he was certain!

He rode over and poked his twin in the ribs.

Brian turned a scowl on him.

"Look," his brother hissed. "Up at the tallest tower."

"Ooohhh." Brian shielded his eyes and looked. It didn't matter whether or not he saw what his brother was telling him to look at, one glance at Brandon's wide eyes had told him what he'd see if he looked hard. He didn't especially want to look hard.

"What is it, boys?" Sir John watched them closely.

"Oh, uh, we were just looking to see if Higgins had put out mother's pennant," Brandon answered.

"I beg your pardon!" Sir John was shocked. A Marchioness was not a personage for whom a pennant was to be flown to show she was in residence.

"Oh, dear." Anne was caught between guilt and laughter.

Sir John turned his full attention on her. His narrowed blue eyes glinted with intelligent interest. His attractive mouth was firmly set. He was clearly waiting for an explanation. And he wasn't waiting any too patiently. Anne felt like several varieties of fool.

"It began as a joke, you see." She smiled at him tentatively.

Sir John didn't look as if he were amused.

Anne sighed. She could guess what his trouble was. He was in the first throes of proving to himself that he was going to be an acceptable guardian for her son who had just become a peer of the realm. Now he'd caught her, the peer's mother, in an act of disrespect for the rank her son had attained.

What a dilemma for the poor Captain. What a dilemma for her!

Reluctantly, she explained. "My husband's pennant flew from the roof when he came to Kent Hall. He did not come frequently, so when he did, the twins were especially curious about all that occurred. When they learned that his pennant was hoisted to indicate that he was in residence, they wanted to know why we didn't fly one to indicate that *we* were in residence." She shrugged a shoulder at him. "They refused to accept the fact that our presence at the Hall was"—she looked Sir John straight in the eye, challenging him—"of any less importance than their father's."

She continued coolly under his unrelenting gaze. "So, Lois and I made a pennant to fly just for us . . . and that is what Brandon is talking about."

"I see." Sir John's voice was devoid of warmth or expression.

"Yes." Anne ducked her head, struggling with her laughter. He looked so prim. "I am quite certain you do."

Brian reproached Brandon. "See what you did."

Brandon looked back at him levelly. "That wasn't what I meant to do, and you know it!"

Anne saw their small quarrel and dove in, more for self-preservation than to keep the boys from coming to blows. It would never do to laugh at Sir John when he was being so stern. "Brandon, Brian, that will be enough."

"But he . . ." they cried in unison, each accusing the other.

Sir John decided he was behaving like a jackass and took a hand. "A soldier does not explain himself unless he is ordered to."

The twins looked at him in utter admiration.

Anne looked at him in utter astonishment.

Sir John merely looked satisfied as the twins straightened in their saddles and put identical solemn expressions on their identical faces.

Anne was momentarily bereft of speech by this display. Then her motherly instincts leapt to life. No one was going to make soldiers of her boys! Why, hadn't she heard that Sir John, himself, had been sent home from the war to recuperate from something or another? She wasn't going to let her precious sons be put in a position where *they* might have something to recuperate from at some future date!

Sir John was slightly taken aback when his hostess turned blazing eyes on him. Gad, the woman was a beauty, but what in hell's name was she so angry about? He sat his horse quietly and waited to find out.

"My sons," Lady Anne told him in sharp, measured bits like broken icicles, "are *not* soldiers, Captain Kent!"

"Really?" He made his voice as bored as he could.

She looked at his amused expression, raised an eyebrow, and ignored his invitation to return to civility.

"No, they are not! Nor do I ever want them to be."

He asked her softly, "Because of the danger, Lady Anne? Are you intending, then, to raise a pair of cowards?" His voice strengthened as he finished his sentence.

Anne gasped, "No . . ." Of course she didn't want her sons to be cowards. Granted, she never wanted her sons in danger, but she certainly wanted them to be brave. She wanted them to be the best they were capable of becoming, and the fact that she now realized they could never attain that goal without taking risks upset her.

She was upset, too, to be forced to consider anything of this nature right now. She'd just been granted the freedom to decide anything about herself and her boys, and she wasn't ready, not so quickly, to agree that they had to be treated as young men. She didn't *want* them to grow up. Not yet, not now. Not when she hadn't even begun to chart a course for her life and theirs. Sir John, unknowingly, was forcing her to face all this too soon.

She glared at him, and Sir John glared back. Instantly she recognized him as the driver of the coach that had nearly crashed into hers in London. "You! You were the driver of the coach with which we nearly collided in Town!"

His cheeks flamed scarlet. If she hadn't been certain before, she was absolutely certain now.

Sir John, embarrassed to have to admit that his debilitating fever had wiped all memory of his entry into the capital from his mind, said stiffly, "I have no recollection of the incident, madam."

"How dare you deny it," Anne flared at him.

Suddenly she couldn't bear his company a minute longer. Glaring at the man, she spun her horse away and told the twins, "I shall see you at dinner." Her eyes blazing defiance at the handsome intruder, she added, "I'm going back to the castle to see to it that our pennant is flown!"

Chapter
Twelve

Anne was still furious when she stormed into her suite and flung her veiled hat onto the nearest chair. Slamming her riding crop and gloves down on her dressing table, she began snatching pins from her hair.

"The idea! The very idea," she muttered at the young woman looking back at her with flushed cheeks and angry eyes. "Just who does he think he is, coming here and upsetting everything this way?"

"Just who does whom think that he is?" Lois let herself in and closed the door quietly behind her.

"That man. That Sir John Kent. That Captain Sir John Kent!"

"My, my." Lois's eyebrows were almost in her hairline. "It sounds to me as if you know very well who the man is. You've just named him twice."

Anne whirled to face her friend. "He wants to make soldiers of my boys."

"There are a great many worse things to be, you know, Anne."

"Lois! Sir John is himself home recovering . . . probably from some wound he received in the war. How can he think any mother could possibly wish such a career for her sons?"

"I'm certain that he hasn't given that any thought at all. Soldiering is an honorable profession, and I assume he merely feels that every little boy wants to grow up to be a soldier."

"But that's not all. Do you realize that he was the driver of the coach we nearly hit in London?"

"No. But I didn't see the driver, you know."

"Well, it was he. I'd never forget those eyes. He was gaunt and disheveled then . . . like so many of the men coming home from the wars . . . but when he glared at me today, I recognized him instantly."

"At the time, you said there was no harm done. Why are you so angry now?" Lois thought that maybe there had been a little harm done. To Anne's heart. "Never forget those eyes" sounded rather promising to her.

"That's not the point. The man had the effrontery to say he had no memory of the incident."

"Perhaps there's some explanation for that, Anne."

"Hmmpf!" Anne tossed the brush she had been dragging viciously through her hair back down. "How can you defend such an attitude? You'd never have let me hear the end of it if I'd been guilty of such."

Lois looked pensive. "Boys somehow seem to get themselves excused from a great deal more than girls do. Do you suppose there's a valid reason for that?"

"Surely!" Anne spoke with some heat. "It's their world,

and they are sometimes excessively stupid and need excuses made for them. There!" She stamped her booted foot. "Now stop trying to change the subject, Lois. Help me find a way to stop Sir John from interfering in my life. Help me find a way to get him to leave my sons alone."

Lois looked at her long and hard. "Anne, you know the best way to get a man to leave a thing alone. You grew up with brothers."

Anne jerked her head up and scowled. After a moment she said, "Yes, I know, I know." She sighed and stated more calmly, "If you want a man to leave something alone, the best policy is to let him have his way about it. That way he'll become bored, and that'll be the end of it."

"Exactly. Opposition merely firms their purpose."

"Oh, Lois. I've had my sons to myself all their lives, and the interest Sir John is taking in them—which I admit I should appreciate—is only irksome to me." She flung herself down in a chair and said on an explosive sigh, "Men!"

Marie, Lady Anne's maid, entered then with a foursome of footmen bearing deep copper vats of steaming water for Anne's bath. Anne and Lois's conversation was at an end.

Lois thought, however, that unless she was very much mistaken, Anne wasn't going to have any peace of mind as long as the dashing Captain was in the castle. Sir John was disquieting enough to cause her own heart to flutter, with his devilish good looks and his impressive war record.

There was nothing like a hero to give a female heart palpitations, she observed smugly. And Anne was showing dangerous signs of palpitations.

"I shall see you at dinner, dear." Lois followed the four footmen from the room to permit Marie to get their mistress ready for her bath.

As she went, she began weaving lovely daydreams. Perhaps she'd soon be able to forget her concern about Brandon and Brian growing up without a suitable male to set them an example. To her mind, Captain Sir John Kent would make a splendid one.

Suddenly, a rude shock halted her dreams for Lady Anne and the handsome Dragoon Captain. Dearest Lord! She still didn't know whether or not the man had a wife and children stuck away somewhere! Just because he hadn't spoken of family, other than his parents, didn't mean there wasn't a family of his own making waiting at home.

Perhaps she'd better seek out the man Danvers, right now. She'd missed him on her first foray to the kitchens. She'd better try again. Then, when she cornered him, she had only to inveigle from Danvers information about the Captain's married state.

If it turned out that Sir John were as eligible as she hoped he'd prove to be, perhaps she could even enlist Danvers to aid her in drawing their two young people together. Danvers would make a most useful ally, *if* he could be persuaded.

She headed down the centuries-worn stone steps to the kitchen. Arriving there, she found Danvers seated comfortably by the long, well-scrubbed kitchen table, his feet propped on a stool and his pipe in his mouth. Smiling at something the cook was telling him when Lois entered the cavernous room, he looked almost handsome.

Danvers saw her immediately and rose hastily. "Miss Carswell!" He was startled to see her in the kitchen. "Please, excuse my pipe." After hastily knocking it out in the fireplace, he put the offending article aside on the kitchen mantel.

Cook looked up from the vegetables she was preparing and beamed with pleasure. "Miss Carswell, 'tis a pleasure to have ye in me kitchen again. Will ye take tea?" She gestured toward Sir John's valet. "And meet Mr. Danvers, Sir John's man."

"How do you do, Mr. Danvers. As you seem to know, I am Lois Carswell." She turned and told Cook, "I should love a cup of tea, Mrs. Beaton, thank you."

Danvers hurried to pull out a chair for her. As she sank gracefully into the chair he held for her, he breathed deeply of the fragrance she used and smiled inside. Old memories of his gentle mother and the rose scent she'd worn came to him. He stood a moment, awash with a nostalgia he hadn't known for years.

Lois said quietly, "Thank you, Mr. Danvers." Then, risking being thought bold, she said, "I hope you will take tea with us. I should hate to think that my unexpected arrival had interrupted your conversation with our Mrs. Beaton."

"Of course he'll have tea," Cook spoke with far more than her usual heartiness, a grin splitting her round face. She knew a smitten man when she saw one, she did. Fancy the cool Danvers speechless.

Just wait till she told Higgins; that old stick would drop his teeth! She swallowed a giggle and applied herself to doing her best at being hostess. "Maybe if you asks nice, Mr. Danvers, Miss Carswell would let you finish your pipe."

That brought Danvers back to himself. "I have finished it, thank you."

Lois, finding his stern face oddly appealing, said, "I wish you'd load it again, then, Mr. Danvers, for I saw you knock it out as I entered. My father smoked a pipe, and I love the aroma of tobacco."

Cook plunked a basket of potatoes onto the table. "You heard Mrs. Carswell, Mr. Danvers. Light up and oblige the lady."

Orders Danvers could understand. He rose immediately

and got his pipe off the mantelpiece. The familiar ritual of filling it calmed him, and by the time he'd finished tamping the tobacco, he was himself again.

Cook brought two cups of tea and sat down to peel the potatoes for supper. "Well, I do declare this is nice. 'Tisn't near often enough I have company while I fix dinner for the folks abovestairs."

Danvers sat drawing on his pipe, watching Lois Carswell from the corner of his eye.

Lois stirred sugar into her tea and wondered how she was to go on. She could hardly ask outright if Sir John Kent were a married man, in spite of everyone wanting to know.

Finally she said, "Have you been Sir John's valet long, Mr. Danvers?" She was pleased to hear that her question sounded as if she were only making conversation, and began to relax.

"I was his batman throughout his service, Miss Carswell. And proud I was to be." He smiled wryly. "I only took on this valet label when the Captain came home and became a civilian."

Lois smiled at the obvious disgust he felt to find himself no longer a military orderly. "I've heard that the Captain was quite a hero."

"That he was, Miss Carswell. There were a few who equaled him for valor in the face of enemy fire, but none who surpassed him. The men used to say they'd follow him anywhere." His eyes took on a faraway look that tugged at her heart. His voice grew hushed with remembering. "And they did."

Lois experienced a thrill at his words. It was as if she could hear distant shouts echoed, the thunder of cannon, and the drum of horses hooves as they charged because Danvers heard them. "His family must be very proud of him," she said in a voice soft with admiration.

"Yes."

It took moments for Lois to recall that she was here expressly to learn just what comprised Sir John's family. With a little difficulty, she called herself to order and set about doing so. "Children need a father they can look up to," she hazarded, feeling rather ashamed now to be playing this game.

"Aye, that they do. And Sir John's will have plenty of reason to be proud of him."

"Do you mean that they aren't already?"

"No," Danvers laughed, then caught himself. "Forgive me, Miss Carswell. I shouldn't have laughed, but the Captain has no children." His smile was apologetic. "Not yet. The Captain is not wed, do you see. His wards, the young Marquess and his brother, will have to be the ones to do the looking up for now."

Lois felt herself blush, but for her life she couldn't decide whether it was from triumph or for shame. She'd learned what she'd set out to learn, but she'd learned it from such a proud, kind man in such a devious way that she felt rather angry with herself. She buried her nose in her teacup.

Tom Danvers looked at the top of her pretty little lace cap and thought how lucky he was to have even this brief time in the presence of such an attractive lady, hard-bitten old soldier that he was.

Cook looked from one to the other with a secretive smile. How nice it was that this was happening in her kitchen! What a fine thing it would be if, just for once, these two stopped always thinking first of their respective employers and took a look at each other. A little romance around the castle just might make the gloomy old place a whole lot cheerier. *Yes,* she thought, plunking a peeled potato into the pot, *a whole lot cheerier.*

"My! Isn't that refreshing." Cook beamed as a cool breeze fanned her. "Kitchens are always too warm, I say. I wonder where that nice coolness came from?"

Dammit. I didn't come to make a cook cooler! Jared moved closer behind her chair, nevertheless. If the poor woman got comfort from his presence, who was he to deny her it? Heaven knew nobody else did.

But what the devil was going on here? It was obvious that Anne's companion was on the verge of simpering at the valet. And the valet was about to burst his buttons just to be sitting at the same table with her. Jared was confused. Was this the couple who were supposed to fall in love? Were these two the two he was to help unite?

Feast or famine! For a hundred years, there had been no one, not a single eligible candidate to help him break the curse. Now there were four. *What the bloody hell was a poor ghost to do?*

Chapter
Thirteen

"It's cold in here."

Brandon looked at the fire blazing merrily in their fireplace and agreed with his twin, "Yes, it is."

"Maybe Sally left a window open." Brian's eyes were not looking toward the windows, they were searching the shadows, his body tense.

"Hell, no!" The voice racketed around the room. *"Your nursemaid did not leave a window open!"*

Brandon clutched his twin and tried to say with dignity, "There's no need to shout."

"Ah. Yes, lad. Yes, there is." The ghost's voice was quiet now. *"When you haven't been heard by a living soul for almost a century, it becomes imperative to shout."* He noted the wide eyes of his new friends and added gently, *"Just once."*

Brian gulped and stood up straight.

Brandon said, "Yes," and added gravely, "I suppose there is truth in what you say, but I'm glad you won't do so again. It's most disquieting."

Brian chimed in, "Indeed! I came up here quite sleepy, but your shouting has me wide awake." He looked more than a little reproachful.

His Lordship failed to look repentant. *"Good. I didn't come in here to listen to your snores. I have need of your council."*

Both twins looked highly gratified. "How may we help you?"

"Good God! Do you do that often?" The ghost had materialized enough so that his scowl was clearly visible.

"What?"

"That. You just did it again."

"Oh, you mean speak in unison. Yes, we do occasionally."

They could see the ghost smile. The smile looked a little sad.

"Forgive me, lads, if I'm sometimes a little harsh. I had time to sire but one child, and she was a girl. My Celestine."

Brian smiled dreamily back at him. "Celestine is a beautiful name. We had a great-grandmother named Celestine."

Jared St. Legere was suddenly alert. Could they possibly be his descendants?

Could it be kinship that enabled them this communication? Excitement seized him. His heart—for he still had all the sensations he'd had as a living man—quickened its beat. Could the boys before him be his precious little Celestine's great-grandsons?

Holy God! If they were, then they were certainly his own kin, his own blood. Then their mother would be his great-granddaughter! He would have at his fingertips the means to break the curse! He didn't have to worry about Lois and Danvers. It was as clear as daylight which couple he was to unite.

He laughed then, a joyous laugh. From somewhere on high, certainty filled him. He knew in his heart these stalwart boys were indeed his descendants. The thing he was growing more and more certain was about to happen was within his grasp!

The boys stood looking at him expectantly. They repeated, "How may we help you?"

"God bless you both, you can be my hands. You like Captain Kent, don't you?"

"Oh, yes!"

"Then you must help me get and keep him with your mother. When they are by chance alone in a room. I can blow the door shut, but I'll need you to turn the key or shoot the bolt home." He looked from one to the other of them. *"Are you willing to do that?"*

The boys' faces filled with happy determination. "Just tell us what you want us to do."

For the first time in a very long while, Jared let himself regret yet again his absence of corporeal ability. He longed, with an intensity of yearning that threatened to unman him, for solid arms with which to sweep the children—his great-great-grandsons—into his embrace.

The next morning was bright and clear, and spirits were high throughout the castle. The long run of sunny days brought out the best in everyone.

Sir John could hardly stand still long enough to be helped into his coat. "Hurry, Danvers, we must be about it!"

"About what, sir?" Danvers smiled to see his friend so full of life.

"Plans, Danvers. Plans." With that cryptic reply, he was on his way, his grin the last thing Danvers saw of him.

In another part of the castle, in the room Lady Anne wanted to turn into a study, Higgins held a five-branched candelabrum high to give her the light she needed.

"I think that this will be a pleasant room, once we let in some light." She moved toward the narrow window. "This room does overlook the meadow to the west of the castle, doesn't it, Higgins?"

"Yes, milady, I believe that is correct." He pulled the draperies back for her, coughing slightly from the drift of dust that swirled down on them. "My sincerest apologies, milady!" he tried to fan the dust away from her.

Lady Anne smiled, sneezed twice, and laughed. "Thank you, Higgins, but I hardly think *you* are responsible for this dust." She brushed it from the front of her muslin day gown.

As Higgins muttered unkind things about the skeleton staff that had been in charge of the castle before his own staff's advent, Anne worked the catch on the casement window and leaned out. "Yes." She craned out a bit more to see the foot of the wall. "Look, Higgins, there'll be room for a pleasant garden here, then a low wall to separate it from the meadow." She moved so that he could lean out. "I can sit there on nice days, and the children can ride in the meadow where I can watch them."

Higgins placed his candelbraum on a nearby table and stuck his head out the window. "Yes, milady, I see."

Jared toyed with the idea of blowing out the candles. Just for practice.

"Isn't that someone out there in the meadow, Higgins?"

Jared floated up to where he could see over their heads. *Hmmmm. The person in the meadow was Sir John. But how to get them together?*

Higgins moved closer to look out the narrow aperture again. "Indeed there is, milady." He squinted his eyes and stared for a moment. "I believe it's Sir John Kent."

Anne snuggled into the window embrasure with her father's butler. "What in the world is he doing?"

"It looks as if he's searching for something in the grass, your ladyship."

"Yes, it does, doesn't it?" A slight frown marred the smooth surface of her forehead. "I wonder what it could be?"

"Perhaps he lost something while he was out riding this morning. Old Parsons said that your late husband's stallion gave the Captain the very devil of a ride, begging your pardon, milady. Maybe he bucked something out of Sir John's pockets."

Anne, who'd cut her teeth on Higgins's pocket watch, took no offense.

Jared closed his eyes and concentrated. As strongly as he could, he sent a message to Anne. *"Go help him. He's your guest."*

"I suppose I should go offer to help him find it. Dratted horse. I wish I hadn't brought him down from Kent Hall."

"Better wear a hat, milady. There's a great deal of sunshine today."

"Yes, Higgins."

The butler stood looking after her fondly as she left the dark, ugly room. He grinned. The Captain's presence was not without some influence on her. She was certainly livelier than she'd been before his arrival.

How good it would be if something were to come of this

visit of Sir John's. Something special. Then the prayers of Lady Anne's family for her happiness would be answered. So would Miss Carswell's.

Higgins picked up the five-branched candelabrum and walked to the door. "So would mine," he admitted softly.

In a complete reversal of his usual policy, Jared stood back to keep his frigid presence from disturbing Higgins. *"So,"* he said with a great deal of satisfaction, *"I have an ally in you, do I, Higgins? Good man!"*

Chapter Fourteen

Sir John walked the meadow enjoying the soothing warmth of the sun on his shoulders and the heady, sweet smell of the tall, thick grass and the wildflowers that grew in it. Inhaling deeply, he swept off his hat, threw his head back, and turned to face directly into the wind coming in off the Channel.

Dear God! How long, how indescribably long, had it been since he'd simply stood out on a wide field in full view like this? How long since he'd heard no more than the song of the wind singing through the tall grass of an open space? No whistle of shell, no screams of wounded horses?

Peace poured through him. This was what he'd been fighting for . . . this was England. His England.

He whistled, and a large dark horse being exercised at the far end of the meadow lifted its head. Danvers let it off the lunge line he was using to work the kinks out of Sir

John's charger after the trip from its home stables. It cantered over to his master. Sir John was glad he'd sent for the newly arrived big gelding. After his wild ride this morning, he appreciated the steadiness of his charger.

"We're home, Hercules. We made it." The horse pushed its head against the man's chest and rested it there while John scratched gently behind its ears. "Funny, I don't think I thought we would."

The horse pulled away, nickered softly, and watched him with liquid brown eyes.

John laughed and scratched it under the chin. "So. Did you know we would? Or are you agreeing with me?"

Hercules snorted, shook his mane at his master, and dropped his head back to the grass.

John put a hand on the strong-muscled neck and finally relaxed. Just as he'd felt a draining of tensions when he'd first ridden out on the cliffs, now he could feel his interest in life stir in him. He could feel it returning full force.

Until this moment he hadn't realized how firmly he'd kept it banked down. He'd kept his feelings repressed so he could survive the carnage of war and the death of comrades. Now, though, life, strong and questing, flowed back into him. His senses reeled under the impact.

He drove his booted feet deep into the resilient grasses, drew a long breath, and stood absolutely still, feeling the sun on his head like a benediction . . . the healing touch of a benevolent God.

Moments later, he sent Hercules back to his exercise with Danvers and returned to his inspection of the footing in the meadow. It was good to be alive!

When he straightened to rest his back, he saw a slender figure at the far side of the lakelike expanse of grass. It was his hostess. She was fighting the breeze as she attempted to tie the ribbons of her wide-brimmed garden hat. It looked as if there were a chance he might have a moment alone with her. Good. He'd checked with Danvers and his coachman and knew now what had happened when they reached London. If Anne did come out to where he was, he was in for a snack of humble pie.

As he watched, she began to struggle toward him. He saw her stagger now and again and knew that the grass was catching at her feet. Her long skirts hampered her.

He debated whether to walk to meet her or simply to stand and enjoy the sight of her. He watched her a few moments. Pride in her determination rose in him, and he went back to his own task, refusing to diminish her effort.

As Higgins had warned her, the sun was indeed bright on the meadow, and Anne was glad she'd brought her wide-brimmed hat. She stood a moment, fighting to tie its ribbons before the wind off the Channel snatched it away. What in the world was her unwelcome guest doing out here?

It didn't matter. She was glad he'd furnished an excuse for her to come out. She'd been in the stuffy gloom of the castle long enough.

As she finished tying the broad ribbons under her chin, she reveled in the freshness of the day. The breeze off the Channel was cool, the sun's warmth welcome.

She plunged off the terrace into grass that was well above her knees and started for the Captain. The meadow grass smelled sweet in the sun. It was a wonderful day.

Her long skirts impeded her way through the tough grasses. Still, she was glad she'd come herself instead of sending a footman.

*   *   *

Sir John stood easily, watching her come. He enjoyed the sight—she was a beautiful woman. She was bold and brave, too. He grinned to recall how she'd left her sons and him to gallop over rough terrain back to Castle Caldon to see to it that her unorthodox pennant was flown. She was a spirited woman. He had to admit that he admired that quality in his women . . . as well as his horses.

She must be amusing too. He chuckled, and another shot of pride in her surged through him to see her whimsical pennant flying from the flagstaff on the roof over the castle's entrance even now.

Squinting against the brightness of the day, he could just see the damned thing. It was a frivolous slap in the face of masculine tradition. If he'd been closer, he knew he'd have been able to make out the rocking horse of one twin mounted by the teddy bear of the other. They were appliqued in the flower-filled pennant's center, in honor of the twins. He knew because, burning with curiosity to see what form her rebellion against propriety had taken, he'd made a special effort to see it after their ride.

It flew just under the pennant that had once flown for her husband and flew now for her sons.

He had to approve as he thought of her designing the boys' pennant. Anne was a very special woman to have designed that bright banner. Clever, caring . . . and spirited.

For just an instant, the face of his former fiancée flashed across his memory. Felicity was spirited, too, but Felicity wouldn't have thought of making a pennant to ease the hurt caused by a neglectful father.

The remembrance of the jilt brought a momentary frown to his face. Then wryly he admitted the truth of the matter. He was relieved to be free of her. His reason for becoming betrothed—the matter of securing his lands by producing an heir—was no longer urgent now that he wasn't in imminent danger of getting his head blown off. He was home safe and whole from the war—which seemed to be concluding nicely without him—and he had a project worthy of his attention in the form of the twins. Felicity could have her Duke, and be damned to them both.

The twins had become a real concern to him. Last night when he'd paid a visit to their nursery, he'd found no toy soldiers, swords, or guns and no toy castles to besiege. He scowled. Obviously, Anne didn't realize the importance played by dreams of glory in the life of a boy.

It was damned lucky he'd come to remedy her defect in this area. Knowing he'd take care of the problem filled him with a sense of satisfaction.

It also gave a much-needed purpose to his life at present. He missed the war.

His plans pleased him. The day was perfect and here was Anne.

Even as he watched her, she almost fell; caught herself with a staggering step, and came on. Immediately, he walked to meet her. Along the way, he picked her a bouquet of the wildflowers in the meadow.

"Lady Anne," he called to her, "you shouldn't be out here. Walking through high grass is too difficult dressed as you are."

She stopped in mid-step and glared up at him. Her mouth was set stubbornly, her brows were drawn down in an annoyed frown. Determination glinted in her eyes.

He was fascinated. She was even more beautiful than he'd thought. He looked closer. Could she be clenching her pretty white teeth?

John stopped dead in his tracks, struggling not to grin. He handed her the bouquet with a flourish. "For you."

"Are you laughing at me," she demanded, "when I have

been at such pains to come to assist you!" She snatched the bouquet from him irritably.

"God, no, Anne. I was thinking how damned beautiful you are!"

Anne looked at him in astonishment. She knew she should reprimand his use of profanity, but she couldn't. This was the first time a man outside her immediate family had told her she was beautiful without meaning her bank balance.

"I was also hoping my bouquet would serve as an apology for my telling you I didn't recall our first encounter." John watched her intently. Her eyes fascinated him. Their violet-tinged blue had changed hue several times since she'd met his gaze. "I checked with Danvers and my coachman, and they tell me I behaved rather badly to your driver."

"Were you foxed?" She asked without rancor, wondering if that explained the brightness of his eyes at the time. Then she remembered that drinking dulled the eyes of the men of her acquaintance, and was completely puzzled. Unable to stop herself, she asked softly, "What was the matter with you that you don't remember?"

He frowned in annoyance, but she knew it was for his indisposition, not for her question.

"It was the tag end of a fever I'd picked up somewhere on the Continent. I was a fool to try to drive, and stupid not to remember nearly hitting you. Can you forgive me?"

"Of course." She let it go at that, knowing he wanted her to. "I came out to ask what it was that you'd lost, and whether you might like some of the servants to help you to look for it."

It was his turn to be astonished. She'd struggled across this vast sea of grass to ask if he needed servants to help him. Her unselfishness surprised him. Suddenly, he wanted to please her. "I was walking the meadow to be certain it was safe to teach the boys riding on."

"Oh."

Looking down at her, something stirred in him. He was glad of his decision to stay at the castle . . . and not merely because of the twins.

She couldn't object to his presence. It was a large castle, after all.

Besides, it belonged to him.

Standing there in the open with the sun shining down, he was tempted to tell her the whole truth behind his inspection of every inch of the meadow . . . that he wanted to be certain the footing was good because he was going to be teaching her sons to ride a cavalry charge full tilt. Fortunately, he resisted the impulse. Telling her all of the truth wouldn't be wise, no matter how appealing he found her standing there quietly in the shade of her broad-brimmed hat.

She might look all compliance, but he'd already discovered the fine steel in her. Anne would be easier to handle if she wasn't in possession of quite all of the facts.

If he did his training when the beautiful Lady Anne was busy tearing out some wall over on the far side of the castle, it'd be so much the better.

It seemed completely reasonable to him that if he didn't protest her mutilating his castle, she shouldn't mind him training her sons. When all was said and done, while the twins were hers, the castle was unquestionably his, and both were worthy projects. Wisdom, however, kept him from making an issue of it.

He bowed and offered Anne his arm. "I'm content that the meadow is safe enough for your boys to ride in."

Anne slipped her hand through his arm. How thoughtful of him to check the surface of the meadow to be sure Brandon and Brian would ride there safely. She turned back to the castle with a lighter heart.

They'd taken no more than a few steps when she realized how much easier it was to walk through the heavy grass with the support of Sir John's firm-muscled arm. She was so glad he'd told her about his fever. Now she didn't have to worry that helping her through the tall grass of the meadow might worsen a wound. She didn't even mind when he clasped his arm firmly to his body, securing her hand and giving her even greater assistance. Walking was made much easier by this closer contact with her masculine guest.

Why then, she wondered, was she experiencing even more shortness of breath?

Sir John smiled down at the top of her Milan straw garden hat and imagined the earnest face under it. Damn, it felt good to walk with her beside him, her soft arm clasped in the crook of his own strong one, her hip lightly brushing him when the ground was a little rough.

When she brought his bouquet up to sniff its fragrance, his day was complete.

Maybe being left a huge bother of a castle and two wards in the form of irrepressible little boys wasn't going to be as onerous as he'd first thought.

Chapter
Fifteen

"Permit me," Sir John murmured as he reached forward to open the narrow door that would let them into the long west wing of the castle. As she walked easily under the arm that braced the door, he breathed deeply of her fresh scent and stood smiling down at her.

"Thank you," she acknowledged his courtesy. Then she earnestly told him, "I want to thank you for your care in inspecting the meadow, Sir John. It was truly kind of you. Mothers do worry about ponies taking a tumble." She tilted her head back so that she could see him from under the wide brim of her garden hat. "Thank you, too, for your willingness to improve my sons' riding. They're becoming wild Indians in the saddle as things are."

"I'm happy to be able to teach them riding, Lady Anne."

And probably a great deal more, he thought with an inward grin. It had been too bloody long since he'd trained raw recruits into troopers. The schooling of his wards would fill that gap nicely. He was eagerly looking forward to it . . . especially now that he'd been given permission to go ahead with it by their unsuspecting mother.

He glanced back over his shoulder at the length of hall they'd traveled since entering the castle and found the distance satisfying. If he did all his training in the west meadow and on the western walls of this vast edifice, chances were that Anne would never know an instant's uneasiness.

Anne pulled her hat off to carry it in her hand. Now she could look up at him without breaking her neck. "Thank you, Sir John. I hope they won't try your patience."

He looked at her lovely, too-serious face and suddenly found he wanted to make her smile. He wanted to hear her laugh. "In the army, I had an officer who sometimes shared his opinions with me." He smiled down at her. "The Colonel used to say about our recruits that 'Every one of them would try the patience of a saint.'"

He was successful. Anne, expecting a reassurance to the contrary, was startled into laughter. He chuckled, enjoying the sound of it, then caught his breath. Her lovely eyes were smiling, the wary expression gone from them. The trusting way she was looking up at him stirred his blood.

He was compelled by something deep inside him to offer a warning. "Rest assured, however, Lady Anne,"—his eyes looked deeply into hers, his voice grew husky,—"I am no saint."

Both stopped. They turned to face each other as if bidden to do so by some force outside themselves. For a long moment they stood gazing into each other's eyes.

"Ah. This is most promising." Jared smiled widely. He

was glad now he'd waited at the door for them. Maybe he could help start the wooing.

Anne found she was having difficulty with her breathing again. In fact, she seemed to have stopped breathing altogether. Her lips parted on an indrawn sigh.

"Kiss her, you block!"

Sir John fought an absurd impulse to sweep Anne into his arms and cover that soft mouth with his own. The urge was so strong it amazed him. His body ached with it.

Sharply, he called himself to order. What the devil was happening to him? Did he really think he could snatch this woman into his arms and kiss her until she was breathless just because he wanted to? Damnation! He'd be given his walking papers, whether he owned this castle or not!

With a mighty effort, he checked his involuntary move toward her. Where the hell was his much-vaunted self-control? Damn and blast!

"Damn and blast!" Jared echoed his thought. *"I'm sorely disappointed in you, Sir John!"*

John drew a deep breath to clear his head. As he did, he breathed deeply of her elusive perfume. That didn't help matters. It had teased him all during his walk with her through the meadow. It had filled his senses when she'd passed under his arm as he'd held the door. Now, it tormented him.

"What are you going to teach the children?" Anne recovered with an effort and forced herself to keep her tone casual. Inside, she told herself she was uncomfortable with the knowledge that she'd almost been kissed. Then admitted that she was really rather elated. But she wasn't going to give up control of her life by losing herself in this man's embrace, no matter how tempting that embrace seemed.

As if by mutual consent, they walked on. Her voice

sounded faint to her. The Captain was having a startling effect on her senses. She would take care to guard against him in the future. She'd definitely had the strongest feeling that the Captain had been about to kiss her! Too strong a feeling to ignore the warning it brought with it. Anne fixed her mind on what he intended to do for her sons and ignored the fact that she could feel her cheeks burning.

Sir John was still deviled by his urge to kiss her. He damn well wanted to kiss her, and he had every intention of doing it. This just wasn't the right time. He'd have to wait. Anne wasn't a barmaid to be seized and thoroughly kissed just because a man hungered to.

Waiting wasn't what a soldier did best, however, and his arms ached because he wanted to hold her. Soldiers were good at ambushes, though. With a grin, he took comfort in that. He knew he'd have to keep his urge to kiss Anne firmly in check. He'd get himself thrown out of his own bloody castle if he didn't watch it.

Waiting for that kiss would be easier if he could tear his gaze from her lovely face. But she was so blasted beautiful, how could he resist? Her eyes were lively with interest. He felt as if he were scrambling to keep from falling into them.

Jared snorted in disgust. Nothing was happening here that suited him. Now his senses were telling him something was happening outside the front of the castle. Damn, he needed to concentrate all his efforts here. This was no time for an interruption.

Nevertheless, he shot ahead toward the great hall.

As John spoke, he made a superhuman effort to look away from Anne. "The boys have asked that I teach . . . " He interrupted himself. "I say, isn't that Higgins?"

He gestured in front of them toward the end of the hall,

and Anne looked away from him. It was a relief. Not only did her lovely eyes captivate him, but he'd be in the soup, and so would the twins, if Anne found out they were going to practice headlong, neck-or-nothing cavalry charges. Damned if he hadn't been on the verge of blurting it out to her. The woman must have a spell on him.

He made a mental note to invent an excuse to give the provident Higgins a half crown the next time he found him alone.

Anne was listening intently. Vaguely the sound of carriage wheels crunching gravel came to them. Anne started quickly forward. "Someone must have come! It's probably the Athelstains."

She quickened her pace, leaving Sir John to trail along and thank his lucky stars for the diversion. In his present mood, he might tell her anything.

They arrived in the great hall just in time to see, through the door Higgins held open, a stylish maroon traveling coach pulled by four grays draw up to the broad front steps. The Athelstain crest was painted on the door. As the coach came to a complete halt, a tall, slender man dressed in the latest fashion jumped down and stood to one side while a footman turned down the steps.

A lovely woman in her middle twenties appeared and placed her hand in his to be helped from the coach. She'd barely put foot to ground before two boys erupted from behind her and ran ahead up the steps to the door.

Sir John scowled and watched with narrowed eyes as his hostess hurried forward. He resented this intrusion. He wanted Anne to himself.

Anne was glad, truly glad to see her friends. She needed a woman to talk to, and who was better than her dearest friend, Becky?

She wanted to discuss the strange longings the Captain aroused in her, and she didn't want to do it with Lois. Lois might be shocked, her worldly-wise Becky, never.

"Becky, I'm so happy you are here." She embraced her friend affectionately and was hugged enthusiastically in return. Then she turned to the man at whom Sir John was almost glaring. "Lord Robert. How nice that you've come." To the boys she said, "George, Luther, welcome to Castle Caldon. I know the twins will be glad to see you."

"Where are they?" They spoke together, but not in the flawless unison of the twins. It brought a gurgle of laughter from Anne. Before she could answer, their father reprimanded them.

"Gentlemen!" Lord Robert called them to order with the single word, and both boys apologized for their rude eagerness like the little gentlemen they'd been called. Grinning, they stepped back to wait, squirming impatiently until all the greetings were out of the way.

Listening to the pleasantries with half an ear, Sir John watched the boys. If these two were to stay any time at all, he'd add them to his brief list of troopers. A little military discipline wouldn't come amiss where they were concerned.

Anne turned to introduce him, and he suspended his observation of the sons to inspect the father. The pleasant-looking man hadn't changed appreciably since he'd last seen him before leaving to join his regiment on the Continent. "Athelstain." Sir John spoke with no particular enthusiasm. "Nice to see you again."

Then he bowed over the hand of his acquaintance's attractive wife, wishing them both at Jericho. He wanted Anne to himself, blast it. "Milady."

"Oh, Sir John." Lady Rebecca's gamin face glowed.

"How very exciting it is to meet one of England's heroes. My husband has told me much of your exploits. He always reads the dispatches they print, you know."

Sir John looked startled.

Lord Robert said, "Don't embarrass the man, m'dear."

Anne graciously took the attention from Sir John by saying, "Here are the footmen to take your luggage."

Her eyes showed him that she was amused by his embarrassment. He slanted her a threatening glance and made himself a promise to kiss her all the longer when he finally got to it.

Further diversion came in the form of four men in Kentwell's blue and gold livery who walked past them on the way to the traveling coach. Sir John, marveling at the strong effect Anne was having on him, gave the men good marks for their bearing and the fact that they walked in step.

Anne told her new guests, "I've put you in the east wing, so you'll be nearer the rooms we live in. You'll be comfortable, but the renovations are far from being done. You'll have a lot to put up with, but I'm so glad you have come."

Becky Athelstain shivered and drew her shawl closer. "Never mind the renovations, my dear. I just thank you for giving us rooms that will keep me from having to pass through this chilly hall again."

"Yes." Her husband looked uneasily over his shoulder. "How the dev . . . er . . . how do you account for the cold in this place? You have four fireplaces going, and still it's as cold as a miser's charity in here."

Anne looked a little uncomfortable. She, too, had a problem with the cold that pervaded the great hall in spite of all they could do to disperse it. "It must be the height of the ceiling and our proximity to the sea," she murmured as she herded them off toward the spacious chamber she'd had converted to a drawing room. "Let me give you sherry and port while your things are unpacked. We'll all be more comfortable in here, I assure you."

Sir John, following behind the little group, could feel the hair stirring on the back of his neck. It signaled danger. All his senses went on the alert.

He was acutely conscious of a mass of frigid air that seemed to be following them from the great hall. Following them purposefully.

With the sixth sense that had kept him alive on many a battlefield, he knew there was someone behind him! He stopped suddenly and glanced back, his hand slapping down across his body to the hilt of the saber he no longer wore.

No one! The hair stood on the back of his neck.

He shrugged uneasily, refusing to disbelieve his senses.

There was nothing there to explain the cold air that surrounded him. Not one of the tall windows that began above the level of his head and went the whole long way up to the roof was open. The heavy door to the gardens behind the castle was closed, and he distinctly remembered not only closing but bolting the door through which Lady Anne and he had reentered the castle from the west meadow.

Blast and damn! Try as he would, he couldn't explain the cold draft. With a final careful look around him, he shrugged again and followed the others down the wide passage and into the drawing room.

In the shadows that swirled in the great hall, Jared St. Legere stood narrow-eyed and grimly smiling. *So. It would appear that Sir John Kent is not completely unaware of my*

*presence. Interesting. The man's a true warrior. It'll be a
challenge to have him here. He's a fit mate for our brave,
lovely Anne.* He laughed exultantly. *"Ah, my treasured
Bethany! Here is our chance. Here, at long last, are two
people who have the power to reunite us."*

His expression softened. His voice was tender as he
whispered, *"Dearest Bethany. Oh, God, my love. For the
first time, I have hope!"*

Later that evening, after a sumptuous dinner, Anne's
guests all adjourned to the drawing room.

"I say, Anne." Athelstain warmed his hands briefly at
the fire. "Jolly good of you to let us come. The boys have
missed your twins quite a bit, and Becky has had a strong
desire to see Castle Caldon ever since she discovered
Kentwell won it from old Halperin. Becky's gr—"

"How you do run, Robert!" His wife, resplendent now
in an emerald-green moiré taffeta evening gown that
matched her fabulous jewels, smiled at him from her chair
by the fireplace. "I should think that instead of prosing on
about me, you might thank Anne for letting you have your
after dinner port in here."

"Good God, yes. I do, Lady Anne, I most sincerely do.
Believe me, much as I might have enjoyed Sir John's company and a good cigar"—he bowed to the only other male
present—"I should have hated the two of us being abandoned in that stone cavern you call a dining room." The af-
fable Lord Robert shuddered. "Enough to give a man
nightmares."

His wife admonished him with a mild, "Robert," her
green eyes regarding him fondly.

Anne was used to Robert Athelstain. One of the things
that endeared him to her was his habit of saying exactly

what he thought and giving it a touch of whimsy. She was glad that Becky didn't really mind him doing so.

She smiled and told him, "When the new windows are in, it will be a delightful room. You saw by the marks on the wall where they will be. I think they will make the room a very light and pleasant one. Don't you agree, Becky?"

"Indeed I do, dear. You have a real talent. There are not many people who could have changed that awful old Kent Hall into the pleasant place you made it."

Sir John frowned. The thought of Anne having visited Kent Hall disturbed him. The fact that she'd been forced to live in the cold, ugly old mansion appalled him. He kept his voice mild as he said, "I remember Kent Hall from when I was a boy." He was looking directly at Anne. "I remember being extremely uncomfortable there. Don't tell me that's where Kentwell took you as a bride."

Anne's luminous eyes seemed to grow to fill her face. Remembered pain was so plain in them that John cursed himself for every kind of a clumsy fool.

Athelstain broke the moment. "Yes, he did. Stuck her out there in the middle of nowhere in that nasty old house with not a soul but the servants to keep her company. Bad show I called it then, and bad show I still call it." He lifted his wineglass to drive home the point.

Sir John just kept staring at Anne. She must have been a mere child then. He'd heard his cousin had robbed a bride from the schoolroom. He'd felt sorry for the unknown girl then; he felt savage now to know it'd been Anne.

Hell and damnation! Kent Hall hadn't been fit to live in!

Anger toward his dead cousin grew in him as he looked at her. Too bad the bastard was safely dead.

Anne was still facing him. She knew she should pay attention to her other guests, but she seemed unable to tear her gaze from Sir John's. She saw blazing anger replace the shocked pity in his eyes and found she much preferred it.

She didn't want anyone to pity her. She'd endured, and in her own way, triumphed. Having found it impossible either to interest or to love her husband, she'd turned the soul-sapping energy of her sorrow into positive works. She'd achieved a victory over the gloom and discomfort of the house her husband had made her prison.

She wanted to remember that . . . not her defeats.

Proudly she lifted her chin at Sir John. She dared him to pity her, dared him to belittle her achievements at Kent Hall. They had kept her sane.

Sir John's eyes glinted as if he understood her challenge. *My God, if she can do that to Kent Hall, she can work miracles!* New respect for her was born in him.

Deliberately he moved forward and took her hand from where it was fisted at her side. Turning it palm up, he forced it open and looked long at the little crescents her nails had dug into it. A glance at where Lois kept the others' attention, and he placed a lingering kiss in the palm of her hand.

An electric moment passed between them, as his gaze held her own, unblinking, praising. Then he lifted his wineglass. "To the extraordinary woman who found it within herself to make Kent Hall a pleasant home."

"Hear, hear!" Lord Robert tore his attention from his wife and Lois and jumped to his feet. "I'll certainly drink to that. One of the nicest places I've ever visited, Kent Hall. Becky assures me it's the same with her." He beamed in Anne's direction. "To Anne, our talented friend." He quaffed the rest of his port in her honor.

Finally, Anne could look away from Sir John.

Becky laughed. "Well said." Her eyes were bright with what she'd seen pass between the handsome Sir John and her dearest friend.

John kept his gaze on Anne. He'd seen the shadow of past sorrows in her eyes. He thought with cold fury, *I bloody well hope you're toasting nicely in hell, my cousin.*

Then, with genuine interest, he asked, "What are your plans for Castle Caldon, Lady Anne?"

"I suppose you would be interested. It is your castle, after all."

"Consider it your own, Lady Anne." His voice held a hint of amusement. Acceding to her wishes in the matter of the renovations was the only sensible course open to him. He'd come to realize that trying to turn Anne from her plans would probably be like trying to turn a cavalry charge of greatly superior numbers.

Anne looked at him sharply. "Are you saying you don't mind my cutting windows in the walls of your fortress, Sir John?"

Soldier he might be, but Sir John didn't care what she did with Castle Caldon. He'd been garrisoned in too many freezing stone piles to have any affection for this one, his or not. He saw an opportunity to get her alone, however, and the idea appealed strongly to him. He hadn't forgotten the kiss he wanted. "How can I know, milady, when I am completely in the dark about them?" He gave her his most winning smile. "Suppose you tell me about your plans." He set his wineglass on the mantelpiece and came away from where he'd leaned there. Offering her his arm with a bow, he said, "Or, better yet, show me?"

Anne looked up at him and saw the mocking lift of his

eyebrow. Accepting his challenge, she slipped her hand through his arm. "Won't the rest of you join us?"

"No, thank you!" Lois and Lady Becky chorused, then laughed.

"No, indeed." Robert settled himself more comfortably in the tapestry-covered wing chair he occupied and strengthened his refusal by holding his glass out to Higgins for refilling. "I've had quite enough of your drafty castle for one day, m'dear."

Sir John was pleased. His plan for another walk alone with Anne was succeeding.

The cold draft that had followed him from the great hall was also pleased. As Lady Anne left the room on Sir John's arm, Lord Jared St. Legere was close behind.

Chapter
Sixteen

Higgins, his face stern with disapproval, maneuvered adroitly to intercept Lady Anne and Sir John at the door of the drawing room. His tall frame blocked their exit without seeming to do so. He'd seen that gleam in the Captain's eye!

"Would you like me to accompany you with a branch of candles to light your way, milady?"

Sir John answered him, "A candelabrum is an excellent suggestion, Higgins, but I think I can manage to carry it. We'd hate to take you from Mrs. Carswell and Lady Anne's guests."

The amusement in his voice didn't escape Anne's notice. Neither did the bad grace and sour expression with which Higgins handed Sir John a five-branched candelabrum.

Higgins gave the Captain the heaviest that came readily to hand. He hoped the hideous thing would tire the young officer's arm quickly. That way he and Lady Anne would return to the drawing room sooner.

"Thank you, Higgins," Anne told her old friend. She was careful to speak with grave courtesy.

Higgins stepped away from the door with a "Very good, Your Ladyship," from which they could have chipped ice.

Out in the wide passageway, Anne drew her Kashmir shawl more closely up around her shoulders, shivering slightly. Behind her, Jared St. Legere, disgusted as usual by the odd cold he seemed destined to trail around with him, dropped back several yards.

"I hope to replace most of the wall along here with windows"—Anne gestured gracefully—"to let light in and to give us a view of the Channel over the road along the shore. It'll be the same view you get from the overlook you passed on your way up the drive."

"Hmmm."

"There will, of course, be sturdy support columns between the windows."

"I'm glad to hear it." He looked at her seriously. "You'll have to watch you don't collapse any walls, Lady Anne. Remember, this is an ancient fortress. Not only are its stone walls of immense weight, but you can't know by looking at them how or where they may have been weakened by the siege machinery of past centuries."

Anne was thoughtful. "Yes. Yes, of course. I hadn't thought of the injury that might have been done the walls by catapults and such. Thank you for reminding me."

"Not at all." He lifted the massive candelabrum, ignoring the twinge its weight caused an old wound in his shoulder. "Hmmmm. Certainly these walls look sturdy enough to stand forever." He turned to grin down at her. "Unless, of course, you tear them down." He wanted to see her smile again. Beautiful when grave, she was utterly enchanting when she smiled.

Anne obliged. "I've employed an engineer to investigate the walls so that I don't bring them tumbling down on us with my renovations. He should be here from London any day now."

"And he's good?"

"He's reputed to be the very best man about such things. As soon as he's determined the state of the walls, I'll make all of us thoroughly miserable with the din and clatter of my workmen."

John heard the note of excitement in her voice. Obviously she enjoyed her renovations.

"I imagine that Castle Caldon has had more than its share of din and clatter, milady. I doubt that there's much one lone gentlewoman can do it."

Anne looked up at him, all interest. "You sound as if you know something of the castle's history."

"Yes. I made it my business to learn all I could when I was told I'd inherited it."

Jared St. Legere's interest was caught by the officer's comment. Could it be possible this young warrior knew something of the castle's history that might include his own story?

Eagerly, he came nearer the couple. The chill of his presence swirled around them. *"He knows my story?"* Then he scowled. *"Knows what history tells, more like. Damn the man!"*

Anne shrugged deeper into her shawl. She hadn't missed the note of reluctance she'd just heard in Sir John's voice. "Tell me what you know of Castle Caldon."

Sir John frowned. "It has a bloody history, Lady Anne. One you might be more comfortable not knowing."

Anne gave him a level look.

Sir John stared at her a long moment. A grin grew slowly on his sensual mouth. "No, by God," he murmured as if to himself, "you're a brave one, aren't you?"

Shaking his head in wonder, he began the story. "The castle was built by a Knight named Caldon. It withstood two sieges under his rule. Then he was murdered for it, and a French family—the Des Jardins, if I remember correctly—held it for a number of generations until it was bought from them by old Jasper Halperin fifty or so years ago." His voice sharpened with irritation. "Your husband won it from the doddering old wreck in a card game." In spite of himself, his voice showed what he thought of men who gambled with ancients.

Though she agreed with him, Anne pretended not to notice.

"Just the usual sort of thing for a castle—attacks and a siege or two—up until the eighteenth century."

"What the devil are you going to tell her? Why the bloody hell can't you keep your mouth shut?"

John looked over at Anne as if to determine whether or not to continue.

Anne waited.

"In the early 1700's something happened that led to the present legend that the castle is haunted."

"Haunted?" Anne stopped walking and turned a startled face to him. She hid the shiver that went through her as she remembered the other night when she'd felt there was someone in her room. Common sense came to her aid. Disturbed or not the other night, she knew there were no such things as ghosts. "Surely you're not serious."

"Oh, yes he is." Jared circled them restlessly.

John grinned down at her. "I'm only relating what's been told me, Lady Anne."

Anne's heart skipped a beat. There was such a reckless-ness in his grin.

The grin disappeared, and Sir John's expression sobered. "Then in the early 1700's an obscene act took place here in the great hall." He paused as if he again debated whether to continue.

Around them, the cold sighed softly and twisted closer. Jared growled, *"Just how will you tell it, my handsome young Dragoon?"*

"Please." A sudden premonition made Anne breathless. She could feel the strength of his arm under her hand and was comforted by it.

Sir John scowled. "A condemned traitor to the Crown came here then. Some said to find a document that would prove his innocence. He galloped straight to the door, rid-ing like a madman."

Sir John's eyes looked to Anne as if they were actually seeing the scene he described. His mouth was a grim line.

"Leaping from his horse, he burst into the great hall. The door had been carefully left unlocked for him . . . and he walked straight into an ambush."

Anne couldn't look away.

"The noblemen of the castle had ten men with pikes waiting for the rider. With only a sword and a single shot in his pistol, he fought them." His brows drew down in a fierce frown. "It's said that he did for a number of them be-fore he was weakened by loss of blood." His voice became tight. "Weakened by wounds safely inflicted from behind the advantageous length of their pikes."

Sir John's narrowed eyes clouded. He was seeing a valiant man unfairly fought to a standstill by sheer weight of numbers.

Anne's heart was paining her. She pressed her hands to her chest and waited for him to go on.

"The heroes of the tale," John's voice was hotly scathing, "waited until his wounds had brought him to the point of staggering. Then they called their dogs off and the six of them took on the dying man. They cut him down to lie in his blood here in the great hall . . . to the glory of the Crown." His voice broke under its burden of scorn.

"An ally, by God. This man's an ally." Jared nearly wept with savage joy. He could feel strength rising in him beyond anything he'd felt in the entire time he'd been dead.

Wind from nowhere steadily rose in the hall.

Neither Anne nor John moved or spoke. It was as if they were suspended in time, incapable of doing either.

The cold intensified and broke around them like waves smashing against rocks.

Anne had never felt cold like it. It slashed to the very depths of her being and crept outward after freezing her very soul. She began to shiver under the intensity of it.

Sir John seemed unaffected by the sudden drop in temperature Anne was experiencing. He was still lost in the scene so graphically played in his mind. When he saw her shuddering, he cried, "I've been a brute. Blast me! I've overset you."

Anne shook her head violently. "No. No. I wanted to hear." She strived to reassure him. "It's just that I'm too lightly clad for tales of old horror told in drafty corridors at midnight." She tried to laugh, wanting to put him at ease.

"Give her your coat! Let her feel the warmth of your body lingering in it. Enfold her with the scent of you. Don't just stand there. Do something to snare the wench!"

Anne was puzzled. Surely she had heard . . .

John shook his head as if to clear it. Something seemed to brush the outer limits of his mind. "You're cold. May I offer you my coat?" He flushed slightly and added, "That is, if you don't mind my removing it."

Anne felt shaken loose from the present by the Captain's story. "Could you?" She hadn't meant to refer to the fact that most gentlemen couldn't get out of their coats without assistance. It was just that she wasn't paying attention to anything she said.

Neither was John. Like Anne, he was waiting for something. Waiting with his senses stretched to the breaking point for something they both knew was coming. His mind wasn't on what he was saying, either. It was just important to speak, to hold something at bay. Something that . . . "Soldiers like their coats a little less fitted. It's no fun being helped out of a tight jacket when you've got a shoulder wound, I assure you." His eyes constantly searched the shadows around them.

Anne felt her heart flutter strangely. Suddenly she realized that she hated the thought of him shot . . . nor could she stand not knowing whether he had been. "Do you speak from experience?"

"No, milady." His voice was quiet, his attitude inattentive. "I had them cut my coat away."

"Get on with wooing her, damn you!"

John stopped walking and stood looking at her, stunned. He'd just told a lady about a wound to his body. Bloody hell! He knew better than that. Not even his own mother knew where his wounds were!

Anne was still struggling to come to grips with the story Sir John had just told of the man who had died here in the great hall. That man might have been her own great-grandfather. When Sir John failed to speak, she said, "I'm sorry. That was not polite of me."

"Quite all right." He cleared his throat. "I must apologize . . ."

"No . . . " She felt as if the word had been torn from her by the mounting pressure in the corridor.

Silence hung between them for a long moment, full and heavy, and accusing to them both. With half their minds, they wondered what had come over them. With the other halves they probed the frigid shadows.

Anne denied she was afraid, yet her hands were shaking.

John knew he was as keyed up as he'd ever been for any battle. Against this vague, hostile force, would he be able to defend her? All his attention focused on the empty air around them.

The cold surrounded them on every side, pressing close, and the shadows of the hall seemed to shift and move in the candlelight. There was a third entity in the passageway. Sir John could sense its presence as surely as if it had ridden in on a horse.

He turned to see if Anne were aware of whatever had raised his hackles.

Her gaze locked with his super-alert one. It was obvious that Sir John was experiencing the same odd disorientation she felt, she could see it in his eyes. What in heaven's name was happening? It was as if they occupied a place where all the rules were somehow suspended. It was as if the odd cold that enveloped them had seeped into their minds and rendered them useless. They were left only their emotions with which to respond to each other.

Anne began to shiver uncontrollably. She'd never felt so helpless, so vulnerable. It was as if the cold air in the hall had stripped her of her every long-practiced defense.

Sir John slammed the candelabrum down on an ancient chest so fast that his haste extinguished two of the five candles. He was overwhelmed with the strong awareness that he had to keep her safe. "My God, Anne, what is this?" He ripped off his coat and flung it around her.

"Ahhh. Finally."

She stood with John's coat, warm from his body, around

her. His saber-calloused hands held it closed under her chin, comforting her. She breathed the faint scents of sandalwood and evergreen that came from his coat and clenched her teeth to keep them from chattering.

John moaned deep in his throat and reached out for her.

When he drew her into his arms, Anne went willingly; she rested trustingly against him, her cheek against the firm-muscled wall of his chest.

He was warm and solid under the fine linen of his shirt. His body was the strong body of a warrior, a protector. She listened to the steady rhythm of his heart. She couldn't fight the strange force that urged her into his arms.

Sir John held her gently. He cradled her close against him and breathed deeply of the rose and jasmine scent that had eluded him out on the meadow. Its tantalizing sweetness filled his senses, dizzying him.

His lighthearted plan to steal the kiss he'd wanted was forgotten. Stronger emotions gripped him. Smoothing his hands down her back in an unconscious gesture of comfort, he marveled at the fierceness of his desire to keep her safe.

He pressed his lips to her hair, but it wasn't enough. Unable to resist, he put his fingers under her chin to tilt her face up so that he could kiss away her tears.

"Yes! Yes! Kiss her!" Jared fought to hold in check the power that began to surge through him. This wasn't the time to let it begin altering things in the space around him.

As John's fingers touched her face, he saw the flames of the three candles that remained burning . . . slowly . . . as if they were being drawn down by an unseen hand into the wax of their tips until they could be seen no more . . . disappear!

With a frightened cry at this creeping onset of stygian darkness, Anne threw her arms around Sir John's neck and buried her face against the strong column of his neck.

From nowhere, a wind screamed in the hallway.

Even as his hair rose on the back of his neck at what he'd seen happen to the flames of the candles, desire for this woman he held so desperately in his arms rose in his body.

"Damn!"

"God be praised! That's right. Hold her. Kiss her." He turned to face in the direction of London. *"Bethany!"* he shouted across the miles to his beloved wife. *"Together! They're together! We've won. We've won!"*

He lost all control then, and the frigid winds of his presence gathered force and howled through the corridor like a hurricane. The candelabrum was swept from the chest by its fury, and he could hear the candles rattling away down the hall before the strength of the wind.

"Blast. I mustn't let this damned wind blow the two of them away!"

Sir John chose that moment to lower his head and claim Anne's mouth with his own.

Chapter
Seventeen

In the ugly cavern that was supposed to be a drawing room, Lois Carswell looked across at Higgins. He, too, seemed uneasy about the continued absence of Sir John and Lady Anne.

"Higgins, where do you suppose they've gone?"

"I've been looking for them to return for the last ten minutes. Both of them have a fine sense of what's proper, and Anne has been away from her guests too long."

Lois sighed. "So you're uneasy, too."

"Distinctly."

Lois frowned in concentration. "You're the best one to go look for them. Besides"—she shuddered delicately—"I'm afraid to go out there alone."

"I'm relieved that you can feel it, too, Lois." Higgins pulled out a stark white handkerchief and mopped his perfectly dry forehead in a nervous gesture.

Lois was determined to be cautious. "Feel . . . what?"

Higgins's impatience with her little display of mistrust showed plainly on his face. "The odd feeling this bloody castle has. The way you *know* there's someone just behind you, but when you whip around to catch them, there's nobody there! The way the shadows stir when there are no candles flickering to make 'em." He scowled at her. "You can't mean to stand there and tell me you aren't aware of it, because I've seen you glance back over your shoulder more than once!"

Lois threw a glance over her shoulder then, but the Athelstains seemed engrossed in their chess game. "All right. That *is* why I'm afraid to go look for them. But I'll come with you if you want me to."

Higgins registered the magnanimity of her offer and smiled. "No. One of us should stay. I'll go." He turned to pick up and light a lovely four-branched candelabrum from the table near the door. "Just pray Anne has no plans to renovate the wine cellar. I'd rather take a flogging than go down in that blasted wine cellar!"

Lois's face was full of sympathy and admiration as Higgins straightened his shoulders, tugged at the bottom of his vest, and moved majestically through the open door.

In utter amazement, she heard herself cry, "Wait! I'm coming with you!"

Shouting over the howling of the wind, Sir John ordered, "Stay behind me!" He'd carried Anne, shaking as if she would come apart, to the wall, and put her down with her back pressed against it. He stood close against her with his own hard back a scant inch from her. He spread his arms wide, feeling as if he were inviting someone to disembowel him, and jammed his palms back and flat against the wall. Nothing would get to her while he lived to protect her.

Anne slipped both arms around his waist, clasping him as tightly as she could. If she could have done so, she thought crazily, she'd have become a permanent part of him at just that moment.

Wind, cold and furious, tore around them. Anne could feel her hair whipping free of its constraints and flying over Sir John's shoulders to lash at his face. She cringed and buried her face in his shirt. Her blood ran cold in her veins with fear. She thought she heard sounds in the wind like the sound of a human voice! Wildly, she feared for her sanity.

Terrified, she let go of her protector's waist with one hand. She needed it to cover the ear that wasn't pressed hard into the firm muscles of his back. She clutched all the harder with the one still holding her body frantically to him.

She felt his chest heave as he drew breath. Then he shouted, "Get away, you bloody fool!" Anne could feel the outrage spilling from him. "You're frightening her!"

His voice, the voice he'd used to be heard above the roar of cannon, filled the section of the passageway in which they stood and reverberated off the stone walls.

The fury of the wind increased to blot it out. It shrieked and howled around them. It tore at John's lean body, shaking him. It was as if it wanted to blow him apart.

Then it weakened suddenly and died.

The resulting silence was deafening.

Anne heard a little whimpering sound. It was she! She stopped it instantly. With a great effort, she forced her arm to let go of the Captain's waist. She blushed as she realized—the wind having all but blown his shirt off—that her hand had been pressed hard against the bare skin of his flat, firm stomach.

He spun around as soon as she freed him and grasped her by the shoulders, yanking her to him. "Are you all right?"

"Yes." It was a tremulous whisper.

He cursed himself that he'd been unable to stop whatever had just happened here. God! If only the assault on them had been something that he might have fought to keep from her!

His hands felt down her arms and across her back, then he gently touched her face. "Damn this blasted darkness!"

His breath fanned her cheek. She could see nothing in the blackness, but she felt the touch of his thumbs as he brushed the tears from her cheeks, the gentle clasp of his hands as he cradled her face.

She sensed his mouth close to her own. Very close. His firm lips were only a breath away.

Then they were on hers, and she forgot everything but the sweet sensation of his gentle kiss.

Lifting his head, he kept his mouth only an inch from her soft lips. He was powerless to increase the distance. His mouth hovered just over hers. The sweet scent of her breath filled his nostrils. A wild desire to kiss her again surged through him. He wanted to kiss her until she could no longer think—no longer remember the violent windstorm and the frigid cold that had shaken them both to their very foundations.

He wanted to kiss her until he'd satisfied his burning hunger to taste her . . . if it could ever *be* satisfied!

He had to lean down only a fraction of an inch . . .

"Anne!" Lois's cry echoed through the darkness. "Lady Anne, Captain Sir John, where are you?"

Cursing his foul luck under his breath, he pushed away from the wall to which his body had pinned Anne. "Here!" he sang out in his parade ground voice. "We're here!"

Anne's thoughts were in turmoil. So this was what it was like to be kissed by a man. Never had she felt like this. Her blood ran singing in her veins. How she wished it could go on a little longer. But rescue had arrived.

Her hands flew to her wind-disheveled hair, her fingers trembling as she tried to tuck it back into order. "Oh." She strove for something sensible to say. "Thank Heaven! They're bringing lights." Her voice was as breathless now from his kisses as it had been moments before from sheer terror.

Softly he asked her, "Are you all right? Can you stand alone?" He held her gently by the shoulders.

Then she realized that she was still leaning into Sir John's embrace, her body melting against his. She'd been braced against his long, lean length! Now she was torn between the desire to stay as she was and the urge to jump back from him before they could be seen. Her body throbbing with a poignant intensity of feeling everywhere it touched his, she moved away. "Of course."

Great Heaven! She'd been pressed against him as trustingly as a kitten curled against a mother cat. She didn't even want to think of the way she'd returned his kisses.

She stood as straight as she could, her eyes fixed on the glow from the candelabrum her butler carried, and felt her cheeks flaming with embarrassment. For the first time this evening, she was thankful for the dark.

He felt Anne straighten her shoulders and dropped his hands away from them. His hands felt empty. Turning to face the dawning glow of the candles her butler was carrying toward them, he pushed one long-fingered hand through his own wind-whipped curls, smoothed his tear-soaked cravat, and offered Anne his arm.

She placed fingers that still shook slightly upon it, and he covered her hand comfortingly with his own steady, sun-bronzed one. Together they walked toward the light.

The nearer they got, the more Anne's body sought to betray her. By the time she could see Lois's face, she was shaking again, badly.

Leading her up to her companion, Sir John told Lois, "She's had an unpleasant experience, Miss Carswell. She's chilled to the bone. I suggest hot tea and bed." Feeling his hostess's hand quiver beneath his own, he added very quietly, "And I think it would be in her best interest if you spent the night in her room."

Lois opened her mouth to say something bracing. She took a second look at her employer's face and the words died in her throat. Anne looked as if she'd seen a ghost. Her luminous eyes, deeply lavender with emotion, filled a face pale and drawn with fright. Now and again her slender frame shook.

"Lois," Anne managed between shudders, "I'm perfectly fine. D-don't fuss." To her own disgust, Anne could hear her teeth chattering. She couldn't explain what was happening to her, though. She couldn't tell Lois that she was being torn apart by the idea that the ghost of her own great-grandfather was the force that had attacked them. She couldn't!

Lois was appalled. She drew her woolly shawl from her shoulders and flung it around her friend. Even over the gentleman's coat, it was long and wide enough to envelop Anne to her knees.

"Higgins, give me the candelabrum and go ahead and command water for a hot bath," Sir John ordered.

"An excellent suggestion." Lois threw him a grateful look from where she walked on Anne's other side holding her shawl tightly around her friend.

Together they made their way in silence toward the east wing. Anne was still too stunned by all that had happened, Lois too concerned, and the Captain too deep in perplexing thought.

Chapter Eighteen

"What happened last night, Sir John?"

Sir John stopped tying his cravat and met his man's grave regard seriously. "I'm not precisely certain, Danvers." A frown appeared as he considered his next words.

Danvers waited. The Captain never left questions unanswered. It was his nature to solve puzzles, not to endure them.

Finally he said, "It would appear that Lady Anne and I were the victims of some sort of windstorm in the corridor that leads from the east wing to the great hall."

Danvers saw that his employer's eyes were slate blue, a sure sign that he was troubled. Evidently Sir John wasn't really satisfied with the explanations his mind offered him for the occurrences of the night before.

Danvers prompted gently, "What happened, sir?"

The Captain told him all that had happened to Lady

Anne and him—except, of course, for the marvelously sweet kisses and the sensations that had shaken him—in his customary straightforward manner. He ended his recital with a wry, "So you see, either we have drafts in this place that are strong enough to sail ships of the line, or . . . "—he struggled to bring himself to say it—"this castle is bloody well haunted."

"Haunted, sir?" Somehow, Danvers wasn't as skeptical as he'd always thought he'd be about ghosts. It had a lot to do with the feelings he frequently had that he wasn't alone, that some—thing, he'd have to say for want of a better word—was watching him every now and again as he went about his daily tasks. It was a feeling he'd been unable to shrug off, and an old soldier got to *be* an soldier because he never ignored his instincts. Danvers was an old soldier.

"I know it sounds absurd, Danvers." Sir John spun away from the mirror and paced the room, the ends of his cravat hanging free. "Hell and damnation! It *is* absurd!" He was almost shouting with frustration. He scowled from beneath brows drawn fiercely down. "It was late. We were tired. Some servant slipping out of the castle opened a door somewhere and the draft was magnified by the width of the passageways in this damned fortress."

He stopped pacing and fixed Danvers with a piercing glance. "Yes." He forced himself to accept it. "That's it. These damn passageways were made extra-wide so that large groups of armed men could be moved around the castle double-time. So why the hell couldn't they have ten times the draft?" His eyes were solemn, their blue the almost-gray of a troubled sea. "It was an exceptionally strong draft that frightened Lady Anne last night." He made a decision and his eyes took on a color closer to their natural clear, bright blue. "Hell!" He looked at Danvers and laughed. "It didn't miss scaring the devil out of me by much, either."

He blew out his breath in an explosive sigh. "Yes." He decided it was plausible enough until he could search out the truth behind what had happened. "That's the story. I shall go and tell her so at once. It'll put her mind at ease." He headed for the door in long sure strides.

"Sir John!"

The Captain stopped abruptly and turned back halfway, his face impatient.

The looks they exchanged told plainly that they both understood the need for the Captain's lie.

Danvers spoke on another subject entirely, though. "Perhaps, before you go to find the Marchioness, you should finish tying your cravat."

Anne sat in her bed with her knees drawn up, hugging her arms around them. A cup of gently steaming chocolate was clasped in her hands, as if by holding it she sought to warm them.

"Drink your chocolate, Anne. It's going to get cold." Lois tried to keep any anxiety out of her voice, but she was still distinctly worried about her friend.

Sleeping, as the Captain had suggested, beside her, Lois had felt every movement, heard every murmur from Anne. And there had been far too many of both.

The poor child had spent a dreadful night. Tossing and turning, she'd talked in her sleep almost the whole night through. Now her eyes looked haunted, and there were dark smudges under them that told the tale of a lack of rest.

Still Lady Anne warmed her hands. She'd learned that when she removed them from the cup her fingers trembled.

"Anne?"

She felt as if she were coming back from far away.

"Wha . . . ? I *am* being an awful woolgatherer this morning, aren't I?" She sipped some of her chocolate. How could she help being? Even as she apologized for it, she returned to thinking of the startling events of the previous night. Could what she was thinking about the man who'd been murdered here in the great hall of Castle Caldon be true? After the voice that had haunted her dreams, urging, demanding, granting her no moment of rest as it insisted . . .

There was a quick, purposeful knock at the door. The two women looked at each other, startled.

"It must be Higgins." Lois started across the room to the door.

"That wasn't Higgins's knock, Lois."

"Well, we shall soon see." As she finished her statement, she flung open the door.

Framed against the relative darkness of the hall, Captain Sir John stood almost at attention. "Permission to . . . " He grinned and shook his head ruefully, beginning again. "Would it be possible to speak with Lady Anne, please, Miss Carswell?"

When Lois hesitated—after all, her employer was hardly dressed to receive gentlemen—the Captain explained further.

"I think I've discovered a reason for what occurred last night to frighten the Marchioness," he said in a low voice.

Lois stepped back instantly. Sir John entered the room in a single long stride, then stopped as if he'd run into an enemy's lance.

Anne was sitting in the large bed, surrounded by a froth of white lace and fine lawn that was her multi-pleated nightrail and a sea of small decorative pillows that graced the bed for her comfort. Her dark hair was a sleep-tousled cloud hanging to her shoulders . . . and halfway down her back he knew, as he poignantly remembered last night.

As if he saw it again, he recalled her futile attempt to resecure her hair after the unexpected wind had pulled it loose. Vividly he recalled how she'd tried, with delicate, trembling fingers, to tuck it back into its prim chignon after the wind had set it free. Set it free to fly around his face . . . to caress his lips with its silk and leave behind the fragrance and faint taste of her clean, scented hair.

Her eyes were as wide as they'd been then, too, but thank God they weren't shadowed by the awful fear he'd seen in them last night. The fear that had shaken her as he'd walked her to her bedchamber door had changed the color of her eyes last night. Now that they were clear of their deep lavender shadow, he realized that he'd never seen a more beautiful shade of blue than the violet-tinged blue of Lady Anne's eyes.

Ten minutes later, having heard his softly voiced explanation of the strange occurrences in the hall the night before, Lois closed the door behind the Captain and turned back to Lady Anne. "Well? What do you think? Could his explanation be true, dear?"

Lois hoped with all her heart that her young friend would accept the Captain's solution of the mystery. Desperately she wanted them to remain here at Castle Caldon, whether or not it was haunted. She was appalled to find that she was actually more afraid that Anne would pack up and leave, interring herself at Kent Hall to escape life again, than she was that real harm might befall her.

There at Kent Hall, there'd be no handsome Captain of Dragoons with eyes that devoured her precious Anne in such a satisfactory way. Even more than her physical safety, Lois wished for Anne the experience of this dashing officer's devotion.

"Yes." Anne let the word linger on her lips, savoring the

taste of her deliberate lie even as she silently asked forgiveness for it. She knew that what Captain Sir John had offered was only an attempt to provide a rational explanation for the events of the preceding night. She knew as clearly as if he'd spoken his true thoughts aloud that he didn't really believe his very plausible explanation about drafts magnified by the huge tunnel-like passageways of Castle Caldon. *He* didn't believe it, but he wanted her to. He wanted her to with a desperation she'd easily read in his eyes.

He had such magnificient eyes, clear blue when all was well—as bright as the sky on a summer's day. Clouded, slate-tinged blue like a stormy sea when he was troubled or—she hugged her knees even harder to her chest as she remembered—when he was feeling protective . . . or passionate.

"Be careful, Anne! You almost spilled your chocolate."

Lois's peevish voice brought her back to the subject at hand. Anne, rudely torn from her pleasant musings about the Captain, gulped the rest of her now lukewarm chocolate in a most unladylike fashion and handed the empty cup to her friend. As she pushed the white satin comforter and lace-bordered sheet off and slid out of bed, her mind returned to him.

A blush stained her cheeks and warmth tingled through her as she remembered how he'd held her against him, protecting her from whatever force had assaulted them there in the dark. And there in the dark, she had shamelessly pressed her own body against his long, lean frame and let her senses swim with the feelings he'd aroused in her for that brief moment before fear overwhelmed them.

She was no stranger to the body of a man. She had been impregnated, after all, and knew how it was accomplished. Always before, however, the hardening of a man's body in arousal had signaled degradation and brought her revulsion. Last night, though, in those last brief moments before Lois had called out to them, something astonishing had happened.

Surely the feeling she'd experienced that had held in abeyance the fear threatening to overcome her had been one of longing? Surely it had been a yearning response in her to what she'd felt happening to the body of the man who'd stood embracing her. The man who'd stood defending and protecting her to the best to his ability . . . and possibly to his peril?

Remembering his kisses, and the flame his touch had called forth in her, she shivered once more. This time it was with delight.

She drew a deep steadying breath as those pleasurable feelings flooded her again. When she'd felt the response of his body to her own, she'd felt as if she . . .

Lois spoke sharply. "Anne, why in the world are you just standing there? If you don't get dressed, we shall be late for breakfast."

For the very first time, Anne wished her dear friend was anywhere but in her bedchamber.

Marie came smiling from the dressing room with a morning dress over her arm as if summoned by Lois's wish to get them down to breakfast. "It is unusual to hear a masculine voice in milady's boudoir, yes?"

"Yes." Anne laughed then, and was startled by the joyous sound of it. "Yes, Marie," she said more firmly, "it is." She looked with interest at what Marie had chosen for her to wear. Never particularly interested before, she now found clothes of supreme importance.

Marie noted the change in her mistress's usual behavior with relief. It was time—past time— that the lovely Lady Anne took more interest in her appearance. *"Oui.* That

Captain, he is quite a man, *non*? Ooh-la-la! Such shoulders. Such a smile."

Lois snapped, "Get on with it, girl." The very idea!

Anne quickly approved Marie's choice of clothing. She smiled, ignoring the fulminating glare Lois was giving Marie. Marie had only spoken the truth. The Captain was, indeed, quite a man. She could feel her heartbeat quickening at the remembrance of those broad shoulders Marie admired and the way the muscles in them had moved under her hands as she'd clung to him and he'd tightened his arms around her. She recalled his eyes and the way they'd looked at her as if he were going to . . .

Breathlessly she tore her mind from the Captain and returned it to the business of dressing. She'd wear her hair loose and tied back with the ribbon Marie had found to exactly match the color of her eyes.

Her lips parted softly as she remembered Sir John's face a few minutes ago. She hadn't missed the look on it as his eyes had lingered on her unbound hair. Anne yearned to see that look again. She felt an odd stirring in her chest at the thought of him.

She sighed, savoring each feeling she was experiencing. Never had she had such lovely sensations at the thought of a man. She hadn't known they were possible.

Shaking her head, she allowed Marie to dress her. Suddenly, she was eager to get down to her breakfast . . . and to the handsome Captain who made her heart behave so oddly.

Chapter
Nineteen

" . . . and the Marchioness was scared half to death, I can tell you. White as a sheet, she was, and shaking like a leaf. I doubt she'd a been able to walk if it hadna been for that handsome Captain half-carrying her."

"Shhhh." The woman's friend indicated the half-open door of the twins' bedchamber with a toss of her head. "Not where the children can hear you, Matty."

"Oh! Yes, you're right. You're right. Thoughtless that was. Do you expect they heard?"

"No, I guess not. Tell me more about the Captain."

"Weeelllll." She drew the word out, her eyes twinkling. "He was in his shirtsleeves, he was, with his coat around Her Ladyship, and let me tell you them shoulders of his don't need no padding, me dear. Broad and square, they are, and his chest muscled like he worked in the fields pitching hay." She explained earnestly, "I could see because his shirt linen is so fine. Maude, it was so fine it was like a lady's handkerchief. So fine it clung to him in front, like."

"Just like I'd like to, dearie!" Her friend poked her in the side, grinning.

"Oh, go on with you!" Matty shoved her back, and they moved out of earshot, giggling.

Behind them, standing in the doorway of their room, Brandon looked at Brian. "Something's happened to Mother!"

"We have to find her!" They ran for the room next door. Their mother's door slammed back against the wall as both young bodies hit it.

"Mon Dieu!" Marie threw things all over the room as her hands flew to her ears in startled reaction. "What is it that you do?" She shook a finger at them. "You have affrighted me half to my death. You do not run through doors like little ruffians. You are little lords!"

One glance told them their mother wasn't in the room. "Where is Mama?" they shouted in unison.

Marie scowled fiercely at the two of them and answered in a voice as loud as theirs, her arms rigid at her sides. "Your mama, she is at breakfast!"

As the boys tore out of the room, she started gathering up the things she'd dropped. *"Sacré bleu!* Me, I don' like nothing about this place. No, I *do* not."

The twins didn't hear her. They were halfway to the breakfast room before the disgruntled lady's maid had finished picking up what they'd caused her to drop.

In the breakfast room, the twins found Anne. "Mama!" they gasped in unison, one hanging, panting, from either side of the doorjamb.

"Boys, what is it?" Anne rose to go to them, concerned.

"We heard that something had happened to you last night!" Brandon gasped.

"Oh, my dears." Anne held out her arms to hug them. "I'm fine, as you can see."

Sir John entered the room just then, his short-cropped hair still damp from the bath he'd needed after his ride. He crossed to Anne as if there were no one else in the room. Lifting her hand, he kissed it tenderly, his gaze locked on her eyes. "Good morning."

Anne couldn't help it, she felt her lips part and her fingers tremble in his clasp.

John felt a wild elation tear through him. She was affected by his touch! He promised himself that soon he'd have her clinging to him again, but not in fear this time. His pulse quickened at the thought.

He steadied himself with his duty. "Boys," he ordered, turning reluctantly from Anne, "I'll expect you in the west meadow, mounted, one hour after you've finished here."

The twins' eyes grew wide with excitement. One hasty look at their mother to be sure that she really was all right, and they gave themselves over to the eager anticipation of the treat ahead. "Yessir!" they chorused.

Breakfast passed in a very boring fashion for the twins.

The Captain looked so long at their Mama that they became embarrassed for him, even if they did think he was top of the trees. They pushed aside their plates with one accord and asked to be excused.

"Certainly, dears."

Their mother's dreamy voice didn't even sound right to them. Thoroughly disgusted, Brandon signaled Brian with his eyes in the direction of the tower. Brian's slight nod of agreement was all they needed to take off again at a run.

When they reached the door at the foot of the tower

stairs, they stopped to catch their breaths. "Good . . . thing . . . George and Luther . . . slept late."

"Yes."

They swung the heavy door wide. Cold spilled down the stairwell at them.

"Why are we going to see him?"

Brandon looked at his brother as if he thought him too stupid to instruct. "We're gonna ask him if he scared our Mama."

"Oh." Brian squared his shoulders. "Yes, of course if that is why, we must certainly pay him a visit."

"Good fellow!" Brandon slapped his twin on the back. "Besides. We can hardly go looking for a ghost when George and Luther start getting up early. They aren't the sort to have the proper respect for a gentleman ghost."

"Quite. And besides, they'd tell."

"Yes, and that would spoil everything."

With firm tread they ascended the deeply worn stone steps of the tower.

The ghost was there. In the shadow of his presence, he was a vague, forbidding form, his features indistinct as he stood looking out across the water. There was a purpose about him that the twins hadn't noticed before.

When he didn't acknowledge them, Brandon cleared his throat. Brian added a discreet cough behind his free hand.

"Aye, lads. I see you." Slowly the ghost took firmer shape, and as he became more and more human-looking, and definitely much less ghostlike, the boys relaxed a bit.

Jared noted the tenseness in Brian's shoulders and the purpose on Brandon's face. *"Yes."* He decided to put them out of their misery by disposing of the subject at once. *"I fear I did frighten your mother rather badly last night."*

The boys' faces became identical angry masks.

Jared raised a hand. *"Not on purpose. Certainly not on*

purpose. A gentleman does not distress a lady, even when he's dead."

"Then what happened?" Brandon demanded. "The maids said Mama was scared half to death."

"It was an accident brought about by your friend Sir John's knowledge of the history of this castle. Your Captain told the story of my murder here with a sympathy I never expected to hear, and then . . . " He could hardly tell them that he'd lost control of his powers at how pleased he was that Sir John had kissed their mother. *"Then, I . . . forgot myself."*

His proud face looked just the faintest bit apologetic. *"It was not my intention to frighten your lady mother."*

The boys looked as if they were reserving judgment until they'd heard more.

Having suffered a century deprived of human company, St. Legere was willing to comply with their unspoken demand for more information. *"Did your mother tell you what happened here in the great hall? No? Then permit me to tell you my story.*

"It's a rather complicated tale, and one that is, perhaps, not for the ears of children." He saw Brandon stiffen and added, *"But I shall tell it if you wish."*

Brandon said firmly, "We wish."

"Very well. Be it on your own heads if you have nightmares."

The boys nodded, accepting the condition.

"Long ago there was a very great fool named Jared St. Legere, who wanted to be a powerful man."

Brian was staring raptly at the storyteller. It was as if he were being told a fairy tale.

Brandon watched with narrowed eyes, certain that the tale was to take a dire turn.

"In his zeal to serve his King, St. Legere uncovered a plot against the Crown."

Both boys were wide-eyed now.

"St. Legere was an arrogant fool. Despite the wise counsel of his dear, intelligent wife, he accused the plotters, but, more fool he, he did it privately, for the sake of their families. He demanded that they leave England, never to return. He swore he would expose them in court the very next day if they didn't comply."

The boys nodded their approval of his plan.

"The next day at court the six traitors informed the King that they had information about a plot against him . . . by His Lordship Jared St. Legere, Fifth Earl of Mannerly."

The twins gasped in shock.

"Jared St. Legere alone!"

"What rotters!" Brandon burst out.

"How could they behave so dishonorably!" Brian gasped.

The ghost of the Fifth Earl of Mannerly smiled cynically. *"That traitors are never honorable men was something that St. Legere learned to his sorrow."* A moment passed, then he said quietly, *"It was just as his beloved Countess had warned."*

"What happened?" the twins asked in one voice.

The ghost shrugged and floated off the chair he'd seemed to occupy. Moving to his customary arrow slit, he leaned there in the embrasure and stroked his chin. The light from outside made his long fingers transparent.

Brian slipped closer to Brandon.

After a minute, the ghost went on with his story. *"St. Legere was arrested on the spot, of course, and thrown into the Tower of London."* His transparent fingers clenched into a fist.

"That's awful!" Brian's indignation brought a tight smile to the ghost's grim visage.

"In the Tower, one of the traitors, Henry Des Jardins— the owner of the castle on the coast to which the King was to have been lured to his death—came to visit the prisoner."

"Did he come to help him?" Brandon couldn't contain his excitement. Brian straightened beside him. Both boys were eager to hear of a rescue.

"No. Not to help him." The ghost sighed wearily. *"Not to help, young gentlemen. Far from it. He came to taunt St. Legere. He told him that he'd received a letter from the leader of the traitors."*

"A letter?" The boys, with unsullied, youthful trust in the goodness of man, hoped against hope.

The ghost nodded. *"A letter that contained the details of the plot against the King and the stated intention to make it look as if I, Jared St. Legere, were its instigator and sole perpetrator. Further, Des Jardins told me that the letter would easily clear my name, and for a moment . . . for one sweet, blessed moment . . . I dared to hope."* The ghost's voice grated now, as if his next words choked him. *"Then, as he left, Des Jardins smiled from the safety of the other side of the bars and told me that unfortunately he'd decided it would be wiser to keep the letter to safeguard himself against possible betrayal by the mastermind of the plot at some later date."*

"How dreadful," Brian breathed.

"How dishonorable!" Brandon asserted.

Both boys were quiet. There was no doubt in their minds that they were in the presence of a terribly wronged man. When he didn't speak for longer than they could bear, Brandon whispered, "So then what happened, sir?"

The ghost drew himself up to full height, and cool air

began to stir in the tower room. His face stark with memory, he told them, forgetting to speak impersonally, *"Then I escaped. By bribery and brutality I won free of the bloody Tower of London. Stealing a fast horse, I made for the coast."*

"Were you running away?" Brian asked the question as if he didn't believe he could possibly get an affirmative answer.

"No. I was running to the castle on the coast to wrest from the treacherous Henry Des Jardins the letter that would prove my innocence and clear my family name of the stain of treason.

"But life is never as simple as it seems." He leaned forward, speaking carefully to the children. His eyes bored into first one and then the other. He willed them to learn so that they would never have to experience betrayal for themselves. *"The people who'd helped me to escape were not my friends, as I had supposed, but my direst enemies."*

There was a startled gasp from the twins.

The ghost of St. Legere nodded. *"Yes. It was all a plot. A magnificent plot, if you will. With me dead, my honor gone, there would be no one to raise the question of anyone else's involvement in the plot against the King."* He lifted an eyebrow at them, his smile a bitter twist. *"Do you see the beauty of it?"*

"Nooo!" Brian cried out his protest. "There wasn't anything beautiful about it. It was horrible and ugly."

Brandon drew him down again and told him quietly, "Brian, be still." Then to the ghost, "Yes." His voice took on a cynical tone far beyond his years. "I see. I see the *beauty* of it."

"Yes." St. Legere's eyes glittered with appreciation. *"I believe you do."* He smiled a tight cold smile, made as if to

clasp the young Marquess's shoulder but withdrew his ghostly hand. *"To go on with the story. I rode here . . . "*

"Here? This very castle?" Brian's voice was full of awe, but Brandon merely nodded.

The tall, vague figure continued as if the younger twin had never spoken. *" . . . as fast as the horse could be pushed. Maddened with righteous anger, I threw myself against the front door."*

He was silent, remembering.

Brian started to speak, but Brandon silenced him with a gesture.

"They'd left it open. Sixteen men waited in the great hall."

"Sixteen," Brian said the number in a whisper full of wonder.

Brandon grated out, "Dastards! You never had a chance!"

"No."

"Did they kill you?" Brian wanted to know.

St. Legere smiled, and the cold that followed him everywhere intensified and filled the room with a frigidity that set the boys' teeth to chattering. *"Yes,"* he told them quietly. *"They murdered me here in the great hall. It's the remembrance of that foul deed that renders the hall so chill, even now."*

"And you never found the letter." Brandon made it a statement, his tone infinitely sad.

"No. And I have searched for it through almost a century."

Brandon peered at him intently. "Can you move things?"

"No."

"Then it might be here, still. In a chest or in a drawer that you've been unable to open."

"Surely, if it were in so obvious a place, someone would have found it by now. And they have not."

"How do you know?" Brian queried.

"Because I keep watch over this castle. Nothing occurs here that I do not know. Of that you may rest assured."

The boys sat and looked at the ghost. There was nothing they could say, nothing they could offer. Except their friendship.

Just then, the mellow bong of the newly repaired clock in the southwest tower sounded the half hour. Both boys got to their feet. "We must go, sir."

The ghost stood silent, light beginning to show through his figure.

"May we come again soon, sir?" Brandon was spokesman. "We should like to visit you again."

"Come when you will." His voice lingered on the mist that was all that was left of his image.

Then it too trailed away, and St. Legere was gone.

Chapter Twenty

"Charge!" The Captain's shout rang out over the thud of galloping hooves. "That's it, men! Sabers forward! Charge!"

Four boys flew over the bright meadow, faces determined, lips drawn back from clenched teeth. They held their yard-long sticks pointed rigidly forward as they thundered down on their imaginary enemy. Leaning from their saddles they slashed off the heads of the straw dummies Danvers had constructed for them. With whoops of triumph, they decapitated them all.

"Well done!" Jared shouted from above them on the battlements.

The Captain smiled and sat enjoying the sight of the boys pushing their ponies close to pound one another on the back. After a moment, he shouted, "Attention!"

As the boys lined them up facing him, he assessed the

condition of the four ponies with a practiced eye. "That's it for now, men. Your mounts are tired. Be sure you cool them out thoroughly. We'll begin again after luncheon."

"Don't mollycoddle them, blast you, Kent. There's still plenty left in those ponies. There's been nothing interesting going on here at Castle Caldon for almost a century, and now you want to stop for lunch! Damn and blast!" He turned and slammed through the tower wall, grumbling.

Below in the meadow, Luther asked as the boys walked their ponies, "Do you do this every day?" He slashed the flower from a field daisy. Then he said slyly, "Your mother is very good to let you do such things."

"Mama doesn't—" Brian began.

"Mama doesn't mind us learning things from someone as thoroughly knowledgeable"—he borrowed those two impressive words from something Lois had said—"as Captain Sir John Kent," Brandon stated almost at the top of his lungs. He grimaced fiercely at his twin, his eyes full of menace.

"No," Brian agreed weakly, "Mama doesn't mind." Then a little more strongly, "Sir John is a very great hero, you know."

"Yes," George chimed in. "Papa and Mama told us so."

"Ad nauseam." Luther decided to show both his new Latin skills and his boredom with his parents' lecturing in one phrase.

The rest of the way to the barn, Luther, by unspoken common consent, was banned from their comradery.

The Captain and all four boys appeared at the table for luncheon clean-scrubbed and glowing with the touch of the sun. Anne looked at them curiously. There was no way she could miss the lingering excitement in the boys . . . or the way the sun had turned the Captain into a golden Greek god.

"What did you do to entertain your guests today, Brandon?" Her smile encouraged him.

"We went riding, Mama. With the Captain."

Luther blurted, "Oh, I say. It was a very great deal more than that!"

Brandon glared at Luther and signaled him to keep his mouth shut.

Captain Sir John offered mildly, "I showed the boys a bit about riding." He leaned easily back in his chair and smiled lazily—possessively—at Anne. "Just as you asked me to."

"Yes, of course." Anne spoke reluctantly, wondering if she were going to regret her request. She looked from one to the other of the boys. Every face was angelically innocent. Obviously, something was going on that they didn't want her to know.

Lady Rebecca told Sir John, "We hope our sons aren't a bother."

His smile was a crooked grin. "No worse than any other raw recruits, milady."

The boys seemed to swell with pride at being likened to raw Dragoon recruits.

Lord Robert laughed out loud.

Anne turned to the Captain. She ignored the invitation in his eyes to remember the day in the meadow when he'd shared his colonel's comment with her. Instead she asked, "You aren't allowing them to do anything dangerous, are you, Captain?"

Sir John quirked an eyebrow and smiled reassuringly at her. "Of course not, Lady Anne." His voice was a caress. "I don't, however, do my training on lead lines."

"Lead lines?" Lord Robert looked up from his plate, startled. What's this about lead lines?"

Sir John shot a meaningful glance at Anne before he lied for her. "Nothing at all." He saw the twins relax. "Merely an expression."

"Just what *are* you doing with the boys, Kent?" Lord Robert didn't look half as interested in the answer to his question as Anne felt.

She watched the former captain of Dragoons closely. Just what *was* he—a man who thought it overcautious to have put lead lines on her sons' ponies when they were riding in a strange place—doing with the children?

"Teaching them simple saber strokes, how to charge in a line." He looked approval at his students. "The boys are doing very well. You should be proud of them."

Every one of the boys sat up straighter.

Lord Robert smiled, pride shining in his eyes.

Becky asked, "Shall we see them one day?"

"Oh, yes, Lady Rebecca. The boys are already eager to demonstrate their new skills. We're only waiting until they're proficient in all of them."

Anne couldn't stop herself. "All of them?"

"There are a few more skills to being a soldier, Lady Anne."

She fought an impulse to demand a list of them for her approval. She was certain that if she did, he would reel one off right here at her table. She was equally certain that she would make a scene, ranting at him about any point of his plans that she felt was not safe for the boys.

Anne took a deep breath. Better to wait until they were alone to demand that he tell her his plans. Surely she could devise some excuse for being alone with him. Then the peal she'd ring over him wouldn't disturb her other guests.

There was no doubt in her mind that she'd be telling him she didn't approve of his schedule for her sons with some anger. She'd come to believe that Captain Sir John was an

overly brave and reckless man. The chances that he'd be
teaching her sons to be properly careful were nil, she knew.
Thank Heaven no one had been hurt already.

She cast about in her mind for a way to get him alone.
The maze. She could get him to go into the maze with her,
and while they penetrated its secrets, she could find out just
what he was up to with the boys.

She congratulated herself on thinking of it. It would be
perfectly proper, for she would issue a blanket invitation.
She'd be safe in doing so, because she knew Lord Robert
and Becky would decline. She could count on the fact that
they were both totally disinterested in anything that even
vaguely resembled physical exertion.

Her voice was bright as she announced, "One of the gardeners tells me we have a maze here at the castle."

"Really? Where?" Brian was all curiosity.

"That tall, dense hedge that seems to fill the center garden is a maze."

Brandon poked his twin. The look he gave him to go
with the poke kept Brian from begging to go. It also
brought back the ghost's plans for getting Mama and the
Captain together. Maybe they could get them lost in the
maze. They had to go find their great-great-grandfather.

Brandon asked, "May we boys be excused, Mama?"

"Yes, dear." She watched fondly as the four boys tried
not to rush from the room. "Well? What do you think of the
castle having a maze?"

Sir John's eyes were alight with interest. Anne was jubi-
lant. Obviously he was willing to accompany her.

She looked at Becky and Robert. She knew just what to
say. "Won't it be fun to find our way to the center? It
should keep us occupied for hours."

"Hours!" Becky pretended to shudder. "Walking around
in circles for hours? Anne, you know how devoted I am to

you. You've been my dearest friend for almost six years. Our friendship might stretch to me going to the guillotine for you, Anne darling, but it does *not* stretch to wandering about in a hedge full of insects for hours!"

Lord Robert grinned at her. "Thank you for your splendid invitation, m'dear, but unfortunately I have a previous commitment to my lovely wife for just exactly that time—whenever it may be."

Anne's laughter rang out. "You're frauds, both of you. You pretend friendship but refuse to go with me on the smallest adventure. For shame!" She didn't see the distress her comment caused Becky.

Lord Robert laughed with her. "No, no. There's no shame to self-preservation. You might be lost in there forever."

"Ninny!" Anne chuckled. "I shall take a ball of yarn. There's absolutely no chance of my getting lost in the maze." She turned to Sir John, bright-eyed. "You'll be brave enough to be my escort, won't you, Captain Kent?"

"Put that way, how can I refuse?" His eyes teased her.

"How ungallant! One would hope you wouldn't refuse no matter how I phrased my invitation."

"I stand chastised. My most humble apologies." What was she up to? he wondered. It was clear to him that she wanted to get him alone. He wished with all his heart that she had dalliance in mind, but he'd discovered Anne was no Felicity almost as soon as he'd met her. So what did she want? If he were back in his regiment making a wager, he'd bet it had something to do with her boys.

He made a mental note to concentrate harder on his training. If Anne were uneasy about the children, it would be the quickest way to reassure her. The boys were learning fast, and having the time of their lives. Stepping up his program wouldn't be difficult.

Once they held the graduation ceremony the boys planned, their very proficiency would reassure her. Seeing how well they handled their ponies at the charge should clear up the lead-line question, and watching them carefully and intelligently scale a wall should take care of any other motherly qualms she might have. Anne would be able to trust her sons to manage themselves in any situation.

Anne straightened her shoulders. "Well, Sir John. Will you mind acting as my escort to the heart of the maze when I go?" In silent challenge, she lifted her chin ever so slightly in the Captain's direction.

He bowed. "I shall do so with pleasure, milady." He hoped she couldn't read in his eyes the heat her challenging look caused to flare in him. If she could, he'd probably find himself escorting her companion, Lois, as well.

Escorting Lois Carswell, pleasant as he found her, had no part in his plan to steal a kiss. He hoped it wouldn't be long before Anne decided to explore her newly discovered maze.

In London, at St. Legere House, luncheon was also in progress—in the servants' hall. Bethany was so lonely that she'd wandered down to be with the staff. She stood disconsolately beside the table, wishing there was someone, anyone, who could see her.

The butler was saying, "I don't suppose the master will be returning any time soon, but we must not let down."

"Surely not!" The head footman was in perfect agreement.

The others all had something to add.

"His nibs must be enjoying a bit of that sea air, eh?"

"Do him a world of good."

"*Oui,*" the cook chimed in, "the air of the sea is most salubrious."

One of the grooms chuckled. "Salubrious?"

"If you wish dessert, you will not again laugh at my English."

They bickered on good-naturedly.

Bethany liked them all. Sir John's secretary had chosen the staff well. After a while, however, she got bored and wandered away.

St. Legere House was terribly lonely for Bethany since Sir John had gone. It had been weeks since Sir John and she had first talked, but it felt like years.

She sighed. It would almost have been better if he'd never come into her life . . . *"Oh, dear."* She almost laughed. *"I mean, of course, into my death."* She frowned. *"How very many turns of phrase one must change after one dies. It's really quite annoying."*

She floated back to her own part of the house, frightening the cat on the way. How she hated that. She'd quite liked cats when she'd been alive.

She settled lightly on a chair by the window. Looking out into the bright day, she wondered where Sir John had gone and if he had found his Forever Love yet? She missed him rather dreadfully.

How she wished she could have gone with him. She was so tired of being here. One hundred years was truly a long time to be cooped up in a house, and it was seeming longer every day.

She perked up a bit. Jared had called out to her across the long miles just the other evening. Her heartbeat quickened as she remembered. For the first time, he seemed to be hopeful.

Perhaps there was a chance of lifting the curse at last. She closed her eyes in anticipatory bliss. If they could fulfill the conditions, they could lift the curse. They could be together again. *Oh, wouldn't that be wonderful!*

* * *

After lunch at the castle, the training resumed in the meadow. Sir John sat his charger, Hercules, and marveled at the clear sky.

"Watch the demonstration carefully, men." And then, "Danvers!" Sir John drew his saber. Shining and sharp, it hissed from its scabbard with a shivering snick.

Danvers, a seasoned campaigner for long years before retirement had forced him to accept the position of batman to Sir John, drew his own blade.

The two men charged each other with a fury that left the boys gasping with eager anticipation of spilled blood. Not one of them even blinked.

Shoulder against shoulder, the war-scarred horses under the men rammed together. Grunting, they tore the surface of the meadow with iron-shod hooves as each strained to unbalance the other.

Over their heads the sabers clashed and rang in sun-catching arcs as each man narrowly missed cutting the other down.

It was over almost instantly, leaving the boys round-eyed and breathless.

"Very well, men." He looked at each boy in turn. "Do you want us to do that again more slowly?"

The boys, with the exception of Brandon, were still staring at their elders, slack-jawed.

"Hmmmm. I see that you do." He turned to an amused Danvers. "Again. Very slowly, if you please."

They repeated the exercise and then shepherded the boys through it one step at a time until they had it down pat.

Sir John signaled the charge with a down stroke of his glittering saber.

Manfully, the boys sent their ponies dashing at those of

their assigned opponents. Flailing and hacking, they strove to copy the sequence of saber strokes they'd just learned.

When they finished the drill, all four boys waited, panting, for their Captain's comments.

"Well done, gentlemen," he told them solemnly. "Quite commendable for a first attempt." While the boys happily congratulated one another, he ran an eye over their mounts. "All right, lads. The ponies look fine, but there's nothing more we can do with sticks for sabers. We'll have to wait until Danvers and I can rearm you."

"Can we have *real* ones?"

Sir John heard Danvers murmur, "Not bloody likely, you little savage," and saw Luther grin as if he'd received a compliment.

Anne was spending her afternoon in the north end of the east wing with the engineer she'd hired. He'd arrived from London late this morning and had gotten right to work. With him, Anne had inspected the far part of the east wing that he'd wanted to show her, and had agreed to more bracing for that part of the corridor. Her mind, however, kept leaping ahead to the time she planned to spend alone with Sir John. Sternly she told herself that she wanted to be with him because she needed to ascertain that his training was safe for her sons. The way her heart was behaving, she could almost think she was foolishly hoping for another of his kisses.

"While most of the northeast wing is sturdy, milady, the very end of it seems of much more recent construction. Little more than one hundred years old, I'd say." He rubbed his chin. "This part of the castle is simply not as well built as one could wish, Lady Anne. Notice how you can hear the sounds of the sea more clearly in this passageway than in any other part of the castle." He cupped his ear and leaned toward the sound. "We'll have to go more carefully here than in the older sections."

Trying not to laugh at his pose, Anne told him, "Please take every precaution. I don't want any of the workers hurt." She became serious. "And if you think this part of my plan might be hazardous to execute, just let me know, and I'll abandon it."

"That would be a pity. The view you hope to achieve will be spectacular. I'd hate to see you have to forego it." He spoke confidently, "Never fear. With great care and the proper bracing we'll be able to finish the project safely."

Anne was glad to have his assurances. She was also glad to leave his company. Being with another man only sharpened her longing to be with Sir john. It was a longing that was becoming more difficult to deny.

Chapter
Twenty-one

The weather was beginning to change. There were clouds gathering on the horizon over France. Everyone at the castle was suddenly struck with a sense of urgency to finish their current projects before rain and fog sealed them indoors for who knew how long.

Sir John spent the time between luncheon and tea in the armory. Anne was going to explore the maze today and planned to do it before time to dress for dinner. Since he'd promised to accompany Anne on her exploration between teatime and dinner, he was in a hurry.

"Damn!" He fought to stifle a sneeze. "Where the blazes does all this dust come from?" He snatched out his handkerchief; he'd be ready for the next assault.

Irritably he searched the long-closed room. He was looking for things that might serve safely as sabers for the boys. He yanked open and slammed closed drawers and cupboards with a force that increased in direct proportion to his disappointment at finding nothing that would serve as a mock weapon.

Finally, he strode out of the armory to go find Danvers. He'd send him to ask how near the sabers they were having carved were to completion. In his mind, he formed quick plans for the boys to scale the northwest tower until their wooden sabers were ready.

The Athelstains took their sons, Luther bitterly complaining, for an excursion down the coast to look at historic ruins.

Anne was looking through her wardrobe for a sturdy dress. She needed something that wouldn't be reduced to rags by pushing through overgrown hedges.

Amazed, her maid was telling her, "Sturdy, *madame*? Sturdy? *Mon Dieu.* I have thought all this time that it is the boots who are sturdy."

The twins, taking advantage of George and Luther's absence, headed for the southeast tower.

"Are you here?" Brian's voice shook a little.

The ghost's laughter rang out. Jared thought how much more pleasant it was to know that he had kinfolk again. *"Yes, I'm here and glad of your company. Come. Sit, lads. And tell me what you were up to in the west meadow today."*

The twins eagerly complied, faces aglow with the pleasant memory of it all.

When they'd finished, the ghost asked them, *"You are absolutely certain you like this Captain Sir John Kent then?"*

"Oh, yes!" They spoke in unison.

The ghost smiled. Their odd habit was getting less annoying to him as his fondness for the boys grew. *"Good.*

And your mother? Are you positively certain she likes him, too?"

Clouds arrived on the sunny faces. The boys were unsure.

"Well?" The ghost could feel impatience building. He'd already waited a century!

With the boys so slow in answering, his impatience spilled over. *"Dammit, boys. Your mother can't help but be impressed by that handsome officer. He's a fine figure of a man, and brave to boot. She can't be indifferent to him. I won't hear of it!"* He began to pace furiously. *"Your mother and Sir John constitute the first blasted chance that's presented itself to me in my whole death! The first chance I've had to satisfy the curse."*

"The curse?" Their eyes widened in unison, too.

"A condition. An irksome condition that keeps me bound here in this blasted castle and away from my wife, Bethany." He slammed the fist of one hand into the palm of the other. *"Damned if I'll stand for it! Your mother must have some feelings about Captain Sir John! She must!"*

Brian cringed a little at the thunderous look on the ghost's face.

St. Legere took a couple of turns around the tower room, the skirts of his gold brocade coat swinging with every change of direction.

"The problem dates back to the moments immediately after my unfortunate death almost a century ago." He frowned as he remembered, saying brusquely, *"As I've already told you, I foolishly refused to go to my rest. Dammit, I'd died without proving my blasted innocence! A stain rested on the honor of my family, and my children and my children's children were destined to bear the shame of a guilt that was not mine! The idea was unbearable."* He

looked at the twins as if they couldn't fail to understand his reasoning, then began pacing again.

"So, I defied the Angels!" He stopped in front of the boys, his eyes full of anguish. He shook his head at his own folly. *"God, what a pitiful fool I was!"* His shoulders slumped and he straightened them with a jerk. *"Now, because of my own stubborn arrogance, I'm not permitted to leave this place until I have found the letter that will prove my innocence"*—he lifted his right hand toward them, index finger raised, to be sure of their full attention—*"and performed one other task that will wash away my presumptuous anger in their"*—he threw a gesture skyward—*"sight."*

"And what is that?" Brandon was the one who asked. Brian was too mesmerized to utter a word.

"I must help to unite two living humans in true love." He scowled, and his voice went hoarse. *"According to the Angels' dictates, one of these humans must be my descendant."* He laughed. It was a tight, bitter sound that spoke volumes. He ran his fingers distractedly through his hair. *'I've had no information about my family since I died . . . but I've come to suspect—to hope—God, how desperately I hope it . . . that your mother may be my great-granddaughter."*

Shooting to his feet, Brandon cried, "Why, that would make you our great-great-grandfather!"

"Yes."

"Oh. Jolly good! I don't know anybody who has met their own great-great-grandfather." Brian's innocent excitement kept Brandon from jeering at him.

Even so, he muttered, "Nobody's ever seen their own great-great-grandfather, nodcock."

Lord Jared's smile was like sunlight spilling into the

tower room. *"Will you help me then? Will you help me get your mama and Sir John to fall in love?"*

"Yes!" Both boys thought His Lordship's suggestion was capital. If it worked, they'd have the Captain for a papa. Nothing could be better than that. "We'd be glad to.!"

The dead nobleman, struggling with emotions that threatened to overcome him, did the only thing he could do. *"Thank you,"* he told them gravely. *"Thank you both."*

Then he whirled away from them and began pacing furiously. When he spoke, his voice rang with joy. *"We must make plans! We must get them alone together and keep them that way for long enough to fall a little in love, at least. We have to do this as many times as it may take. Are you with me?"*

"Oh, yes!"

"Good! Remember. We are agreed. If they go into a room, I blow the door shut and one of you will throw the blasted bolt."

"Yes!"

"And there's the maze, too," Brandon offered eagerly.

"Yes," Brian joined in. "Mama has just discovered that there's a maze in the center court."

"How would we get them there together alone?"

"Oh, that's easy." Brian's excitement sounded in his voice. "Mama is eager to explore it. Lord Robert and Aunt Becky are too lazy to go. So, we have only to distract Lois and it'll just be Mama and Captain Sir John!"

Brandon forgave Bri his earlier stupid remark.

"Good! Now, we must devise a way to keep them there."

Then they were all lost in laughter. It was a long minute before they could go on with their plotting.

On their way down from the tower room, Brian asked his

brother hopefully, "Do you really think we can help him do this?"

Brandon sensed his need to be reassured. "Of course we can. Besides, we promised."

Brian shook his brother's arm. "I just had a thought. We could get in terrible trouble promising a ghost something that maybe we can't do."

Brandon was stung; Bri was being stupid again. "Nobody made you promise anything, Brian. You didn't have to promise just because I did!"

Immediately behind them a footfall sounded. "Promise who what?" Luther demanded.

Brandon jumped and spun around. "Luther!"

Brian looked back over his shoulder as if afraid of what he might see. Seeing only Luther, he turned and stood staunchly beside his brother.

"I asked who you made a promise to." Luther's expression was truculent.

"It's nothing that concerns you." Brandon's voice was firm. "And it's whom, not who."

Brian knew just how far *that* was going to get them with Luther! George had warned them about his brother long ago. Luther would keep after them like a terrier after a rat. If they didn't want him finding out about their ghostly friend in the tower, they were going to have to do something to throw him off the scent. Brian thought frantically. "We promised one of the grooms . . . " He cast about in his mind for something that they might have promised one of the grooms. ". . . that we'd try to bring him a pastry. He likes them, don't you know."

"A pastry." Luther sounded like he didn't believe Brian. "For one of the grooms."

Brandon was as piqued by the older boy's attitude as he was dismayed by his twin's lie. He dove in to support his brother, disliking Luther too much to let him gain the upper hand. "He likes the pastries Cook makes." There. That was an easy statement. Everybody on the whole estate liked the pastries Cook made.

Luther regarded them for a long moment. "Very well." He said it as if he were excusing them from some wrongdoing.

Brandon bristled. As if anyone cared *what* the unpleasant Luther thought!

Brian was just greatly relieved. He tugged at his brother's sleeve. Brandon turned away with him, and they left Luther standing there staring after them.

Luther leaned a shoulder against the cold stone wall of the passageway and watched them walk off. He squinted his eyes as he cudgeled his brain seeking to penetrate the twins' secret. His instincts told him that something was definitely up—something that Brandon and Brian wanted to keep to themselves.

That wouldn't do. He just didn't think that would do at all.

Luther decided that he'd have to keep a much closer eye on the Kent twins.

Chapter
Twenty-two

Sir John hid his impatience poorly, Anne was delighted to see. All through tea, he kept glancing at the ball of yarn on the table beside her.

Anne kept glancing at him. He was especially handsome today. The sun had darkened his face until his eyes were the brightest blue she'd ever seen. She was glad he'd been a soldier and spent his time away at war. If he hadn't, he'd never have remained single so long. Long enough for . . .

She frowned a little. What in the world was she thinking? She had no intention of giving up her independence. Marriage, with the subsequent loss of the right to make her own decisions, had no place in her plans. Why, just the other night, hadn't she said she'd never have another man in her bed? And, of course, she'd meant marriage.

She knew herself too well to think she would risk sullying her reputation with an affair. She had her sons to think of, after all, not to mention the fact that she'd find such an arrangement demeaning.

She smiled softly to herself. A few kisses, however, couldn't hurt anything, and she had a distinct desire to be kissed again. To be kissed when she wasn't so frightened that she had no time to enjoy it.

And, she admitted to herself, she wanted those kisses to come from Sir John Kent. She wanted to savor the feel of his lips on her own, the strength of his arms around her . . .

Becky cried, "Anne, are you all right?"

Startled, Anne pressed her hand to her heart and hastened to reassure her friend. "I'm fine, Becky."

"Looked like you were having a heart attack for a minute there, old girl." Lord Robert's eyes held concern.

Anne laughed. "No, I'm fine. Truly. It's probably only that I need a little exercise." She felt foolish. She'd be careful not to fantasize about kisses in the future. Not while her dearest and best friend was around, anyway.

She looked hard at Becky, and her friend caught her meaning. One glance shot Sir John's way, and Becky gave way to peals of laughter.

"What do you find so amusing, m'dear?" her husband asked.

"Not amusing, delightful. You must forgive me, I was merely"—her gaze caught Anne's—"imagining something delightful." She raised her teacup to her lips, and just before it hid them from her best friend, mouthed the words, "Good hunting!"

Anne choked on her own tea, trying not to laugh.

"Don't mind them, Sir John," Athelstain said in a bored drawl. "They've done this for years. Some kind of silent communication. So as to drive us men mad, I think. Best just to ignore 'em."

Sir John smiled and lifted his own empty cup to Lord

Robert in silent agreement. His regard touched Becky, a hint of amusement in his eyes, then turned to Anne, and the look in them warmed considerably.

Anne's pulse quickened. She could feel her breath start to catch and strove to breathe naturally. She didn't want him to have any idea how strongly his slightest glance affected her just now when she had his kisses so firmly in the forefront of her mind.

He was so devilish handsome. If she was going to learn more about kissing, she was glad she planned to learn it from him. He'd not be averse to teaching her, she'd wager. She doubted that all the enthusiasm she sensed in him was because he wanted to discover what lay at the center of the maze. She hoped that, like her, he was glad of the opportunity to be alone together. In order to speak privately, of course. She mustn't forget that she intended to demand of him just what it was he was training her sons to do. She was the one responsible for their continued safety, after all.

She watched the way his long fingers toyed with his cup. The delicate china seemed even more fragile in his hand. "Would you care for tea, Captain?" How silly that it was impolite to ask if he wanted *more* tea, when she was the one who'd poured his first cup. Anne was becoming impatient with the constraints of society.

"No, thank you, Lady Anne." His eyes were intent, urging her to get through this ceremony and get on with it.

She smiled. "Becky? Robert?"

Becky murmured, "No, thank you, dear."

Robert, his eyes bright with mischief, glanced from her to the impatient captain. "Shouldn't you two go on if you're to finish your exploration of the maze in time to dress for dinner?"

"Yes." Anne kept her voice perfectly serene. "I suppose

that might be wise." She rose and looked at Sir John. "Are you ready, Captain?"

"I'm always ready."

Lord Robert choked on a sip of his tea.

Suppressing a twitch of his lips, Sir John solemnly offered his arm to his hostess.

Anne picked up the ball of yarn, hesitated for an instant, then slipped her hand into the crook of his elbow. She almost jumped as she felt the spark of electricity that flashed between her fingers and his sleeve.

"Until dinner," she told her friends.

Sir John managed the huge door to the center court with only a little difficulty, and Anne and he passed through into the quiet green world of the garden. Paths ran down each side, paths that Anne had previously thought defined by the tall hedges. She said as much. "You know, I thought these hedges were merely overgrown borders of the two paths to the outer garden. I had no idea that there was a maze here."

John smiled at the excitement in her voice. "I imagine it was laid out hundreds of years ago to judge by the density of these hedges. See how interlocked the branches are and how large. If we lose our way and our patience, it will take a strong man and a sharp axe to get us out."

Anne laughed up at him. "Oh, no. That would be a desecration! And there will be no need, for I have my trusty ball of yarn." She held it up for him to see.

"You needn't show me. I've looked at little else this past half hour, hoping to hint you away from your tea tray."

She laughed, and Sir John's smile widened. She had a delightful laugh, as free as a child's just now. Had she put aside her concerns for the twins for just this small slice of time? He hoped so.

He didn't think they'd remain in the distance long, however. Unless, of course, he could distract her. "Shall I tie the end of your yarn here for you?" He held out his hand for the ball of wool.

"No, thank you," she told him firmly. "I'm in charge of this adventure." She found the end of the yarn and pulled it free from the sphere.

John pushed aside the leaves, and she tied it firmly to the bough he exposed. He was intrigued by her mood. She was almost—he searched for the word he wanted—mischievous? Or was it—his mind hesitated over it—provocative?

"Look at the size of these branches." Her voice was soft with awe. "I can't remember ever having seen a hedge so ancient."

"Possibly there isn't one. This maze has grown here in the shelter of these walls and been watered all its life by fogs and mists from the sea. Other hedges throughout England, whether mazes or not, have had to survive both drought and the full force of storms."

Anne turned from her finished task and looked at him seriously. "Funny. I've always thought life's storms made things stronger."

He looked deeply into her eyes. His voice softened. "I've always found that to be true for people, at any rate."

Anne watched the clear blue of his eyes change. It darkened and grayed to the slate blue of a turbulent sea. Her pulse sped again. Unless she was very much mistaken, Sir John was a man with a mission. For the first time, she questioned the wisdom of coming here alone with him.

Sir John saw her begin to doubt. She was questioning whether she should be exploring the maze with him. Damn and blast! He'd no intention of having her change her mind and go back for Lois. Pleasant as he found Lois Carswell, her presence would certainly put a crimp in his plans to steal a few kisses. "Here." He held out his hand. "Shall I play out your yarn for you? I assure you I make a most excellent reel."

His foolishness reassured her. Of course he was perfectly safe company. No doubt he'd kissed her that night in the hall just to calm her. Kisses simply didn't mean as much to men as they did to women. Certainly he'd given no sign that he even remembered the incident. And if her pulse fluttered wildly just to remember his lips on hers, well, then she would just have to be certain that she didn't think of it.

Besides, she'd sought this opportunity to find out what his training of her sons consisted of, hadn't she? Yes, she had, and she'd every intention of discovering it before the day was done. The idea that she might want him to kiss her was absurd.

She put both thoughts from her mind for the time being, however. Time enough to discuss a subject that might turn acrimonious after they'd reached the center of the maze and discovered what awaited them there. She had no desire to spoil that pleasure.

She surrendered the ball of yarn to him. "Very well, make yourself useful."

They moved forward into the dimness of the maze. Frequently they found places where the hedge had grown together overhead and shut out all the light. Anne moved hesitantly when they came to these places.

"Here, Anne." He used her first name without her title without even thinking about it. "Why don't you let me go first?"

"I'm all right."

"Spiders?"

She swung around him like a child swinging around a post. "You go first."

He chuckled and handed her the wool, his fingers lingering on hers as she took it. "Now you're the reel. I'll need both hands for some of this."

"As long as you're the first to run into any spiderwebs."

"Webs do no harm."

"Spiders do."

He chuckled again and told her, "Better stay close then."

She moved forward and gently clasped the back of his coat.

A few feet farther along, he stopped abruptly for no other reason than to feel her bump lightly against his back. "Sorry." He lied, "Spiderweb." He made a sweeping gesture as if he were clearing one away. "All clear now."

He stopped again after a few feet.

Anne was careful not to bump into him this time. "Why did you stop now?"

His back had felt like a wall. Anne found herself recalling the nightmare in the windy corridor and the way she'd pressed against his back then. The way she'd decided that his body was the strong body of a warrior. That he could protect her. That he was deliberately exposing himself to danger by doing so. Her breath shortened.

He turned to face her. "Dead end. We'll have to try another way. Reel in your yarn."

Anne was glad of the excuse to retrace her steps with her back to him. Her face must be flaming! She took a deep breath. It was easier now she couldn't see him. Expertly, she wound up the wool.

Suddenly his breath was warm on her neck. "Are you all right, Anne?"

She took a long stride forward, the last thing she needed was to have him find out how easily he affected her. "I'm fine. I was just sighing because we have to turn back." She sighed again, on purpose. "But that's what a maze is all about, isn't it? Trying first this way and then that until you discover the heart of it?"

She'd babbled herself a safe distance from him and could relax. Relaxing a bit made it possible to think again. Maybe she'd better begin discussing military training with him, after all. And right now might be the time to start.

"Dead end." She'd blundered almost into the dark green wall ahead of her before she registered it. Definitely coming in here alone with Sir John had not been a good idea. Not if it was going to turn her into a henwit every minute or two.

"So it is." There was laughter in his voice. "Would you like me to go first again?"

"No, thank you, Sir John. I haven't seen any spiders." She was beginning to wonder if he had.

She hoped they found the heart of the maze soon. Sir John's presence behind her was beginning to feel larger than life. A little farther along, the hedges grew so close that now and again he had to reach over her shoulder to hold back a mass of branches so she might pass. Every time he did, he brushed against her.

Before long, she was walking in a haze of sensation that had nothing to do with the hedge touching her body.

"Anne?" His voice was just a little husky.

"Yes?" Hers was breathless.

"Won't you call me John? Haven't you noticed I've been calling you Anne since we came in here?"

Anne stopped stock-still. A few feet ahead of her the hedge made a cul-de-sac in which stood a low stone bench. She almost sat down on it, her knees having gone strangely weak. "Another dead end."

She could feel him inches behind her. It was as if her every sense had been sharpened where he was concerned.

She was grateful that he stood absolutely still. If he moved, she'd probably tingle to death.

"I hadn't noticed you'd neglected to use my title." Warily, she turned to face him. "Now that you've pointed it out, though, I suppose the proper thing for me to do would be to reprimand you for it." She tried to look as if she were completely indifferent to him. "I'd rather just call you John and have done with it, however. After all, you *are* the boys' guardian, and I suppose you will be around for a long time."

His eyes burned into her own. "For the rest of your life, Anne." His voice was a low rumble. Intimate. A little frightening.

She bit her lower one to stifle the *Oh, dear!* that rose to her lips. Her heart felt as if it were going to pound itself out of her chest. This man had the power to stir her emotions to an extent she felt unsafe. Instead of *Oh, dear,* she said, "How very nice," as if she didn't mean anything of the sort, and he laughed.

Turning, he got back to pushing his way through the overgrown maze. "Follow me, Anne."

Half an hour passed with them rerolling the wool on the ball as they went down more and more false passages in the leafy green dimness.

"It's amazing that there is such a length of pathway in so small a space." Anne could hardly believe it.

"It's because the hedge is so thick. We've doubled back and around more times than I can remember. It's a good thing you brought the yarn."

Anne minded terribly when their intrusion into the pathway made it necessary for John to snap branches off. He reassured her with a terse, "They'd have to be pruned back anyway," and they pushed on. Still they hadn't found the center of the maze.

Jared St. Legere called to the twins, *"They're far enough in now. Quickly! Snap the yarn and run it into the maze as far as you can without being seen."*

"How will we find our way back out?" Brandon was always practical.

"I'll lead you out. Hurry."

The boys snapped off the yarn their mother had tied at the entrance to the maze and ran into the dim greenness with it. When they heard the voices of their Mama and the Captain, they dropped the loose end and scuttled back to the entrance guided by the faint mist that was their great-great-grandfather.

"What good will that do?" Brian was full of curiosity.

"We don't know yet, Brian. We're hoping that if they're lost in the maze alone together for a while, nature might take a hand."

"You mean like make it rain?"

St. Legere and Brandon merely exchanged a look.

Chapter
Twenty-three

"Oh, look!" Anne peeked over John's shoulder, her voice throaty with excitement. "We're here. We've found the heart of the maze."

A stone structure resembling a miniaturized ancient Roman temple stood in the center of what had once been a round clearing. The soft gray of the stonework was covered by a heavy patina of green moss, and vines twined around the temple, creating deep shadows in its interior. The stonework of the structure was visible only in the several places that were bare where the vines had fallen, dragged down by their own weight as they tangled together to reach toward the sun.

"I'll reconnoiter. Wait here."

She smiled at his unconscious use of the military term. Obviously he expected to be obeyed, but Anne wasn't one of his troopers. She followed along close behind him. All her instincts told her this lovely place was safe.

"And well they should, my girl. If I do nothing else today, I intend to convince you that the safest place of all is in your handsome Captain's arms."

Jared was ecstatic. They'd fall in love here in this magical setting, he was sure.

He hoped the twins would keep quiet where he'd left them hiding at the entrance to the maze. This temple wasn't far from that spot, as the ghost flew.

When John came out of the small temple, Anne was there at the entrance waiting, a soft smile on her face. "Isn't it beautiful?"

"Very beautiful." But John wasn't talking about the temple, and his warm regard made that perfectly clear.

"Is that the best you can do?"

Anne refused to let him see her blush. Instead she bent down to touch a small flower growing in the crack where the mortar that had once joined the first and second steps had fallen away. "Oh, look. Isn't it dear?"

Sir John didn't answer. They were all alone here. There was no one to see that he didn't observe the inane rules of society and respond to every comment to avoid being thought rude. If things went as he hoped they might, Anne was probably going to consider him a great deal worse than rude. Here in the green depths of the maze they were no longer Lady and Sir. They were simply Anne and John, and John had made up his mind that he was going to satisfy his craving to kiss Anne before he let her go from this place.

Anne looked up at him expectantly, and he was forced to speak. "Very pretty." She heard the words as a low rumble, and again she was sure he hadn't meant the flower she was pointing out. His gaze locked with her own, and she was powerless to look away.

"Hell and damnation! What the blazes are you two doing? You've been in here the best part of an hour." Jared stormed up and down the edge of the clearing, his fulminating gaze scorching the couple on the steps of the temple.

The dark cloud that surrounded him echoed the skies above, darkness lowering. Jared's cloud was lit now and then by flashes of his angry frustration. *"What the bloody hell is your problem, you blasted twit! Kiss the girl!"*

Still muttering, he turned his face skyward. *"You wanted me to engineer this. How about a little help? The least you could do is give me a storm or something to keep them here since you've saddled me with such a pair of backward slowtops!"*

A searing flash of lightning split the sky. A shattering crack of thunder shook the temple. Anne startled into John's arms, and he drew her back with him into the interior of the vine-covered building. Heavy raindrops spattered the steps.

"That's more like it." Jared spoke with a great deal more respect than he'd used a moment before. He wasn't entirely certain whether he'd gotten assistance in his endeavor or a severe reprimand.

'*Apologies, my Lord God,"* he mumbled, ashamed of having been disrespectful—and even more ashamed to have to apologize.

Finally, the rain began to dissolve him, and muttering curses, he sprang into the air and took refuge in the castle. He saw the twins run in beneath him. Just the sight of them cheered him. *"Ah, well. It's obviously not permitted for me to leave the actual castle. I should be glad that I was able to stretch to the center court even so briefly."*

Flying to a window, he strove to see what was going on in the maze. No sign of the temple was visible in the greenery. *"Damn and blast!"* His habitual irritability returned.

"You mean you're not even going to let me see what happens?" Clamping his mouth shut on words he knew might force him to apologize again, he turned and shot off to his tower to sulk.

Anne stood quietly in the circle of John's arms. She knew propriety dictated that she should make some maidenly comment and move away from hm, but she had no intention of doing so. She'd had a brief taste of what it was like to be held in his arms that night her great-grandfather had frightened them, but she'd been too terrified to enjoy it.

John held her close and bent his head to speak softly into her ear; his low voice was audible under the sound of the thunder, the drumming of the rain. His lips brushed the shell of her ear; his breath was warm on her neck. Tingles rushed up and down her spine. "Are you all right, Anne?"

When she merely smiled into his cravat and declined to answer, he gathered her closer. "It's only thunder, Anne. Down here in the center court we're safe from the lightning. It's only noise, Anne. Don't be afraid."

She pulled back from his chest then and looked up at him. "I'm not afraid." Her eyes were full of mischief. "But I thank you for your concern."

John stood there like a statue. He was having a little trouble coming to grips with this situation. If she wasn't afraid, why had she so readily accepted the comfort of his embrace? Was this going to be easier than he'd thought?

Grasping her by the shoulders, he looked down into her face. By the light of a hissing flash, he saw she was perfectly calm. Perfectly calm. He felt as if the ground had been cut out from under his feet.

Like any good military man, he'd planned his campaign here carefully. He'd planned to work up to the kiss he'd been longing for slowly, and follow it with as many more as she'd permit. Now he felt as if the situation had subtly changed.

There was nothing for it but a frontal assault. He lowered his head and gently claimed her mouth.

Anne stood there, quiet and accepting.

"What the devil?" He thought he'd only breathed the words, impossible for her to hear, but she answered him.

"Perhaps a tiny little devil, John." Her eyes were frank. "I'm indulging myself, you see. I've had the oddest craving to see what it would be like to be kissed when I wasn't frightened half out of my mind." She looked him straight in the eye and waited a moment before she went on. "I'd never been kissed before you kissed me, and I certainly haven't been kissed since. So I hope you don't mind my maneuvering you into this position on the off chance that I might persuade you to kiss me again."

He stood there like a statue, his mind whirling. He couldn't have been more stunned if he'd been hit by the lightning that played around the towers of Castle Caldon.

Was Anne actually telling him she had *deliberately* gotten him out here alone in the maze with her? He heard his brain form the words into the question, but his mind was having difficulty grasping it.

"You see," Anne was saying, "I knew perfectly well that Becky and Robert wouldn't come with us, and I'd only to give Lois a pleasant chore to keep her out of the way. That was how I guaranteed that we would be alone." A tiny frown gathered on her forehead. "I hope I haven't shocked you. I really was hoping you wouldn't mind." When he still didn't answer, she added, "Awfully."

John's mind exploded. She *had* shocked him. He was having trouble believing she'd deliberately done this. She'd outwitted him and gotten him out here in the maze with all the skill he and his comrades had used time and again to lure pretty young maids to trysts.

A frown creased *his* brow. He wasn't sure he liked the idea of being on the other end of things this way.

"Does it offend you to have me apply to you for kisses?" Anne asked him softly. Then she sighed and moved a little away from him. "Yes, I can see that it does."

He made a strangled sound that was meant to be one of denial, but he didn't seem to have proper control of his vocal cords just at the moment.

She blushed a little and told him, "It *is* a very unusual circumstance, I admit, but you see, until you kissed me the other evening, I'd never been kissed. I'd rather like to see if it's as pleasant as it seemed to be then."

He felt as if he were moving through dense fog. The meaning of her words was clear to him; it was their feasibility that seemed confusing. Was she actually inviting him to kiss her?

She blushed a little more and looked away from him out into the tall hedges that seemed to shape and reshape in the fitful lightning. "Of course, if you'd really rather not . . . "

"Rather not!" He was amazed. "A man would be a fool not to want to kiss you." Her preposterous inference brought him out of his daze with a thud. "My God, Anne, you're the most beautiful, most desirable woman I've ever met." He saw the satisfied smile on her face and added, "And the most exasperating!"

Reaching for her with the reckless grin that always melted her, he pulled her to him and kissed her. When she didn't pull away, but made a little sound of contentment low in her throat, he kissed her again and again. Slowly, at first, then with a mounting fervor that left them both breathless.

"God, Anne. You must be insane to lure a man out here and invite such advances."

She pulled away a fraction. "Surely I am safe with you, John?"

"Any man," he growled, warning her. Blast! He must be the one who'd gone insane. He was actually scolding her for making herself available for just the thing he'd intended to trick her into.

He shook his head. "Anne, my lovely. Being here alone with me isn't the safest thing you've ever done."

"Oh, John, can't you leave off the lectures and kiss me again? I've lived all my life without kisses. Can't you just let me worry about what you tell me I should be worried about and you get back to kissing me?"

He looked at her in utter amazement. What the deuce! Nothing in all his male experience had prepared him to cope with this. He gave it up. With a low growl, he swept her back into his embrace.

His lips covered hers, gently at first. He had every intention of remaining the gentleman. She trusted him, after all.

Then, as her softness and closeness began to heat his blood, and her eager response drove him nearer the edge of his restraint, he found himself kissing her more demandingly. At his insistence, her lips parted, and he gave in to the urgency he felt to taste the sweet interior of her mouth.

Anne felt John's tongue enter her mouth to caress her own. For just an instant, she thought she should draw back from such intimate invasion. Then she remembered that she was safe with him, and that the feelings she was experiencing now would probably have to last her for the rest of her life. These wonderful sensations would probably be the only ones from which her dreams would be fabricated until she was no more.

Anne gave herself up and luxuriated in the sensations he

was bringing her. "How pleasant this is," she murmured against his lips, lost in sensation. "Let's do go on."

Her head began to swim as he kissed her long and coaxingly. Then he slid one of his hands from her back to her rib cage. She could feel the heat of it through the fabric of her gown.

John leaned back against the pillar in front of which they stood. He held Anne against him, reveling in her closeness. Still plundering her mouth, he moved his hand to cup her breast.

Wild desire shot through Anne, hot and bright as the lightning that played over their heads when she felt his arousal. Instantly she jumped a little away from him.

Passion exploded lights behind his eyes. He snatched her back to him again and kissed her bruisingly. Elation swept away caution. Anne was going to be his! He thought he'd died and gone to some voluptuous pagan heaven, and Anne was the sweetest houri of them all.

Masterfully, he cupped her breast again as he drew her closer, raining kisses down on her, her eyes, her throat, the swell of her breast. He pressed her hips against him, comforting his need. She was his. In a moment, she would be completely his.

Anne shoved away from him with all her might. She felt as if she'd been set aflame. Her own body was on the verge of betraying her. She must stop this.

She managed to gasp, "I think we should go back in now."

"What?" He spun down out of his heaven to see Anne fling herself out of the temple and run back down the leafy pathways of the maze.

Anne didn't even watch where she ran. He'd touched her breast. Did he think she was a loose woman? Did he think of her as a common strumpet? Anger filled her. Through tears she saw the yarn and followed it until she was blinded by them. When she could see no more she fled on, heedless of her direction. By some miracle she stumbled out the opening.

Sir John was right behind her. When she flung herself, sobbing, against the heavy wooden door to the castle, he caught her. She slapped his hands from her shoulders. "Leave me alone!"

"Anne. Anne. I didn't mean to frighten you." John strove to ignore the torturing ache she'd created in his loins and tried to comfort her. How could he have been so stupid! She told him Montague had never kissed her. He should have known from that that he was moving too fast. That he was rushing her. "I didn't know you didn't understand how easily things can get out of control with a man. I should have . . ."

"You should open this wretched door and let me out of your loathsome presence." Her eyes were lavender in the eerie light of the truncated storm.

"I had no intention of upsetting you, Anne. In fact, the only intention I had when I came into this blasted maze was to steal a kiss or two." He could feel his temper slipping. "*You*, Lady Anne Waring Kent, are the one who melted against my aching manhood and sighed that this was so pleasant and suggested that we just go on!"

"I didn't mean go on that far!"

"Well, where the bloody hell far did you think we were headed?" He slammed open the heavy oak door as if it were nothing.

Anne stopped and stared at him, aghast. "You thought that I . . . you accepted my invitation to come explore the maze because you thought that we might . . ."

John's temper had flown. "Make love! Say it, Anne. Stop avoiding the phrase. Yes, dammit, I want to make love to you!" He shook his head like a wounded bull and tried to get things straight. "That is, after you invited me to with your little statement that you wanted to go on. Then I thought that you . . . I thought that we . . . "

Anne's outrage knew no bounds. She stood panting with the strength of it. "You *cad*!" she gasped. "You dastardly cad! You actually thought that I would . . . "

"Make love!" He shouted it at the top of his lungs. "Why can't you say it?" He gulped air, and when he spoke his voice was scathing. "Yes, blast you. After you'd set my senses spinning out of bounds and gotten me so hot and bothered that I could hardly stand up, it did occur to me that you had something more in mind."

She looked at him standing there with his head lowered like a bull about to charge, a tumble of dark curls fallen down on his forehead, and hardened her heart against him. Regally she drew herself up to her full height and walked through the door and away from him down the long hall to her room.

"Dammit!"

The huge oak door slammed with a shattering boom that echoed and reechoed through the castle.

Chapter
Twenty-four

Later that evening in the dimly lighted drawing room, Lady Anne and Lois sat in a circle of soft light beside the fireplace. Anne was aggravated. She *still* didn't know *his plans.*

"Lois." She spoke quietly. She didn't want to disturb Becky and Robert. Dinner had been difficult enough with the Captain conspicuously absent, and she didn't want to make things even more uncomfortable for her guests. "I'm worried."

Lois looked up from her needlepoint, startled. "Worried? Whatever about? The twins have never been so happy, your guests are all having a wonderful time, and your renovations are going along beautifully."

Anne frowned. "Yes, I know it seems foolish, but I'm concerned about the boys.

"Captain Sir John is so strong and able." In a flash she

was remembering the strength of his arms around her, the power in the press of his firm, lean body against her own out in the maze . . . and the angry words they'd exchanged. She pushed the breathless thought of the effect he'd had on her out of her mind firmly and concentrated on her anger. Her words to Lois were calm and reasonable in spite of her inner turmoil, though. "He can't possibly know how delicate young boys are. It's just possible that he's requiring of them things that are too difficult for them to do."

Lois understood. Anne was being overprotective—again.

Delicate, indeed! Those two were made of spring steel. Yes, and ripe for trouble if something wasn't done to channel their natural male recklessness into safe and acceptable occupations. What the Captain was doing with them might result in a bruise or two to their young bodies, but the good he was doing their youthful spirits outweighed even a broken bone in her own opinion.

Lois held back a sigh. She wasn't the least surprised to hear Anne's proposal when it came.

"Perhaps we should go watch whatever Captain Sir John is doing with them in the west meadow tomorrow."

Lois noted Anne's elaborately casual tone. She hid her own true feelings and merely looked thoughtful. "Very well, if that is what it will take to calm your fears, Anne." She calculated quickly, determined to manage things for the best outcome. "Suppose we go just before it's time for the boys to come in for their baths. Surely it would be best not to interrupt them before that. You know how much they enjoy their training."

"Good idea." Then she looked thoroughly disgusted with herself. "They'll consider me an interfering spy, won't they?"

"Hmmmm."

"And Sir John will think me an overprotective mother?"

"Hmmmm." Lois refused to confirm the obvious.

Anne made a face. This was what she got for not keeping her mind on the business of finding out just what it was that Sir John was teaching her children. If only she hadn't been so willing to have him kiss her. If only she had . . . Well, it was too late now. "I can't help it, Lois. The twins are all I have."

Lois decided not to tell her friend what she was thinking. Later, when the moment was more propitious, she'd lecture Anne that it was high time she had more in her life than her sons. Now she said, "I think the most natural thing would be to go for a ride right after nuncheon that ends in the west meadow at just before time for the twins to come in to bathe for tea, don't you?"

Anne chuckled. "Thank you, Lois. That's a splendid plan. And thank you, too, dear, for being kind enough to suggest it. I know how you hate to ride a horse. I appreciate your sacrifice, truly I do."

Lois rose and folded her needlepoint. She put it carefully away in her workbasket and pushed the basket back out of sight. "You're welcome. Now, I think I shall go find Cook and have a cup of tea to fortify me for tomorrow."

"I can ring for tea, Lois."

"Ah, yes," Lois told her, "but *I* can't complain about having to ride a horse tomorrow if I drink it with you!"

Lois hurried to the kitchen, her shawl clutched tightly around her against the cold . . . and against the eerie feeling she got walking these ancient, vaulted halls at night! She breathed a huge sigh of relief when she reached the warm, bright domain of her friend the cook. "Thank heavens!" She spoke with more enthusiasm than she'd intended. "You're here."

Jared hung back a little, interested to see what had sent

Anne's companion flying to the kitchen like an arrow from a bow.

Danvers leapt to his feet. "Is something amiss, Miss Carswell?"

"Yes! No! Well, not yet, but it may certainly get to be."

Cook took one look at her flustered friend, threw up her pudgy hands, and went for the tea, clucking like a mother hen as she went.

"Here, Miss Carswell, permit me." Danvers seated Lois at the long, scrubbed table and hung over her solicitously. "Are you comfortable?"

Lois smiled up at him and embarked on her mission. "Please, won't you sit with me, Mr. Danvers?"

Danvers was momentarily dazzled. With flushed cheeks, he fumbled his way into his own chair.

"Your pipe has gone out, I'm afraid, Mr. Danvers." Lois nodded at the object in question, thoroughly enjoying his confusion. "As I have told you, I do so enjoy the smell of pipe smoke."

Danvers looked at his pipe as if he had never seen it before. "Are you certain you don't mind?"

"Please do." Lois smiled faintly to herself. It was rather pleasant to find she could reduce a seasoned soldier like Mr. Danvers to such a satisfactory state.

Cook came back to the table with the teapot and three cups on a tray. One look at the two people at her table, and she gave her friend Lois a meaningful glance with more than a hint of mischief in it.

Before Cook sat down, she removed the remains of her own supper and Danvers's from the table. Her hands free of those plates, she returned for a third. Lois was quick to guess the last plate must have been that of Captain Sir John. Long familiar with Higgins's habit of eating with his footmen in the servants' dining room, she knew Sir John had to have been the third person at the kitchen table.

Lois filed away the fact that the Captain had deliberately avoided Anne's table for future speculation and buried her nose in her teacup, thinking furiously. She couldn't betray Anne by telling Danvers outright about her intention to spy on the Captain tomorrow. She had to devise a way to let him know about it that would keep her integrity intact, and still keep Anne from spoiling the wonderful things that were happening for the twins. Testing the waters, she said, "We missed the Captain at dinner this evening."

"Well, er, yes. Captain Sir John had a quick bite here this evening. He had to go see to his plans for new sabers for the boys, don't you see?"

"New sabers!" Lois used her best shocked-lady tone, liking the effect it had on Danvers.

His face reddened again, and he told her hastily, "Not real sabers, of course. But carved wooden ones instead of the sticks I brought them out of yonder woods. They broke too readily."

Lois took pity on him. "Of course I knew you wouldn't give the boys real sabers. I was merely surprised for an instant."

Cook generated a sound exactly between reprimand for the trick Lois had played on a good man and approval for her letting him off the hook.

Lois shot her a quelling glance that promise explanations to come.

"How is the Captain getting the sabers, Mr. Danvers?" Lois was beginning to see a way to accomplish her plan to warn the men. "One does not quite see in one's mind a picture of Sir John whittling, after all."

Danvers threw back his head and laughed. "No, Miss. I'm certain that's the truth. He's hired old Fartherington

down in the village to shape 'em for him. The man's a ge-
nius at such, and is happy for the money."

Lois led the conversation to the critical warning carefully. "And will the boys be using them tomorrow?"

"I doubt they'll be ready for tomorrow, Miss. Probably
the day after."

"Oh." Lois sounded disappointed because she was. The
sabers would have been the perfect excuse to come watch.
But their absence would serve as well for the warning. "I'm
so disappointed. I would love to have seen them."

Danvers was suddenly alert.

Good, Lois thought, pleased that this very nice man was
also proving quite intelligent.

"Lady Anne has invited me to go for a horseback ride
with her tomorrow." She completely ignored Cook's snort
of derision. She kept her eyes meaningfully fixed on those
of the retired Dragoon as she gave him the information he
urgently needed. "We plan to end our ride in the west
meadow at a little before the time you usually send the
boys in for their baths." She smiled at him sunnily, then
took a sip of her tea.

Danvers sat still as a stone. Clearly, her remarks had him
thinking very seriously about tomorrow afternoon.

Lois gave a little sigh of satisfaction and settled back in
her chair to enjoy the rest of her tea and a conversation with
her friend the cook. Neither of them was a bit surprised
when Danvers begged them to excuse him.

When he was gone, Cook turned to Lois and said, "That
was very well done, Miss Carswell. I think you can be certain that Lady Anne will not see anything in the meadow
tomorrow that will upset her."

"Thank you, Mrs. Beaton, It's always reassuring to have
someone support your conclusions in such matters."

The fire crackling merrily in the huge fireplace was the

only sound as they sat smiling for a moment. Then they
lifted their teacups to each other in a toast to a disaster di-
verted, and settled down to catch up on their gossip.

Hmmmm. How can I turn this situation to my advantage?
Jared wondered, approaching Cook's chair to give her a hit
of cooling after her long day in the heat of the kitchen. He
shook his head. *Anne's snooping sounds more likely to
drive a wedge between them than to help. Blast but she's an
unmanageable wench! I still haven't found out what happened in the maze. Lord knows they came out of it fighting
like two cats, but still I feel that some progress was made,
in spite of that.*

"Women!"

Danvers headed straight for the barn, saddled a horse,
and was off to the village that hugged the shoreline at the
foot of the long castle drive. Before Lois and Cook had finished discussing their first subject, the Captain was in possession of Miss Carswell's warning.

"Damn and blast! Why the hell doesn't the woman keep
to her renovations and let me teach my wards something
about being men?"

Old Fartherington looked up from sanding a half-scale
wooden saber. "She do be a gentle soul when it comes to
her boys, Cap'n. Her Ladyship is wanting them safe all the
time." He chuckled. "We here in the village learned that
from her servants when one of the boys in the public house
laughed at them twins being led around on their ponies by
grooms holding onta lead lines. 'Twere a rare fracas."

"That's exactly what I'm trying to overcome." Exaspera-
tion was plain in Sir John's words.

"Wal, now." The graybeard shook his head. "Just you be
good and sure to keep in mind that nature don't have a

much fiercer beast than a mother defending her child. Don't you go and get yourself mangled, Cap'n Sir."

Sir John had to laugh. His last parting with Anne rose to mind. "Aye, Fartherington. You truly have the right of that." He clapped the old man on the shoulder. "Thank you for your warning."

He grinned as memories flooded into his mind of his own diminutive mother all but attacking his six-foot-three father when he'd brought their only son back with a broken arm from his first fox hunt.

His frustration at the beautiful Lady Anne's planned interference in his schedule for the boys' training left him. If his father could manage his mother, then he could handle Anne.

He turned to his former batman with a grim smile. "We'll just have to outwit her, won't we, Danvers?"

Chapter
Twenty-five

Anne had led a grumbling Lois over the easiest terrain she could find for the past forty-five minutes. It was fortunate indeed for Lois that she was so fond of her.

"Anne, my leg is going to drop off. Couldn't we get down for a few minutes?"

"Of course, if you'd like to." Anne reined in her mare.

"No. On second thought, I wouldn't. It's too difficult to get up again." Lois looked down as if measuring the distance to the ground. "I'd never manage to remount without a groom to toss me up."

"Would you like to go on to the meadow now, dear? I don't mind if we are a few minutes earlier than we'd planned."

She didn't either. If it would help Lois, she'd be content to do it. Besides, it would give her a few more minutes to observe the boys' activities and decide whether or not she would let the Captain continue with his program.

She wished she hadn't thought about Sir John. Thinking of him set her body tingling again. Oh, when would her conscience stop tormenting her for having wanted him to kiss her just a few more times?

"No, let's go on with our ride, Anne. I'm all right. It's just that riding isn't my favorite activity, you know."

"Yes, I know."

"There's no need to depart from your original plan." Lois knew she sounded a little anxious, but she wanted to keep her unvoiced promise to Danvers. She didn't want Anne to arrive at the west meadow before the time Danvers and the Captain were expecting her. She knew, even if Anne did not, how much good the Captain's training was doing the children.

Anne wanted to go now, however. She was eager to accomplish her purpose and return her poor, complaining friend to the comfort of her hearth . . . before she drove her over a cliff in a fit of sheer frustration.

The meadow was still a few miles away, but they'd be there well before the time she and Lois had planned to be. It would still be at least three quarters of an hour before the time the boys usually came in for their baths.

Well, she couldn't help that. The fault wasn't in her planning, it was in her choice of companions. Much as she loved having Lois with her in all other endeavors, she wished she'd asked Robert to ride with her instead.

As matters stood, she'd risk being thought a spy to shorten both the time her dear friend had to spend in the saddle and the time *she* had to spend feeling guilty for having put her there.

Two miles away, out on the meadow, Sir John watched

dark clouds gathering out over the Channel. He scowled when he saw random winds ruffle cat's-paws on its surface in the middle distance. Sunlight lit the west meadow still, but he'd have to keep a careful eye on the approaching storm.

He cursed the towering clouds roundly. If the weather took a turn for the worse, it might be days before he and Danvers could work with the boys again. It would also put him in close contact with Anne, not something he wanted, with her in her present mood.

Danvers called over to him, "Better get 'em up and back down again quick, Captain."

John nodded. An errant gust of wind blowing his hair, he turned to the boys. "All right, men. You've practiced enough to do this without a hitch. Are you ready to try?"

"Oh, yes!" Brian's golden curls bounced as he and George answered simultaneously.

Sir John threw back his head and laughed. "Strip down, then," he ordered.

"Boots off, too, lads," Danvers told them.

The boys dropped their coats, weskits, and fine linen shirts to the grass of the meadow. Boots were piled on top with no regard for the pristine linen, and they ran over to Danvers at the foot of the tower to have their safety lines tied around their waists. They were eager to tackle something more challenging than the low garden wall they'd been taught to climb on.

Luther looked up and blanched.

George said, "Gracious. It looks so *high*."

Brian added, "And so smooth."

Brandon was the only one to maintain his enthusiasm. "The Captain will show us how." He threw back his head and squinted up at the top of the tower. "And just think what a splendid view there will be from the top!"

Sir John hid a grin as he stripped down. Pride filled him to have Brandon Kent as his ward. Bare-chested and bare-foot, he slipped the coil of rope Danvers handed him over his head to rest slantwise across his chest.

Luther Athelstain stared at Sir John's shoulder where a ragged white scar bloomed like some exotic flower. "I say, Captain! Is that a wound from a musket ball?" He pointed.

Brandon slapped his hand down. "Be quiet, Luther."

Danvers stood in tight-lipped disapproval.

After a moment, Sir John said calmly, "Yes, Luther." Then he added with equal disinterest, "The scar along my ribs is from a French saber. So's the one on my back." He was teaching them the skills of war, it was only fair that he teach them the cost of war.

Danvers sensed his discomfort and called the boys to order. "Watch the Captain carefully. You'll be going up after him in a minute or two."

The boys watched intently as Sir John moved to the foot of the stone tower and began to scale it with a skill that left them breathless. Clinging to irregularities in the wall they couldn't even see, he made steady progress up the vertical surface. Muscles they aspired to have the like of someday rippled across his back as he pulled himself higher and higher until he was a dizzy distance above them.

"Watch carefully." Danvers spoke quietly. "See how he makes use of any little outcropping, any place where the stonemasons let the stones get out of line enough to give him a hand- or foothold. It's just as you learned on the garden wall."

"Yes," they breathed as one child.

George whispered, "But so much higher!"

"And there is nothing to catch him." Luther was fascinated.

"*He* won't fall." Brian's voice was worshipful.

"Neither will we." Brandon's voice was calm and confident.

Danvers said, "You climbed the garden wall, here you can do the same. The difference will be that the coil of rope that the Captain has over his shoulder will be tied to the ropes around your waists for your safety."

Even as he spoke, a piece of the stone Sir John had placed a foot on broke off. Cords of muscle stood out along his arms and across his back as he caught himself and felt for another foothold.

The boys continued to watch tensely, and in another moment, Sir John was safely over the parapet. Immediately he removed the coil of rope from his shoulder and sent one end of it swishing down to them. Danvers grabbed it and tied the end to the rope belt he'd tied through Brandon's legs and around his waist earlier. "Remember, now, Your Lordship. Test your holds before you put your full weight on 'em, and always be ready for one to betray you. You saw what just happened to the Captain."

"Yes!" Brian blurted. "And he didn't have a safety rope!"

"I shall be careful, Danvers," Brandon promised, his eyes steady, his voice edged with excitement. Going to the foot of the wall, he looked up, studying the surface for a moment, then began to climb. When he hoisted himself over the parapet at the top, The Captain grinned and clapped him on the back, and the boys sent a cheer ringing up from where they stood on the ground below.

Luther came up next, white-faced and moving at a snail's pace. Once they heard him whimper, though he was obedient to Danvers's stern command not to look down.

George followed him, scampering up the wall like a monkey, determined by his own fearless climb to remove the stain he felt his older brother had placed on them by his whimper.

Brian was the last to attempt the ascent. Sir John felt a breeze ruffle his accursed curls and looked quickly out over the water as Danvers prepared the youngest Kent for his climb.

The dark clouds he'd observed earlier were nearer, almost on them, and there was a great deal of movement in their towering columns. They turned and twisted with the force of the winds in them, roiling ever closer.

For a moment, he thought to postpone Brian's attempt on the wall. One look at the boy's eager face, though, changed his mind. They had time, if only just barely. If the storm arrived more quickly than his practiced eye told him it would, he could always send the boys down the tower stairs.

"Come on, Bri," he called down to the waiting boy.

Brian looked up at him with a shy smile and manfully attacked the tower. Halfway up, a heavy gust of wind preceding the storm caught and tore him loose from his holds on the wall. Scraping against the rough stones, the boy squeezed his eyes shut and clenched his teeth. He swung like a pendulum halfway up the tall tower.

"Hang on, Brian!" The Captain swung a leg over the parapet.

"Wait, Sir John!" Brandon was holding out the leftover end of the long rope securing his twin.

"Good man." Sir John belayed it around a crenel even as he congratulated the boy. He flung himself out into space on the rope and slipped instantly down to Brandon's twin.

"Steady, Bri." He reached out and stopped the child's swinging.

Brian offered him a frightened smile. Trust blazed in his eyes.

Sir John eased the child into a position to find a foothold

and steadied him as the boy regained his courage. Then, they were climbing side by side, the man encouraging the boy every step of the way.

With a mighty sigh, Brian heaved himself over the parapet and stood trembling a little but bursting with exultation. "I did it, sir! I did it."

Sir John stood smiling down at him. "There was never a moment's doubt that you would, Brian." He stuck out his hand. "Well done!"

Brandon grabbed his twin in a bear hug as soon as he'd shaken the Captain's hand, and all four boys congratulated themselves and each other in an excited babble.

Suddenly there was a cry from below. "Captain! There are the women! They're early!"

"Damn and blast!" Sir John looked out across the meadow. In the near distance he could clearly see two graceful figures on horseback, the skirts of their habits blowing in the quickening breeze.

The riders were headed into a slight depression. Good. They'd be unable to see the tower for a short time.

Sir John swung into action. "Quickly, men. Down the stairs or down the ropes, but be quick about it. The Marchioness is coming."

Brandon made a distressed sound and scrambled over the low parapet to walk down the wall with the rope.

Brian, his eyes wide as saucers, gulped once and followed his brother down the other rope.

Luther yelled, "Come on, George!" and disappeared into the tower to clatter down the steps.

George Athelstain cast one scornful glance in the direction his brother had taken, slid over the parapet, and took hold of the rope Brandon had used for his descent.

The Captain kicked his way down the wall with the rope

Brian had used and reached the ground an instant before the younger Athelstain.

Luther puffed his way out of the door at the base of the tower and ran to pick up his clothing. Every one of them was determined to protect the secrecy of their training from the approaching women.

When Anne and Lois rode up out of the grassy depression they'd entered a few moments before, the boys they'd come to spy on were all shrugging into jackets and tugging on their boots.

Danvers shot a glance at Miss Carswell, and saw her shrug her shoulders and tighten her lips. Evidently all her efforts hadn't been able to keep Lady Anne away from the meadow until time to send the boys in for their baths.

Anne drew her mount to a halt several yards from the group at the base of the west tower. Her gaze locked on the Captain. He stood casually, naked to the waist, stomping his feet down into his boots.

As she watched, he picked up his shirt and matter-of-factly pulled it on. She was aware of a most unladylike surge of disappointment. Still, he didn't succeed in getting it on before her fascinated regard had taken in every detail of his bare chest, shoulders, and back.

With lightning perception, she registered the white star of a scar on his shoulder, the one along his ribs, and the slash mark on his smooth-muscled back. She noted, too, the play of his well-toned muscles over the firmness of his upper body. There wasn't an ounce of excess weight on him.

Her heart began to do strange things. She felt herself growing oddly warm all over. The inane thought, *Thank God he kept his shirt on in the temple,* nearly set her to laughing hysterically. She reminded herself how angry she was with him for the unspeakable things he'd said to her as they'd reentered the castle from the maze. It didn't do to have her pulse racing as she watched him now. Sternly she admonished herself, *This will never do.*

Her body didn't hear a word. It just continued to melt at the sight of the Captain's warrior's body and the memory of the breathless moments she'd spent in his arms.

Chapter
Twenty-six

Anne drew a deep, steadying breath. She was behaving like an idiot. The man was a cad. He'd said things to her no gentleman would say to a lady. Shouted them at her, in fact.

She'd remember that episode. She'd fix her mind on it and keep her anger carefully as a shield against him. Having decided that, she called herself sharply to order.

Lois and she had come here to see that her precious twins were safe, and here she clearly saw . . . as she struggled to focus her eyes on something other than the lithe figure of the handsome Dragoon Captain . . . the boys' ponies unsaddled and tied to what she supposed was a military-style picket line, and ropes, of all things, hanging down from the top of the tallest tower on Castle Caldon.

What on earth could they mean? Their very length frightened her. She must certainly discover their purpose . . . and make very sure that they had nothing to do with her sons. "Captain!" The word was a command.

Sir John registered that with a lopsided grin. So Anne was still angry with him for admitting he wanted to make love to her? Very well, he could handle that. He left his cravat hanging loose around his neck and came forward instantly. Quelling a devilish inclination to salute the little lovely, he bowed instead, smiling up at her. "Lady Anne." He inclined his head to Lois. "Miss Carswell. What a pleasant surprise."

Anne suffered a pang of irritation. Why did she feel that Sir John was not as surprised as he pretended to be? And she knew her visit was more an annoyance to him than a pleasure. She was certain that she detected a slightly mocking tone in his deep voice. She sat frowning down at him. "What, may I ask, are the ropes for?"

He turned to survey the area behind him. "The ropes?" He turned back to smile disarmingly at her. Without a qualm he told her half the truth. "They're to help us when we descend from the top of the tower. By grasping them firmly, one can walk backward down a wall, you see."

Anne's blood all but stilled in her veins. Her eyes flew wide open. "Surely you haven't permitted my sons to do anything so dangerous!"

"Not without a safety line on them, Your Ladyship." His eyes lost their hint of amusement. "Surely you're aware that I would not do anything to endanger the young Marquess or his brother?"

She was silent a moment, her teeth clenched firmly against uttering the truth of how she felt about that. She could hardly tell him right here in front of four listening children that she was indeed suffering grave doubts. The doubts arose not because she thought he'd deliberately endanger her sons, but because she knew that in his mind he'd define as mere play any danger he presented.

He stood there looking up at her. His hand was on her mare's shoulder, scant inches from her knee. His fingers itched to place it warmly over the knee caught over the leaping horn of her saddle. Just a moment's contact would be worth the stinging slap he knew he'd get from her riding crop. He grinned at the thought, but for the sake of the children, he kept his hand where it was.

Being so aware of the nearness of his hand to her knee made thinking difficult for Anne. The glint of amusement was back in his eyes. His lazy smile didn't help any either. It was almost as if he knew perfectly well the effect he was having on her.

She dropped her gaze from his too-knowing eyes, then lifted it again immediately as she realized she was staring at his bare throat. Feeling the heat of a blush rise in her cheeks, she tried to say brusquely, "Perhaps we should have a conversation about this after dinner, Captain?"

Thank God her voice sounded normal—her request, just as she'd meant it to, no more than faintly polite. She just might withdraw from this meadow with her dignity still intact. "Lois?" she turned to her friend. "Are you about ready to end our ride?"

Lois smiled widely. "Heavens yes, my dear. Two hours on horseback are enough to last me for the next two years. Nothing, I assure you, would please me half so well as to end our ride." She turned to the others. "Captain." She nodded to Sir John. "Mr. Danvers." She smiled at the ex-soldier.

Then her expression firmed and she looked over at the boys. Sternly she ordered, "Do not be late for your baths."

"Yes, Lois," the twins chorused, their faces as innocent as Angels'.

Sir John stood and watched Lady Anne ride away. After a moment, he signaled Danvers to wind things up, but he never turned away from watching the retreating form of the slender Marchioness.

The fingers of his left hand still itched with the effort he'd made to keep them on the satiny shoulder of Lady Anne's mare. The strength of his desire to rest them instead on her knee surprised him. Evidently, he was ready to walk into parson's mousetrap.

He'd had a good run. His mistresses, when he'd had time to establish them, had always been the envy of every man who'd seen them. His casual liaisons on the Continent had always been with the women other men most wanted. He could retire from that particular field *d'amour* with honors, and finally he was willing to do it. With Anne.

He felt a grin nearly split his face. Lady Anne was a prize worth accepting. She was intelligent, brave, and beautiful. A man could do no better. In addition, he'd gain two excellent sons of whom he was inordinately fond. God had given him a great gift, indeed. Satisfaction welled up in him. He'd begin his courtship of his chosen bride immediately he saw her again.

Still fondly watching the tall grasses of the meadow spring back up where she'd passed, he gave Danvers the hand signal that ordered withdrawal from a position. Out of the corner of his eye, he saw the ex-Dragoon sergeant take the boys on their way. Still smiling, he continued gazing in the direction in which Anne—his Anne—had disappeared.

Even as he watched, the day darkened ominously. The calm surface of meadow changed. A strong wave shuddered through it as the first heavy blast of wind from the arriving storm washed over it.

The next gust whipped the hanging ends of his cravat out away from his chest, and he knew it was time to go. Putting two fingers to his mouth, he sent a whistle across the meadow. Immediately his charger thundered over to come to a skidding halt inches from him, shaking his mane in protest of the storm that was about to break over them.

Springing into the saddle, Sir John laughed exultantly. He threw his arms wide, embracing the day, embracing the storm, embracing life as he let the big horse gallop off to the barn.

Before they reached the huge, ancient structure, the storm broke, tearing at the two of them with icy fury as they plunged down the last few hundred feet to shelter.

Wind rattled every shutter and screamed around every wall. Gusts of it spiraled down chimneys and filled bed-chambers with the acrid smoke of fires built to warm their occupants . . . not suffocate them. Baths became chilling tortures to endure rather than the warm relaxations they were supposed to be.

Danvers handed Sir John his towel and looked at him closely.

"Leave off, man." Sir John snarled at him. "I'm fine!"

Danvers turned down the covers on his employer's bed. "The doctor said to be wary of chills, Captain."

"What the deuce are you doing? It's not bedtime."

"I'm in hopes that you'll get into your bed until you've recovered from your bath, sir."

Sir John stared at him as if his batman had lost his mind. "Not bloody likely."

Danvers gritted his teeth. "The doctor said . . . "

"Hang the damned doctor. I want my blue superfine coat tonight, Danvers."

Danvers knew he was defeated. With a reproachful glance at his employer he went to the wardrobe. Bringing the coat in question, he began to brush its already impeccable surface.

Something special was up. The Captain only wore this particular coat when there was. It was his favorite of all the coats Weston had tailored for him, and, Danvers suspected, he considered it lucky, as well.

A faint shiver assailed Sir John as he stood in the drafty room waiting to be dressed. Frowning slightly, he told Danvers, "By the way. If I should happen to succumb to the recurrence of the fever, as you fear, I want you to get me home to London without the slightest delay." His frown deepened as if to emphasize his words. "It won't do to have Lady Anne subjected to my rantings. Is that understood?"

Stung, Danvers asked stiffly, "Have I ever failed to understand one of your *orders,* Sir John?"

Sir John had the grace to blush. "Of course not." He raised a hand in a conciliatory gesture. "I'm behaving abominably, Danvers. Apologies."

"Accepted, sir." But Danvers thought the Captain was behaving just as he always did before a bout with illness. Already he was worrying that the color that stained his employer's cheeks might owe something to fever. Though Sir John had been free of it for over a month now, Danvers feared the devastating malady might choose to recur after the Captain's drenching.

Anne, in the meantime, was seeing to the twins' baths. She was aghast at the number of scrapes and bruises she was finding on the slight bodies of her two little boys.

"Rose!" She called the nursemaid to the tub. "Some of these bruises are days old," she said accusingly.

The boys' second nursemaid blushed and said defensively, "The Marquess commanded me not to tell you, Milady."

Anne's gaze shot to her older son. "Brandon!"

Brandon met her regard unflinchingly. "I know that such things upset you, Mama, but men get bruises when they are learning to do men's work." His clear blue eyes calmly challenged her.

Anne sat back on her heels, her mind trying to comprehend this change in her precious Brandon. Never before would he have tried to keep anything from her. It hurt her deeply.

She looked at Brian. He had a dreadful scrape on one shoulder that even now seeped tiny amber dewdrops. "And you, Brian? Were you going to keep this"—she pointed at the scrape—"from me, too?"

Brian's eyes filled with tears, but his face was resolute. "Yes, Mama."

"How did you get it?"

Brandon thought it best that he be the one to answer. "He got it when his foot slipped climbing the tower. He brushed by a bit of rough mortar before the Captain caught him." He regarded her solemnly.

Anne's head spun. "Caught him?" she asked weakly. "Was he falling then?" She felt as if her heart had stopped beating.

"No, Mama. Of course not! Danvers had hold of his safety rope, Brian couldn't fall. The Captain climbed down and caught him to stop him from swinging back and forth."

"I see." Anne tried to speak calmly. More than anything, she wanted to keep the boys from discerning the shock she was feeling at the activities the Captain engaged them in. Otherwise she would learn nothing more, and she had to protect them. "Then you were trying to climb up that tower?"

"Oh, yes!" Brian was bursting to tell her. "We had practiced on the low wall to the garden and learned all about

how to do it. Climbing the west tower was the test of it all."
His eyes shone. "The west tower is the tallest in the whole
castle. Did you know that?"

Anne could hardly speak. "Yes."

"And we all got to the top!" Brandon was excited to tell
her, too, now she'd taken Bri's words so well. "And we'd
have done it again, too, only we had to stop when we saw
you coming."

He explained soothingly, "I think the Captain doesn't
want you to see us until we are quite good at it. Then you'll
be invited to our gragiation ceremonies."

"Graduation," Anne corrected without thought, her mind
numb.

"Anyway, all of us but Luther made it down the ropes
while you and Lois were out of sight down in the swale."
His voice took on a trace of scorn. "Luther went down the
stairs in the tower instead."

Anne was trying to regain her equilibrium. Her head was
still spinning. To think of her two precious babies climbing
a tower was more than she could bear. Inanely, she asked,
"Do you have many other hurts?"

"Aw," Brian told her. "We don't have *any* hurts compared to the Captain. He climbed the tower without a rope
around him, and he got several bad scrapes then . . . when
places in the stonework gave way under his weight—"

Brandon interrupted. "Remember, Bri. The whole time
he was climbing he was instructing us. That must have
taken part of his concentration so that he wasn't paying sufficient attention to his holds."

"Yes, and he already had lots of interesting scars on him
from before."

Anne slipped down to sit flat on the hearth rug beside the
tub.

"Are you all right, Mama?" It was in unison.

"Yes," she lied. "I'm just getting more comfortable."

All right? All right! How could she be all right? She was struggling with the mind-numbing thought of everything that was going on. Not only were her eight-year-old sons performing perilous feats of daring, but now she knew that Sir John had climbed the same horribly high tower *without a safety rope* and while lecturing to her darlings on how to do it.

She could hardly contain the emotions that wracked her. She was caught between warring desires. She wished to faint dead away for the first time in her life to escape the horror of it all, on one hand. On the other, she wanted to see Captain Sir John's brave heart hideously offered to her on a platter.

Confused by conflicting emotions or not, one thing she did know. The next time she could find to be alone with her handsome Captain of Dragoons, she was not only going to stop him from endangering her twins, she was also going to tell him exactly how much she hated him for having so casually done so!

With grim determination, she vowed she would order Captain Sir John Kent to go. And the sooner, the better.

From where he stood, Lord Jared could see the expression on Anne's face. It didn't please him. *"Blast you, woman. What maggot's got in your head now?"*

Though he was the whole width of the room from them in order to avoid chilling the twins with the cold he was always trailing around with him, he could see the anger in Anne's eyes, the tightness around her mouth. They boded ill for his plans for her. And he had such plans for her!

Now there was a special bond between himself and Anne and the twins—their kinship. They were his descendants, bless God! If he could get Anne and the Captain together . . . At that thought, his heart almost beat its way out of his chest—except of course that he no longer had one of either.

But he had hopes. God, yes, he had hopes.

This had to be. It just had to be. Dear God, the remembrance of Bethany in his arms sang through him. Anticipated happiness made his senses whirl.

Then, close on the heels of his joy came frustration. *"Blast it, wench! Get over your pique with Sir John. How the devil am I to unite you and the captain if you sharpen your claws for him every time one of your boys gets a bruise? Why the blazes can't you just see what a man he is and stop fighting my plans for you?"*

In his agony of ordeal, he longed for his wife. Quickly he sent the awesome power of his love flying out over the long miles to his beloved Bethany.

Chapter
Twenty-seven

At dinner, by concentrating on the bruises she'd seen on the young bodies of her twins, Anne was able to erase from her present thoughts the undeniable attraction the Captain had for her. By thinking instead of the twins, she was able to ignore the warmth she saw in his eyes.

She fixed her gaze on her other guests, and her mind on the dangers to which Sir John had deliberately exposed— and no doubt planned to continue to expose—her boys. Soon she was seething to have it out with him about her sons.

Steadied by her need to protect Brandon and Brian from the man, she could even glance his way again. Her eyes flashed every time she looked at Captain Sir John Kent.

Sir John noted her banked fury, recognized it as being about her children, not his kisses, and enjoyed it.

Anne snatched her napkin out of her lap, slapped it down

on the table, and said, "Shall we adjourn to the drawing room, ladies?" She gave the Captain a final glare as a footman pulled back her chair. "I'm certain the gentlemen would like to enjoy a cigar without us."

"But . . . " Lord Robert's protest that he and Sir John had always forgone that pleasure to be with the ladies died in his throat at the look his hostess sent him. As the bewildered women left the room in the wake of their agitated hostess, he asked, "What the blazes did you do to her, Captain?"

The last thing Lady Anne heard as she sailed away with Lois and Lady Becky in tow was the Captain saying with a smirk in his voice, "Not half as much as I plan to."

Out in the dark hall, Brandon and Brian shrank back into the deepest shadows as the three women passed them.

"Whew! That was a close one," Brandon told his twin. "They usually stay at the table longer."

"We'd better hurry up to the tower. Mama looked mad. She might not stay in the drawing room as long as usual, either."

Brandon looked at his brother with approval. Brian was growing up at last. "Come on, let's go."

Hurrying to the heavy door, they pulled it open and rushed up the stairs. They were eager to see what Lord Jared would have to say about their mother almost catching them scaling the west tower. Agreeing earlier that their Mama had taken it all too calmly, they felt in need of wise counsel. They were so bent on their errand that they failed to be cautious.

Behind them, a figure darted from shadow to shadow. Luther, a triumphant grin on his face, was following them. He'd promised himself that soon he'd know the twins' secret, and he was about to find it out.

When he did, then the little snobs would stop looking down their noses at him, or he'd make them sorry!

By the time the gentlemen joined the ladies in the drawing room, Anne was a little more in control of her anger. As Lady Becky and Lois conversed, she planned the conversation she intended to have with the Captain.

She looked at him boldly as he entered the room, Lord Robert companionably by his side. His eyes had a speculative gleam when their gazes met, and it irritated her that he didn't seem to be the least bit repentant.

Didn't he comprehend the depths of his perfidy in allowing her sons to take part in the scaling of the west tower? Or did he think she was such a ninny that she wouldn't find out from the children just what it was that he'd had the poor little dears doing in the west meadow?

Well, Captain Sir John Kent had a very rude awakening coming. And Anne was glad she had found—

Her thoughts were brutally ended. Shattering screams of sheer terror came to them from the hall outside.

"Mama! Mama!" It was Luther screeching at the top of his lungs. Every head turned toward the doorway. His legs pumping for all they were worth, he hurtled past Higgins and erupted into the drawing room. His face was pasty white. His eyes looked as if they would pop out of his head. "A ghost, Mama! Don't let him get me! Don't let him get me!" He flung himself to his knees and clutched his startled mother around the waist.

"What is it? Luther! What's the matter?" Lady Becky was shaken from her usual indifference.

Luther's white face and sobs brought the others from their chairs to surround Lady Rebecca's.

"What is it, Luther? Has something happened to the

twins?" Anne could think only of her sons. Her voice was frantic.

Sir John slipped a supporting arm around her waist, and she leaned into him for comfort.

"A g-g-g-ghost! I j-just s-s-saw a g-ghost!"

Lord Robert, as calm as ever, frowned at his oldest son. "There are no such things as ghosts, Luther."

The frightened boy turned his face to the others. "In the tower. I saw him. I followed Brandon and Brian." He shook as another spasm of fright hit him. "I knew they were keeping something s-secret. I wanted to find out what it was. I didn't know it wa-was a ghost!"

"There, there," his mother soothed.

"It chased me," he gibbered. "It was g-g-going to k-k-kill me!" His voice was a wail.

"He was not!" Brian stood in the doorway scowling fiercely at his cowardly playmate.

"He would *not* have harmed you, Luther." Brandon's tone was scathing. "You'd know that if you hadn't run."

His twin added, "He's just here to find an old letter." Brian wanted to shake Luther. "He's been here a hunnert years, and he hasn't hurt anybody yet. You're just an old 'fraidy cat!"

Anne heard her sons' words and was overcome by a storm of emotions. If Sir John hadn't held her firmly clasped against his side, she'd have had trouble standing. Her anger with him was momentarily forgotten. Ghost. Her mind was spinning. The castle was indeed haunted, then! She'd been trying with all her might to deny such a possibility.

Haunted. That explained the cold in the great hall. The windstorm in the passageway. She recalled what Sir John had told her . . . the story of the man who had been murdered there and the way she'd kept on wondering, unable to dismiss it from her mind. She'd finally accepted the fact that the man had been her great-grandfather, but not that he was haunting the castle, if it could possibly have been . . .

Sir John interrupted her thoughts. "One at a time, boys. Tell us what the devil's going on here. You first, Luther. And pull yourself together."

Luther rose shakily from his mother's lap. "Y-yessir." He swiped at his tears of fright with the back of a grubby hand and attempted to obey his Captain.

"I knew Brandon and Brian had a secret because I caught them talking about it once." He gulped a breath. "So I followed them tonight, and they went up in the east tower." He gulped again, hard, and his eyes grew huge. Looking at the Captain's stern face, however, he struggled on. "When I got up to the room at the top, I heard them talking with somebody. When I jumped into the room . . . "

"Yes!" Brian made known his playmate's utter disregard of good manners. "He just charged in. He didn't even knock or anything!"

The Captain frowned him down and Brandon poked him to be still. Both twins glanced over toward a certain shadowy corner of the drawing room.

Luther went on as if Brian hadn't spoken. "There in the center of the room at the top of the tower, talking to the twins like he was a person—"

"He *is* a person, you lout!" Brandon shouted.

Lois interjected faintly, "Don't be rude."

Luther finished his sentence, " . . . was a g-ghost."

"How did you know he was a ghost, Luther?" Sir John didn't believe in ghosts—except, perhaps, Bethany—but he knew the only way to calm everybody down was to get to the bottom of this.

"I c-could see through him."

"Very well." He could feel Anne's heartbeat speed up. "Go on."

Luther took a deep breath. "And then, he t-turned around and started for me. I tell you, he was going to kill me!"

Brandon couldn't stand it any longer. "Ha! All he did was turn to see who the rudeby was who'd charged in uninvited. *You* nearly killed yourself running away!"

"I did not!"

"No?" Brandon demanded hotly. "Then how come you got here so much faster than we did?"

"Yes!" Brian chimed in. "How come?"

"That will do, men!" Sir John continued with his attempt to get to the bottom of things. "The thing we're trying to discover here, is who this—er—ghost is, and why he's here." He'd never admit it, but he was having a bit of trouble with his own mind just at the moment. He couldn't just write off the twins' testimony, for he respected their intelligence. That fact was making him distinctly uneasy.

"That's simple, sir." Brandon stepped forward. "He was murdered here by men who'd falsely accused him of treason. He's here to find a letter that will prove he's—was—innocent."

Lady Becky said, "Oh, dear," and fell back in her chair.

Lord Robert moved closer and placed a hand on her shoulder.

Anne was looking decidedly strange, and Brandon sought desperately to reassure his mother. "Mama. The ghost is really a nice man. And Brian and I have promised him we'll help him. Luther just . . . " He wrinkled his nose; he didn't want to have to put into words what he thought of Luther's behavior. Not in front of his Mama, anyway.

Sir John took back the conversation. He spoke calmly. "And just how did you plan to help your gentleman ghost, Lord Brandon?"

Brandon shot his Captain a shining look. He'd been addressed as an adult, believed like an adult, and asked his plans like an adult. In front of his mother, too! He stood even taller. "We think that the letter he's looking for must be in some hidden place. A secret room, or something. Like a priest's hole."

"Why have you decided that?"

Anne slipped away from him. Somehow, he'd gotten the whole room reassured and thinking again. Even her. She was perfectly capable of standing alone now the first shock of her young guest's proclamation had passed. Besides, she had no desire to have the perfidious Captain's arm around her!

"Because he'd know if anyone had found it." Brandon was answering Sir John. "He says he watches everything that happens in the castle, and that if the letter had been where somebody could've found it, they would've by now."

"That's certainly sound logic." Sir John let his gaze assess Anne. She seemed all right. He relaxed. "Then the next thing you'll want to do will be to check the plans of the castle for a space that might contain a secret room."

The twins winced. None of the others knew it, but they'd clearly heard St. Legere's ghost bellow, *"Damn you, Captain Kent! Don't you think I've passed through every wall in this blasted castle looking for just such a space?"*

Anne touched her fingers lightly to her ears and shrugged off a vague sense of uneasiness to say, 'I've asked if there are any plans, Sir John. The solicitors assure me they don't know of any."

Sir John looked annoyed. "Well, there are some, Lady Anne. I came across them in the armory when I was looking for suitable weapons to train the boys with."

"Weapons! Surely you weren't . . . "

He cut her off, scowling. The blasted woman was still sure he meant to kill off her sons. "Just now, we're concerned with drawings of the floor plans of the castle, Your Ladyship. Come, boys. We'll go get them."

He headed for the door in long strides, the twins hard on his heels. Luther went back to lean against his mother's knees.

No one spoke while the three were gone. There didn't seem to be anything to say.

And the room was getting chilly.

Five minutes later, Sir John returned with the twins and carrying a roll of dusty parchment. "Here are the plans of the castle." He walked to the table near the fireplace and spread the plans out on it. "Hand me that candlestick, Lord Robert, if you will."

Lord Robert left his wife to bring the requested candlestick to weight a corner of the plans. He helped the Captain smooth out and anchor down the first sheet of the stubborn parchment.

"This seems to be the ground floor of th—"

A woman's bloodcurdling scream tore through the room. "The ghost! There! At the door! The ghost!" Lady Rebecca stood, her eyes staring. She was pointing toward the hall as she clasped her son securely to her.

As a man, they all ran to the door. Sir John snatched up one candelabrum and Higgins a second. Lois and Lord Robert were only a step behind them as they spilled out into the hall. The twins ran with them, looking confused.

Anne rushed to the door and was stopped. She stood, her hand at her throat, staring after them. Every instinct told her to see to the safety of her sons, but she couldn't move! Something was holding her back. Something dragged at her, willing her to remain in the drawing room.

She felt a shiver run down her spine. She knew beyond

the shadow of a doubt that the ghost wasn't out in the hall.
She knew with an awful certainty that the ghost had been,
and still was, in the drawing room. She knew, because she
knew that he was standing right behind *her*!

In that mind-shattering instant, as fear shivered up her
spine in an icy rush, tears of terror and tears of relief filled
her eyes. It was! It had to be! It was the only way she could
explain the presence she so frequently felt near her . . . the
presence that she felt even when no one else could sense it
was her great-grandfather, Jared St. Legere.

Awareness flooded her. She sensed him here. Now. *She*
could feel him when none of the other adults could because
she was of his blood. And her sons. Dearest God! *They*
were talking about the ghost of the long-dead Jared St. Legere as if he were their friend!

Her senses went reeling, the room blurred and began to
fade.

Sir John returned at that moment and swept her into his
arms when he saw how she swayed. "Anne!" His voice was
hoarse with concern.

Anne, resting—for just this one, last moment against his
chest—felt his heartbeat accelerate and his voice rumble as
he demanded, "Did you see him in the hall, twins?"

"No, sir," Brian told him.

Brandon, however, was staring, horrified, across the
room. Suddenly he was dashing toward the fireplace. "The
plans for the castle! They're burning!"

"The devil you say!" John spun around with Anne still in
his arms, his eyes intent on the table where he'd left the
plans.

Anne pushed herself out of Sir John's embrace to shout
at Brandon, "Leave them! Don't try to get them!" Relief
flooded her to see him obey.

It was hopeless. Burning quickly, the ancient roll of the

remaining parchment pages was falling to flaming bits in the front of the fireplace. The pages that bore the plans of the upper floors of Castle Caldon were lost to them forever.

Anne could feel the Captain's keen disappointment.

She went to her sons. They might have suffered a devastating setback in their efforts to help the ghost, but they could still give her the confirmation she knew she so vitally needed. Her voice was a husky thread. "His name. Tell me the ghost's name."

Before she'd finished her question, before her sons could frame an answer, from the shadows just behind her she heard clearly in a voice that rang with pride, *"I am Jared St. Legere, Fifth Earl of Mannerly."*

Anne gasped. She could feel the blood drain from her face. Her sons, the Captain, the whole room swirled and faded. For the first time in her life, Anne knew she was going to faint.

"His name's Jared St. Legere," Brandon supplied. Then he cried, "Mama!"

Sir John spun around. He saw his beloved begin to fall. "Anne! Oh, God! Anne!" The agony in his voice told the whole room what he felt for her.

Springing toward her, he caught her up in his arms just before she touched the floor.

Chapter
Twenty-eight

Sir John strode into the hall with the unconscious Anne in his arms and Higgins and Lois trailing along. Behind them in the drawing room, Lord Robert calmed the excited boys, while his wife stood white-faced and stricken, staring after her friend, and the last fragment of the plans for Castle Caldon flared to oblivion in the fireplace.

Higgins was hard put to keep the candles in his candelabrum alight as he hurried after the Captain. His butler's duties be damned. Lady Anne was his first priority.

Lois fluttered ahead and held Anne's door open for him. Then she ran across the room to get to the bed in time to turn the covers back for him. The moment she had, she went to yank the bellpull for Marie.

Anne moaned and stirred the instant John slipped his arms from around her. "Where . . . ?" She stared up at the canopy of her bed in confusion. Hadn't she been in the dra . . . ? Of course! She *had* been in the drawing room. They had all been in the drawing room. And Luther had come in and . . . She looked over at Sir John. "My great-grandfather. It was my great-grandfather, John. He's a ghost."

"Just lie still, Anne." He was watching her anxiously, his eyes too bright, his face flushed.

Lois shot over to the bed. "Yes, dear. You fainted."

Higgins hovered behind her. "Who wouldn't, with that harum-scarum boy shrieking into the room like that," he soothed.

Anne struggled to sit up. Higgins knew she never fainted.

Lois pushed her firmly back down again. "Just lie still, dear. You've had quite a shock."

"Yes." Sir John's voice held a hint of amusement. "One would."

Irritation rose in Anne. Did he think she'd imagined the voice she'd heard? This time, she did sit up.

Lois was deterred from forcing her back down against her pillows by the look on her face. Recognizing that look, Lois stepped back and murmured, "Oh, dear."

Higgins, who'd seen that same expression many times in the willful turbulence of Anne's childhood, rolled his eyes skyward and muttered, "Quite so." He, too, withdrew to a safer distance.

Captain Sir John, a little dizzied by the first tremors of the fever he knew was returning, missed the little byplay. Unknowingly, he put himself further at risk. "Come, Anne, be sensible."

"Uh-oh." Higgins couldn't help his exclamation. He knew too well the unfortunate effect the word "sensible" had on his mistress.

"Sensible! Sensible!" Anne threw her legs over the side

of the bed and sat bolt upright. "I am perfectly sensible. In the drawing room, the ghost was standing right behind me while all of you were looking for him out in the hall. He was standing right behind me. Close behind me. I could feel the chill of his presence as easily as I can feel these sheets." Her hand swept the sheets she sat on. "I could hear him, too. He spoke with perfect clarity." She was glaring. "And he told me, quite clearly, that he was Jared St. Legere, Fifth Earl of Mannerly, and *that's my great-grandfather, whether you like it or not!*"

"Oh, dear." Lois stood closer to Higgins. "She's shouting. That's a bad sign, isn't it?"

"Indubitably."

Sir John flung fuel on the fire. "Calm down, Anne."

Higgins was unable to suppress a groan.

Lois didn't need to be told that Sir John had chosen his words unwisely. It would have been obvious to a statue.

"Calm down!" Anne slid down off the bed and stood firmly on her own two feet. She could feel her temper rising behind the dam of her will. "Of all the unmitigated gall! Just where, pray tell, do *you* get the nerve to tell me to calm down, Mister Captain Sir John Kent!" She pushed her face forward and advanced on him.

"You come here—*uninvited*—and with your extremely disruptive presence proceed to destroy what little peace I'd been striving to put together. You endanger the lives of my sons with your cavalry charges and your tower-climbing, and then you have the effrontery to tell *me* to be calm?" She all but shrieked the question at him.

Sir John recognized it as rhetorical.

"Anne, you're upsetting yourself." His voice was insultingly calm. "Be sensible."

The damn burst. "Sensible!" Now she *was* shrieking, and she didn't care. It was the word her parents had tortured her with all her life. And after resisting it with all her might, she'd finally been sensible. She'd married Montague . . . and precipitated herself into hell.

Sensible! She *loathed* the word. "Sensible! How dare *you* tell *me* to be sensible! *You* take children up towers hundreds of feet high, and maul your hostesses in mazes. What do *you* know about being sensible?"

Sir John, his face dead white except for the two spots of fever burning on his cheeks, said stiffly. "Very little, it would seem, Milady."

His voice was deeper than Anne had ever heard it. There was a note in it that stabbed her to the heart.

"I had no idea my presence was so distressful to you."

"Well, it is!" She couldn't bear to see the tightness around his mouth, to see the hurt in his eyes. "Oh, why can't you just go."

The heedless girl she'd been before her marriage surfaced in her. She didn't care what she said to him, so long as she didn't have to see the quiet reproach in his eyes.

"Go!" She pointed toward the door, her arm rigid. "Get out of my life. Get out of my . . . " Belatedly she remembered that Castle Caldon belonged to Sir John. " . . . *this* castle! And leave me and my sons alone!"

"Very well, Anne." He bowed again, turned on his heel, and stalked majestically out of the room.

Anne threw herself back down on her bed and gave way to a fit of weeping. Desolation flooded her. He was gone. She'd sent him away. Screaming like a common fishwife, she'd vilified him and sent away the man she loved.

How could he ever think of her again without repugnance? Without disgust? While she . . . while she would never see his dear face in her memory without feeling the excruciating regret that was tearing her apart right now.

Lois and Higgins came up to the bed and stood there,

wanting with all their hearts to comfort her. Lois reached out and stroked her hair. Higgins wished he could.

Anne wailed and burrowed deeper into her pillows. All her adult life, she'd acted with restraint. She'd done the proper thing, even if she'd choked on it. But now! Now, when it mattered to her more than anything in the world to have behaved wisely, she'd acted like a shrew.

She could hardly bear to remember what she'd done. She'd accused him of behaving improperly in the maze. She knew, and knew very well that he did, too, that she had all but begged him on her knees to kiss her. When he'd obliged, she'd melted against him and behaved in a manner that any red-blooded man would have interpreted as he had.

And now, she'd accused him of mauling her. In front of Lois and Higgins. She could die.

She'd seen the look in his eyes and knew that she'd wounded him deeply. He would never forgive her. Never.

Why should he? She'd behaved unforgivably. He was gone. She loved him with all her heart and she'd driven him away. She'd lost him forever. She wept into her pillow like a heartbroken child.

Marie appeared in the doorway. "You rang?"

Chapter
Twenty-nine

Outside the castle, the storm raged on. Waves of green water, unleavened by foam, lashed the foot of the cliff, while the wind howled and drove blinding rain that sought entry through every arrow slit and window, and seeped under the massive front doors.

Sir John stormed out of his beloved Anne's room cursing aloud the day he'd met her. Waves of debilitating weakness washed over him and obliterated his ability to see clearly. Staggering as the fever rose in his blood, he fought his way to his bedchamber, muttering, "Dear Lord, make Danvers be there!"

"Captain!" Danvers's head snapped up from a task as the door slammed back against the wall. Leaping to catch his friend, he got to Sir John just as the uncontrollably shaking man lost his hold on the doorjamb.

Supporting him to the bed, Danvers lay Sir John on it

and piled the covers high. "Do you want water? Can you drink?"

"N-n-no." Sir John was shaking so hard he couldn't speak easily. His jaw locked against the shudders that wracked his body; there was no way he could have swallowed. "Dan-vers!" He reached out desperately and caught his batman by the sleeve, half-rising. Danvers's face swam before his eyes, but he managed to tell him, "Ho-ome. L-london. G-get m-me home!"

"But, Captain." The last thing Danvers wanted for his friend was a long trip in dangerous weather. "The world's gone mad out there."

"It . . . will . . . b-be . . . better when we . . . get aw-w-way from the sea. Get . . . me h-home!" His eyes clouded, and he fell back against his pillows, fainting.

"Aye, sir!" He hurried to the bellpull and gave it a yank that must have sent the bell jangling off its spring below-stairs. Then he began methodically packing Sir John's things.

As he packed he muttered, frowning, "What the devil have you been doing to bring the fever on so fast?" He was almost annoyed. "You had only a touch when I saw you only a few hours ago." His voice was rough with concern.

Leaving his packing, he went to the bed to check on the man who lay there shaking as if he'd come apart. He put his hand against his captain's forehead. "Burning up. Dammit, Sir John, you're burning up! And ordering me to take you out into the coldest, wettest night of your whole blasted visit!"

The door slammed open again, and Sir John's two foot-men spilled into the room. "What's up, Danvers? The Captain never rings the bell like that."

"He didn't. I did. We've got to get him home."

"In this?" The man gestured incredulously toward the window where the night had gone wild. "Are you daft?"

"His orders." Danvers shot them an inquiring look. "Do either of you want to be the one to face him if his orders aren't carried out?"

The footmen shook their heads, resigned to a cold, wet ride to London. Ex-soldiers who had served under Captain Sir John Kent, they'd been among the Dragoons who'd conspired to hide his bouts of fever from Sir John's fellow officers. At about the time he'd left the service because of it, they'd each sustained wounds for which they were being dismissed. Grateful he'd taken them along to become footmen, their loyalty never faltered. If Sir John wanted to go to London in the worst storm of the year, then they'd see to it that Sir John got to London.

They walked over to look down at the man in the bed. Both feared taking him out into the weather when the fever was just beginning. A chill at this point could be deadly. They exchanged worried glances. The taller one murmured, "Orders." The other nodded. Both knew there was nothing more to be said.

On the bed, Sir John twisted and writhed, shuddering hard under the onslaught of the fever. Shouting long strings of unintelligible words, he threw the bed covers to the floor.

As the footmen picked up the bedclothes and tucked them firmly in, one asked, "Why, Danvers? He's not good enough to travel."

"He said he doesn't want Lady Anne to be disturbed by his rantings."

The three men stood regarding one another for a long moment while they registered the significance of that bit of very interesting information. Finally the stockier one said, "I'll go roust out the coachman."

He wasn't gone long, but when he returned with word that the coach would be at the door in five minutes, Danvers was ready. They got Sir John on his feet and bundled him into his heaviest greatcoat. It took all three of them to get the Captain to the great hall. He was worse than deadweight. His helpless body jerked almost out of their hands as the fever wracked his body.

When he met them in the hall, Higgins was appalled by the Captain's condition. "Surely you can't mean to take him out in this! Not with him so ill!" He looked at the valet with outrage. "My God, Danvers, you'll kill him!"

None of them answered the butler beyond the terse word, "Orders." They were too intent on their task. Danvers had to hold Sir John propped against the wall while the footmen and Higgins wrestled with the door.

When they finally got it forced open against the wind, Higgins was surprised to see Sir John's coach waiting, his groom hanging from the bridles of the lead team as the coachman tried to sooth the well-trained but storm-maddened horses. His stentorian voice barely carried to them over the howling wind of the storm.

Danvers and the two footmen lifted the Captain into the traveling coach and piled in after him.

When they'd driven off, Higgins shook his head. As he struggled, in closing it, to keep the door from catapulting him across the great hall in a torrent of wind-driven rain, he predicted, "They'll kill the man!"

Out in the full fury of the storm, the coach rocked and slithered down roads that had become rivers. From the box, the coachman kept up a steady stream of curses while the groom huddled beside him and prayed the horses could see their way more clearly than he could.

Sheets of water followed by sheets of water blew across the winding road down from Castle Caldon as the wind

drove the rain in from the sea. The road became a quag-
mire. Only the coachman's skillful handling of the team
kept it from panicking as the rain lashed mercilessly at
them.

Inside, it took all three of his employees to keep Sir John
from leaping out into the mud of the road. Certain in his
fevered imagination that he was being tortured by the Span-
ish, the Captain made continued valiant efforts to escape
them.

"Hold him!" became their war cry, and every man jack
of them was totally exhausted by the time they arrived at
St. Legere House in London.

Bundling the now semiconscious Captain Sir John out of
the coach was child's play compared to the effort it had
been to keep him inside it. They rushed him past his startled butler and straight up to his bed.

"Thank you, men. I can handle him now." Danvers
began pulling off Sir John's boots.

"Let us know how he fares."

"Aye," Danvers told them as the door closed behind the
pair.

"Anne. Don't go! Anne!" The man on the bed reached
out to someone Danvers couldn't see. "Anne! Where are
you?"

Danvers stopped removing Sir John's damp clothes and
looked pensively at his patient. Sympathy softened his expression. "So that's the way things are, are they?"

Turning that bit of information over in his mind, Danvers
finished getting his friend into the nightshirt Sir John had
taken to wearing since he'd asked about whether or not
there were maidservants at St. Legere House. Then he covered him carefully and pulled a chair over from beside the
fireplace to settle down for a long, hard night.

*   *   *

Back at Castle Caldon, the weather held. Blustery and dark, the day promised no let up in the storm.

Anne had spent a sleepless night, tormented by longings she'd never experienced before in her life. Over and over, she'd relived the passion of Sir John's embrace in her dreams. She had been powerless to stop them, and all night they'd been driving her, tantalizing her. Once, she'd cried out her wanting of him aloud and awakened herself.

Awake, she'd sat up in her bed with her arms locked around her knees and convinced herself that she was angry, not yearning. That the tingling fire that coursed through her was indignation, not passion. She'd fled the flames of her anger by telling herself that he'd endangered her children, and played fast and loose with her affections. That there was absolutely no truth in her later accusation hadn't stopped her from using it to strengthen her displeasure with the Captain.

By the time dawn broke, weak and pitiful thing that it was in the raging storm, she found she was anything but eager to see Sir John again. What could she say him? How was she to behave?

Dressed and on her way down to breakfast, she still had no answers. Her steps slowed. She wondered if it wouldn't be nice to have her breakfast on a tray in her room.

In her mind's eye, she saw Sir John's face and the reckless smile that always turned her bones to jelly. Could she bear to see him this morning? Could she bear to look into those knowing eyes and remember that magical time they'd spent in the maze? Could she bear to see in his eyes that he remembered the warmth with which she'd returned his kisses after the first chaste few? She blushed fiercely to recall her enthusiastic cooperation . . . and she knew she didn't dare see him.

No! She thought not! She turned back the way she had

come so quickly that her skirts swished viciously. Better to have her breakfast on a tray! Returning hastily to her own room, she pulled the bell cord and waited for one of the maids to respond to the tingling bell.

Definitely, this would be better, she thought as she calmed down. This way, she might avoid having to face him all the way until lunch. She'd be better prepared to see him then. Besides, by then the Athelstains would be up and their presence at the table would make things infinitely easier.

By the time a rap sounded on her door, she was even smiling a little. "Come in."

Faintly startled that it was Higgins who entered the room at her call, she told him. "May I have my breakfast on a tray please, Higgins?"

When he didn't answer, she offered an explanation. "The weather is so awful, I thought it would be cozier." She blushed a little. While both her statements were true, she knew her intent was a lie. She'd never lied to Higgins.

Higgins answered her with the familiarity of an old friend. "He's gone, Anne. There's no need for you to hide in your rooms."

Anne saw the strain on his face. "Gone?" She was having trouble understanding. "He can't have gone anywhere in this storm, Higgins. Why, it would be worth your life just to attempt the drive down from the castle to the road in weather like this."

"Nevertheless, Lady Anne, he has gone. I myself was quite concerned. His men said merely 'Orders' when I asked them why."

Anne clutched her midsection as if she'd been struck there. Orders! Oh, dear Lord! She *had* ordered him to leave, but never out into this terrible storm! She *had* ordered him to go. She'd ordered him to get out of her life, and the lives of her children . . . she'd ordered him out of his own castle!

"B-but . . . but the weather. Surely he knew I . . . " She closed her lips firmly on the words she'd been about to say. "Surely he wouldn't risk his horses in this weather, Higgins. Surely you're mistaken."

He offered her the only bit of comfort he could find. "The Captain's team was extremely well-schooled, milady. His coachman seemed quite superior, also."

She twisted her hands and looked at him with eyes that cut him to the quick. "What would all that matter in this horrible storm? They're probably wrecked at the foot of the drive!"

"No, my lady. I took the liberty of sending one of the footmen to the end of the drive to see whether such a thing had occurred. The drive was clear of any signs of an accident, he said."

"Thank God!" Anne's thoughts were in chaos.

"Miss Carswell is waiting for you in the breakfast room, Lady Anne." Higgins had no intention of letting her stay in her room in her present state of mind. "The Athelstains will be down presently."

She moved forward with as much dignity as she could muster to do as he silently insisted and go down to the breakfast room. Her steps might be firmly placed in the drafty, vaulted hall, but her thoughts were on the road to London . . . and they were anything but reassuring.

Chapter Thirty

Sir John moaned and tossed until his bed looked like a battlefield. The terrible, teeth-grinding shivering was over. Now he had only to deal with the pain . . . pain that made it impossible to find a position in which he could rest. His bones felt as if they were coming apart!

Tendrils of a sweet fragrance entered the room and floated to where he lay. Mist drifted through the door from the adjoining suite, hesitated, formed and thickened, and gave off a warm glow. Golden radiance colored the grayness of the daylight that filtered in through the draperies, and Bethany materialized at the foot of Sir John's bed.

"Oh, my dear! You look perfectly dreadful again. What is it that has brought the fever back on you? Were you caught out in this awful weather?"

Sir John stirred and looked up at her. "Bethany?" He frowned, trying hard to remember what he'd wanted so badly to tell her. *What had it been?* He remembered that she would be very glad to hear it, but it danced just out of reach on the edges of his fever-clouded mind.

Suddenly it came to him! He jolted upright, then groaned and grabbed his head with both hands as he fell back against his pillows. "Ahhh, damn!" It seemed he had a headache. "I do beg your pardon."

"Not at all. Of course your head hurts, you've suffered a spell of fever. Think nothing of it. Jared, I promise you, has slipped and said worse many *times."*

Sir John sat up more carefully. He was relieved to find his head didn't explode off his shoulders. "Jared! That's what I'm trying to remember to tell you. I met him . . . or rather, I experienced his presence."

"Jared!" Bethany's hands flew to her breast. *"You've seen Jared. Oh, I am so glad. How was he?"*

"Bethany." Sir John was not at his best. "He's dead."

"Well of course he's dead. I'm dead, too." She was clearly offended.

"I apologize, Bethany. I didn't mean to upset you." What the hell could he tell her? She hardly wanted to hear that her husband was the very devil of a windstorm! "He's fine. Quite—er—strong and—ummm—forceful. I'm sure he is doing well in spite of missing you most dreadfully." He had the most peculiar feeling he was reassuring a wife of one of his troopers. He shook his head to clear it. It wasn't the brightest thing he'd done lately.

Thank God the fever seemed to have abated, leaving only a headache. Thoughts of Jared St. Legere had probably frightened it off!

"Oh, John! For the past several days, I've heard Jared calling out to me. I must go to him. You must take me to him."

"I have every intention of doing just that." He didn't tell

her that currently he was persona non grata in his own castle because he'd met and fallen in love with the most wonderful woman he'd ever met. Nor did he mention that the same woman was being an exasperating henwit right now.

His senses reeled at the memory as he remembered the peculiar fit of temper Anne had had when she'd risen from her bed to order him out of his own castle, and anger stirred in him blotting out the guilt he felt at losing control of himself in the maze.

"Of course, it will be difficult," Bethany was saying, unaware of the tumult he was experiencing. *"I am bound here to St. Legere House. But* you *will find a way. You must!"*

She was looking at him so beseechingly that he couldn't tell her he wasn't welcome at Castle Caldon.

"Please," she begged with tears in her eyes. Holding out her hands to him imploringly, she whispered, *"You must."*

Sir John firmed his jaw. There was no way he could resist her plea, no way he intended to try. He owned the damned castle, and he was going to find a way to take Bethany there. If Anne had any objections she could jolly well . . . learn to deal with them.

Rising carefully while apologizing for his nightshirt—a detested garment that he wore only as a concession to Bethany's frequenting his bedchamber—he tottered over and yanked the bellpull to summon his valet.

Bethany disappeared.

Danvers was scandalized at his employer's orders. "You can't go back to the castle. You've only just got over the fever. You aren't fit to go anywhere."

Sir John, waiting to be helped into his clothes, fixed his valet with a glare. "I need fresh air and a spot of exercise, Danvers. Then I shall be right as a trivet. Meanwhile, you go on to the attics, Danvers. Go and find me something like a chest or good-sized trunk that has obviously been here at

St. Legere House since it was built. Something that is obviously a part of the house, do you understand!"

Danvers shoved the coat onto Sir John's shoulders and turned away rather rudely. He went off muttering, "At least the attics I'm to search aren't to let!"

Bethany materialized the instant the door closed behind Danvers. *"Was he saying you're daft, Sir John?"*

"I think that was the gist of it, yes."

Bethany thought it best to let the matter drop, so she changed the subject. *"You're thinking that if I can get into something that has been with the house forever, I can be transported safely to the castle, aren't you?"*

"I am hoping so, yes."

"Oh, dearest John, I am, too!"

Higgins was glad to see Sir John Kent's handsome dark blue traveling coach roll to a stop on the carriage sweep. Now maybe things would come to a successful conclusion.

Anne had been drooping around ever since she'd learned he'd left, and the twins and the two Athelstain boys had done nothing but quarrel and natter at one another, they missed him so. Unless he was guessing wrong, Lois Carswell had been sighing a bit over the tall, taciturn Danvers's absence, too. Things would be better now.

"Welcome, Sir John!"

Sir John nearly missed the step, looking up startled at the warmth of Higgins's exuberant greeting.

"Thank you, Higgins. Is the bedchamber I occupied before vacant?"

"Vacant and aired and waiting for you, Captain."

"Was I expected, then?" He wasn't sure he liked being taken for granted.

"I only hoped, Sir. John. I only hoped."

So Anne hadn't ordered his room kept in readiness for

his return. She didn't take him for granted. So why was he feeling disappointed?

Gad! Would he ever recover control of his life and get the blasted thing back on an even keel? In his mind, he mimicked the butler, *I only hope.*

He turned to be certain that his footmen were handling Bethany's chest with care, then strode into *his* castle.

"Higgins, will you be so kind as to ask the twins to send Lord Jared to me?"

Higgins looked startled—he'd never been sent to fetch a ghost before—but signified he'd do so. Then, he'd take great pleasure in telling Lady Anne that she had another guest for dinner. With an interior grin that buoyed him along, he went to discharge his commission.

"Danvers," Sir John was telling his valet, "I won't be needing you for at least an hour or two." He thought that ought to give him ample time to reunite the ghostly lovers.

Danvers nodded and headed for the stairs down to the kitchen. He was hoping he might find Miss Carswell there.

Sir John headed for his room right behind the two footmen carrying the chest that Danvers had found for Bethany. As he walked, he wondered how Anne would handle his arrival . . . and just how he would handle her!

In the cavernous, gold and blue damask-hung room that served as his bedchamber, the footmen placed the chest carefully at the foot of Sir John's bed. When one of them inquired whether he wished it unpacked, Sir John was quick to slam a hand down on the top of the chest and say, "No!" Then more quietly, "That'll be all. Thank you, men."

"Yessir." The stockier footman almost saluted. Exchanging puzzled glances, they crossed the luxurious Oriental rugs that lay like islands on the cold stone floor and passed through the heavy oak door.

John didn't take a breath until the door closed behind the men. Transporting ghosts about the countryside in antique chests wasn't a pastime he wished to be caught engaging in, especially not by hard-bitten ex-Dragoons.

He threw back the lid of the chest. "Bethany! Are you all right?"

She stared up at him from the nest of blankets he'd made for her in the bottom of the chest. She lay curled in a tight ball, her soft brown eyes round as an apprehensive child's. Breathlessly she asked, *"Are we here? Were we successful? Am I at the castle?"* She waited for the only answer that mattered.

"Yes," he told her gently. "This is Jared's castle."

She rose from the chest like mist from the surface of a river. The smile on her face was radiant. *"How can I ever thank you, John?"*

He smiled at her gently. "By permitting me to go find Lady Anne—my *own* true love."

"Your Forever Love?" Bethany was glowing golden for him. *"You found her and you didn't tell me?"*

"I must be certain of her feelings first." His voice was husky. "At our last parting, she gave me to believe that Forever has already passed for us."

"What utter nonsense, John. Go and find her. Any woman you have decided is yours will be waiting."

"I would that I were so sure."

"Did you give her my locket?"

He smiled and touched his watch pocket. Under the tips of his long fingers he could feel the locket, safe.

Bethany smiled back. *"Go."*

Suddenly, wind howled in the passageway.

Bethany shrank away from the sound.

"It's all right. Don't be afraid. It's Lord Jared."

With a blast of cold air, the door burst back on its hinges and slammed into the wall.

Sir John bowed to Bethany. "I'm sure you will excuse me, it appears your husband has arrived."

Bethany never heard him. Her eyes were fixed on a spot just inside the door; her face was glowing. Reaching both hands out toward the doorway, she whispered, *"Jared!"*

As Sir John turned and left the room, the frigid mass of air that had always signaled the presence of the ghostly Jared St. Legere sped past him.

Sir John closed the door behind him and leaned back against it, a smile on his face. After almost a century of being apart, the lovers were reunited. He'd not seen Jared's face, but the look on his sweet friend Bethany's had told it all. Happiness beyond expression had shone there.

He sighed. Would that matters would go as well between him and his Anne. Bethany was right. Absolutely right. The love Anne and he shared was enough to push aside all the hurt and anger and foolish pride that stood in their way. Hell, the love *he* felt for her was powerful enough to move the bloody castle!

Now he must set their happiness in motion. He pushed away from the door. He'd only to find Anne and make her see the truth of all that Bethany had told him. He'd do anything it took to make her see.

Then, of course, he had to give her the locket. His hand moved to his watch pocket and he traced the oval shape that rested there. Bethany's locket, given him to give to his Forever Love.

He smiled. He hoped he could make Anne understand. The locket would symbolize the truth that their love was eternal. The locket would make her see what he was trying to tell her as no words his soldier's tongue could find would do.

With determined strides, he set off to find his lovely Anne and give her the precious locket that Bethany had entrusted to him.

Inside Sir John's bedchamber, Bethany stood next to her chest and stared at the dark shadow that was her husband. It had been so long since they'd been together. She looked at him, poised to throw herself into his arms. But he was so dark, so cold . . . so frightening. *"Jared?"*

Slowly he took form, scarcely daring to hope, scarcely believing. He'd answered the summons given him by the twins with scant grace. Angry and in a dark mood he'd stormed down here to freeze some respect into the young Captain who'd had the effrontery to dare send for him.

The last thing he'd expected to find was this, his old campaign chest . . . and his beloved wife. The reality of her presence staggered him.

The aura surrounding him changed. From grays, dark blues, and blacks, he began to glow with the same soft golden light that surrounded his love. Sparks of joy showered from him, lighting up the dim cavern of a room.

"Bethany?" Hesitantly he moved toward her. *"Bethany?"* Scarcely daring to believe she was really here, he reached out to touch her. When their hands met, his breath stopped in his throat and tears welled up behind his eyes.

Tenderly he enfolded her in his arms. *"Ah, God!"* Barely able to believe his senses, he crushed her to him, blinking back tears. *"Bethany! My dearest love."*

They clung to each other, together at last. They kissed and kissed and clasped each other with the desperation born of a century of being kept apart.

"Jared!" Bethany wept the tears, through her joyous

laughter, that her husband could not shed. *"Jared. Beloved!"*

A century of longing lay behind them. Now the loneliness and the yearning were over.

The miracle of another love that had been required of them had been accomplished, and by it, their paths had been cleared. The happiness of all eternity was finally theirs.

Sir John's boot heels sounded loudly against the flagstones of the corridor through which he strode. He could hear the roar of the sea as he approached the passageway where, a shy little housemaid had told him, Anne had gone to check on her workmen. He noted idly that he seemed to be in a corridor of more recent construction than the rest of the castle. He doubted that this section had been built longer than a hundred and fifty or so years ago. Architecture wasn't his interest at the moment, however. Right now, he was consumed by his urgency to find Anne.

Though he'd met several groups of tired workers coming out of this newer section of the castle, he hadn't seen Anne. He was so eager to find her that he didn't notice the little person that was trailing him.

Darting from shadow to shadow, Luther Athelstain was coming along to see just what this man who'd asked that a ghost be sent to him in his room was up to. After all, Sir John was the one who'd found the plans to the castle—plans that might have shown a secret room, priest's hole, or vault, a hiding place of some sort. Luther remembered watching his mother scoop up and throw those plans into the fire right after she'd screamed that the ghost was at the drawing room door and nearly scared *him* to death!

When he'd questioned her, she'd told him that it was none of his business, but that the plans had had to be destroyed for the sake of her family. It wouldn't do, she'd said, for anyone to find the secret room they were looking for . . . or the letter.

He hadn't understood it all, but it had certainly put him on the alert to try to know everything that transpired in Castle Caldon. That was why he was holding his breath and tiptoeing along behind Captain Sir John.

Anne was standing in the dark passageway in a pool of lantern light flicking the last of the stone dust from her gown when she looked up and saw Sir John. Her breath caught in her throat. Her emotions went into maelstrom.

She was so glad he had come.

She was so angry to see him here.

She was filled with an aching longing, a burning, quivering desire to be in his arms.

She was humiliated to recall how easily she had surrendered to his skillful caresses, his kisses.

She was outraged to see him standing there so calmly, his eyes claiming her very soul for his own!

Her head was awhirl with thoughts . . . her body was awash with delicious sensations . . . her temper was flaring.

Why did he have to come back?

What had taken him so long to get here?

Sir John stood watching the play of emotions across her lovely face and drinking in her beauty. She was so beautiful! If she'd been no more than a statue, she was glorious enough to grace the alcove in front of which she stood.

"Well?" he asked her. "Have you made up your mind?"

"What are you doing here?" She stared at him over the rubble-strewn floor of the corridor.

"I've come back for you." He stood quietly, drinking in the sight of her. "I love you, Anne. I want you for my wife."

She knew all the foolish accusations she'd made were forgiven. All the agonies she'd been suffering were over. In one glorious burst of pure joy, Anne's vows to remain independent were forgotten. Reaching out to him with all her love for him in her eyes she whispered simply, "John."

"Anne!" He started toward her, his arms aching to hold her.

Behind him, Luther crept nearer. He hid behind one of the heavy posts that the laborers had put in to hold up the heavy stone ceiling while the work Lady Anne had commissioned was in progress. Hearing the breathless note in Sir John's voice when he called out to Lady Anne, he grinned and leaned forward for a closer look. What fun it would be if Sir John would *kiss* her and he could tell the twins. Boy, would they hate that!

As he leaned his weight against the post, it began, groaning, to slip out of alignment. With a grating sound, it began to move forward at the top. A little stream of dirt and small slivers of stone rained down on the child. Luther screamed in fright and shoved away from the post behind which he'd hidden, running back down the corridor as fast as he could run.

His shove was all it took. The massive post began to shift. The planks it was holding aloft to steady the ceiling began to fall. There was a grinding sound as the stones the planks had braced in place changed the positions they had held for hundreds of years. They began to tumble down.

"Anne!" John shouted her name as he leapt toward her. He was thrown off stride as the first stone fell, striking him a glancing blow on the shoulder. Terror such as he'd never known gave him wings. He must save Anne!

With a grinding roar, the rest of the roof above them caved in.

He smashed into Anne, catching her up and catapulting

them both into the alcove behind her. The alcove wasn't deep. It was hardly any shelter at all, but it was the only thing he could do. There was nothing else. There was no time!

As they crashed into the back wall of the alcove, the whole horrendous weight of the stones spilling from what had been the ceiling of the passageway and the wall to the left of it avalanched down.

Despair tore through him. They'd be crushed! There was no way he could save her! They'd be crushed by the surging tide of stone that rumbled toward them!

Chapter
Thirty-one

The roar of the collapsing ceiling filled their ears. Dust threatened their eyes and nostrils. The grinding mass of debris was being pushed toward them by the weight of the rest of the wall and ceiling that was falling behind it. The whole world seemed to be shifting.

Holding Anne hard against him, he rammed as far back into the arched depression as he could. Desperation added to his strength. Suddenly, the back wall of the alcove against which John pressed was shifting, too. It was moving back in on itself!

John twisted to shield Anne from the drop he feared was coming. Instead of a drop, though, he fell on the sharp edges of the bottom steps of a flight of stairs. Choking and coughing, he scrambled to his feet. Dragging Anne with him, he pushed his way up the steps, striving to get them above the cloud of heavy dust that was threatening to suffocate them!

Climbing up through stygian darkness, Sir John discovered the way blocked by a heavy wooden trapdoor. Frantic to get Anne out of the cloying cloud of stone dust, he shoved at it with all his might. It lifted, and he forced it all the way open. Yanking her up with him, he slammed the door back down, and they could breathe again. He held her as if he'd never let her go.

Coughing, he held Anne as she coughed. Lungs free again, he bent to look into her face.

"Anne! Anne! Are you all right?" In his anxiety, he shook her harder than he meant to, and dust flew from her hair and from her lavender muslin day dress as from a doll that had been too long on a forgotten shelf. "Anne, darling. Tell me you're all right."

She looked at him, wide-eyed. Her voice was a whisper. "You should have run away. You could have gotten away." She reached out to touch his face. "Oh, why didn't you run back to safety?" She didn't try to hide the tears that filled her eyes.

"Run away? How could I leave you, Anne?"

"You would have been safe." It was all that mattered to her.

"I'm safe now. And so are you." He gave her just a little shake this time. "You wouldn't have been. You were just standing there watching it come."

Anne admitted that he was right. She would have stood there and been crushed. She wished she felt less irritated about him telling her so. She sought to divert him. "Where is this light coming from?"

He looked around them. Then he was dragging her up a last, short flight of steps.

At the top of these stairs, they found a long narrow room

with a low ceiling. Standing with Anne sheltered in his arms, Sir John studied their surroundings.

Dust lay on the floor and on the six old Jacobean chairs that stood in a circle in the room's center. There was a low couch against one wall. At the far end of the room was a desk, also Jacobean, and an antique Bible box on bulbous, carved legs.

The light was coming from a series of windows set high in the outer wall. They were long and unusually horizontal. They went the entire length of the outer wall and flooded the odd room with light.

John stood absolutely still. If their situation hadn't been so perilous, he'd have let out a whoop of exultation. They'd found it! Obviously, this was the secret room they sought.

Now if the letter the boys said the ghost was so anxious to find were here, Anne and he would be able to remove any taint of treason from the lives of the twins. They'd also rid the castle of the ghost's frigid presence. Lord Jared would be free to spend the rest of eternity with his beloved Bethany.

"Anne! This is the secret room your great-grandfather was searching for." He took her hand and led her to the outer wall. "See how the windows have been cut so that they can't be seen by anyone outside? They're not tall enough to be seen from below, and they crowd so tightly up under the eaves of the roof above that no one would see them, even from out to sea. Clever."

"Yes. Oh, look." Anne let go his hand and headed for the desk. The desk and the ancient Bible box.

"Oh, John." She was whispering, afraid to speak of it aloud. "Surely, if there is a letter that proves Jared St. Legere was not a traitor, this is where we will find it." She ran her hands over the top of the ornately carved age-darkened wood of the Bible box. She looked up at him. Her eyes were glowing. "It's here. I know it is!"

She was breathless with anticipation. Her fingers trembled as she reached out to lift the carved wooden lid of the Bible box.

Sir John watched her a moment. He prayed that she was right.

He didn't keep looking at her, though. He was busy searching for a means of escape. He still had to get her back to safety. He'd scanned the walls and discovered no sign of any door. The stairwell up which they'd come was clearly the only way in or out, and that was hopelessly blocked. Still he had to find a way to save his Anne.

He leaned as far out the window as he could. First he looked down. Hundreds of feet below, the waters of the Channel whipped themselves to spindrift against the rocks at the base of the cliff on which Castle Caldon stood. He calculated the risk. If they jumped . . . and *if* they survived the fall . . . they'd be dashed to death against the rocks.

Then he craned his neck and stared at the eaves above the windows. The eaves went eight feet out from the wall to shield the windows of the secret room from discovery. There was no way he could reach the edge of the roof. Hope died in him.

Damn and blast! There *was* no way out.

Hating the very sound of the word in his mind, he admitted it. They were doomed.

When searchers came looking for Anne—and for him when they failed to find him elsewhere—it would appear to everyone that they'd been trapped beneath the tons of rock in the passageway below. It would be decided that they couldn't have survived the cave-in.

Even if an effort were made to retrieve their bodies, the remaining structure might not be strong enough to sustain it. Should it be, the tons of rubble at the foot of the secret stairs would take months to remove. He leaned his shoulder against the wall and fought down bitterness. Anne and he would be dead long before they were found.

He closed his eyes briefly, accepting the inevitable. Fury coursed through him that he was helpless to save his beloved Anne.

As if the gods of misfortune had heard his thoughts and decided to taunt him, the floor of the room shifted slightly. He heard a distant rumble, and watched as stones splashed down into the sea hundreds of feet below.

His heart twisted in him, then plunged to his boot soles. Anne mustn't know! There might be no way for him to save his precious Anne, but he vowed he wouldn't let her suffer fear that they might fall into the sea.

Anne hadn't noticed the movement of the floor under them. Her face was rapt with the joy of what she'd found. There in the box, faded only slightly in the hundred years since it had been penned, was the letter she sought! The letter that proved that her Great-grandfather Jared had not been a traitor to the Crown!

For a moment, all that her family had endured, all that she herself had suffered because of the false accusation of treason the real traitors had brought against Jared St. Legere swept over her. She began to shake like a person with the ague.

John had her in his arms before she could draw another breath. "I'm here, my love." His voice shook with the intensity of his love for her. "I have you safe."

She turned in his arms and nestled against him. All the silly, petty anger she'd felt for him completely gone. "Oh, John. Look." She showed him the heavy vellum. It was yellow with age and cracked along the edges, but the writing was plain. "He wasn't ever guilty. It was all for nothing." Softly she began to weep.

He knew instantly what she meant. She was remembering Montague's cruelties. Cruelties she'd had to suffer to win for her brothers a place in society. Cruelties that it would have been unnecessary to endure if only this letter had come to light earlier!

He rocked her back and forth in his arms like a child. Love for her overwhelmed him, filling him with a wild elation he'd never known. She was his, this precious woman. His to treasure for the rest of his life. His. His very own.

Bethany's words came to him, and he knew that he'd found his Forever Love. He kissed the top of her hair, breathing in the smell of wildflowers and roses and feeling a keen sense of loss even as he felt a soaring triumph. She was his. This gallant, dear Anne was his Forever Love.

He took Bethany's locket out of the watch pocket of his waistcoat and slipped its chain over Anne's head.

She looked up at him, her eyes full of questions.

"It was your great-grandmother Bethany's."

"How . . . ?"

"Later. I'll explain it all later." When he spoke his voice was husky with the knowledge that she was indeed his. Forever.

He smiled grimly. Not only was Anne his Forever Love, but it seemed that their forever was very near. The "later" in which he'd explain the locket was going to take place in the hereafter.

Right now, he'd only one thought. He had to keep Anne's spirits up. Softly he told her, "If you hadn't married Montague, you wouldn't have the twins."

She smiled up at him at that. She was puzzled by his words, but certain that Montague had been a small price to pay for her wonderful sons. "Yes," she murmured, trying to follow his train of thought.

"And if you hadn't married Montague, and had my wards, I would never have met you."

"Yes! Oh, yes!" She put her arms up around his neck.

He felt tender desire for her well up in him. Lowering his lips to hers, he kissed her gently.

Even as she returned his kiss, Anne knew they stood on the brink of death, and a gentle kiss wasn't what she wanted. She twisted her fingers into his dark curls and pulled his face harder down to hers. "I love you, John."

"I love you, too, Anne."

Now desperation was in their kisses.

There was a long, low couch against the back wall. It had probably served as a bed before.

He lifted her in his arms and began reciting what he could remember of the marriage ceremony from his Anglican prayer book as he carried her toward the bed.

Anne's lips parted in astonishment and wonder. Love for him so filled her that she was afraid she was going to burst into a million glittering fragments. She smiled. If she did, she was certain that each one would become a star for lovers to watch.

" . . . And thereto I plight thee my troth."

Anne took it up and recited all she could remember from the service, flinching just a little as she said, "Till death do us part." Then her voice strengthened, and she gazed deep into his eyes as she said, "And thereto I plight thee my troth!"

He stood, holding her easily in his arms there beside the couch. "We'd no priest to witness our vows, beloved. Even so, I count you my lawfully wedded wife."

After looking long into his dear face, she reached up to kiss him once more. "I love you, husband."

He felt the floor shift again. This time, his hearing acutely tuned to it, he heard a creaking grind, as if long-joined stones were slowly parting company.

Thank God Anne hadn't been standing on the floor to feel it lurch. He pulled the dust laden cover off to the floor and lowered her to the bed.

She reached for him as he came to join her, pulling him to her as he took her in his arms again. "I love you, John!"

He knew then that she was as aware of the danger as he. Anne suspected they were about to die. Tears momentarily clouded his vision. Not his Anne. *Please, God, not Anne.*

Ashamed of his weakness, he started to blink the treacherous tears away.

"No!" Anne lay a hand along his jaw. "Oh, my dearest love, don't you know how much . . . " She stopped her words. No man could understand what his tears might mean to the woman he loved. She kissed them away and smiled instead.

John didn't smile back. With a fierce groan that was almost a growl, he caught her crushingly to him.

Anne held as tightly to him as she could.

Raining kisses down on her face, he plundered her body with frantic hands. His mind was filled with one aching thought. Suppose they fell into the sea before he could join them into one flesh?

Anne understood his desperation and shared it. With death so miraculously cheated but still hovering so near, she, too, was desperate to love him, to know him fully. Passion flamed in her, and she was pulling him to her, tearing at his clothing as he pushed up her skirt, meeting kiss with kiss, matching the urgency of his demands.

They came together like storm clouds. There was nothing gentle in their union, just a tearing hunger to be joined, to be one. His hands were rough on her body, but the hurt was exquisite. His kisses crushed her lips. She sought to bruise his in return.

Then they were moving together, a single being, their rhythm accelerating wildly. They were striving, for just one time . . . perhaps for one last time . . . to reach the stars before it was too late.

The room jolted, but Anne had no idea whether it really did, or whether the whole universe had moved with the wondrous, explosive climax of their act of love.

Panting, he asked her, "Are you all right, Anne?" He stroked her hair with a hand that shook.

Inside he cursed himself. Damn him! He'd been a beast. Damn him to hell, he'd been as bad as Montague. He'd plunged into her like a virgin boy and taken her as quickly. What must she be feeling?

Anne was feeling a languorous satisfaction she'd never known existed. She'd loved him with the strength and desperation born of the fear that time might deny this union, and John had responded with a wild passion that had left her head spinning and her body both replete and longing for more.

"Anne?" His voice was hoarse with agony. Would she forgive him?

"My dearest love."

He smiled then, and kissed the edges of her smile. Gratitude and an awful humility filled him. She'd forgiven him. Relief flooded him. He was the most fortunate man alive!

Remembering the movement of the room as they'd climaxed, he took a vow. Seeing how the far wall of the room was pulling away from the back wall at its top corner, he'd no doubt, now, that they were going to die. He was going to be denied the lifetime he'd wanted in which to make it up to Anne for all she'd suffered, but he intended to do his best with whatever time remained.

He'd do penance for his rough and thoughtless loving. He'd make her forget his brutality. Thank God she'd forgiven it, but that didn't clear his conscience, now he'd do penance.

Sweet penance. He vowed to pleasure her until the end of whatever time they had left.

He was amazed to discover that she was still almost fully clothed. Leaning down to her, he kissed her shoulder and slipped the sleeve of her gown down her arm. Slowly, tantalizingly, kissing her clothing away inch by inch, he set about seeing to it that there would be nothing between the silk of her body and the heat of his own this next time they came together.

Anne, desire rekindling in her, took his face between her hands and kissed him. Fighting away for just an instant the mindless craving caused by the skillful touch of his hands on her bare breasts, on the silk of her inner thigh, she gasped, "Oh, John, I do love you so!"

Then she was lost, spiraling down in a swirl of sensations, drowning in her own passion.

Chapter Thirty-two

Bethany sighed gently and rubbed her cheek against her Jared's shoulder. *"Oh, Jared, I can hardly believe it's true."* Tears threatened her voice. *"Together again at last."* She made an effort to smile for him, knowing how he'd always hated tears, even happy tears, and forced cheeriness into her words. *"Isn't this delightful?"*

Her husband's arms tightened around her. After nearly a century of planning what he'd say when at last he had her in his arms, he couldn't recall a word. He could only clasp her to his heart and hold her as if he'd never let go.

He pressed ghostly lips to her misty forehead and sighed contentedly. *"Ah, Bethany. It has seemed an eternity without you."*

"Yes, but now we're to have an eternity together, love." She looked around the bare tower room to which he'd brought her. *"But I do hope we shall not spend it here."*

He laughed then, and kissed her again.

"Jared?"

"Yes, love?"

"Why are you so cold and dark?"

"I imagine it's because of the bitterness and resentment I've carried for almost a hundred years." He sighed, suddenly sorry now. *"Perhaps I shall improve with you here to help me."*

She looked at him solemnly. *"We shall have to see to it. Captain Kent tells me you're talking with children. It wouldn't do to frighten children, dearest."*

"Hmmmm." He nuzzled her neck, thankful the twins were a stalwart pair. *"How is it you can speak with Sir John? How is it you can converse with a human?"*

"Sir John was dreadfully ill when he first came home from the war. In his fevered condition, he seemed able to hear me. It was lovely, having someone to talk to."

"Hmmmm."

"Jared!" She was so startled by a sudden thought that she almost floated off his lap.

"What is it?"

"We can touch! Do you understand what this means?"

"Of course." He hadn't until she mentioned it, but now he realized it meant that he'd somehow been instrumental in helping one of his descendants find true love. Smiling, he told her, *"This means that your great-granddaughter has admitted she loves your Captain Sir John Kent."*

"Oh, really? How very nice." Then Bethany was scowling. *"Then that means I didn't have to hide in that awful chest to get here to you. How very vexing! I could just have come to you! I was already free of my bondage to our lovely town house and I didn't even know it.*

"Oh, Jared, we could simply have been reunited be-

cause the condition had been fulfilled!" She floated up into the air a bit and then resettled on his lap.

With the lightning reversal of subject he remembered so well, she said, *"Oh, Jared . . . tell me about her. How wonderful! A great-granddaughter. Is she pretty? Is she kind?"*

"She is very pret—"

The door to the tower room burst inward. The twins dashed in. Their faces frightened the ghosts.

"She's gone! Mama's gone!" Brian was sobbing uncontrollably.

Brandon's face was white and strained, his unnatural control distressing to see. "Lord Jared! There has been a collapse of the extreme end of the east wing." Tears formed, but he blinked them away manfully. "We have not seen our mother since it happened."

Jared offered instantly, *"How may I help?"*

"We know that you can move through walls. Would you please go and look where the collapse has taken place." Brandon put a steadying arm around his brother's shoulders. "There . . . might be some chance." He was gulping his breaths, fighting to get the words out. "A . . . a cave in the rubble . . . some place that she might . . . b-b-be keeping safe." He began to sob.

At the end of his courage but not at the end of his duty, the child spoke between sobs. "And . . . if n-not . . . you can tell us where to . . . c-concentrate . . . our efforts t-t-to recover h-her." He was crying as hard as his brother now, his eyes pleading. "And can you hurry, please. Already b-bits of the castle are falling into the s-sea."

St. Legere ordered, *"Stay here with your Great-grandmother until I return!"* He was gone the next instant, leaving the twins quietly crying in a golden glow that seemed to be trying to comfort them.

In the secret room, Anne lay in John's arms and sighed. John kissed her forehead.

"We're going to die, aren't we?"

His eyes closed in pain. He was unable to answer.

"It's such a pity when we have just found each other."

"My good, brave girl." His arms tightened about her. He'd gladly give his life to save hers.

He smiled a tight, rueful smile as his soldier's grim sense of humor came into play. He was going to give it, anyway . . . but it wouldn't save his beloved Anne. His gut twisted at the thought of something so bright and beautiful as his precious wife being taken from a world in such need of her and those like her.

They lay silent for a long moment, just holding each other close.

He cleared his throat. "Anne. Before I met you . . . "

"Yes, John?" She pulled away a little to look into his face.

" . . . I took the liberty of having a legal document drawn up appointing my best friend guardian of your children in case anything happened to me."

Tears filled her eyes, and she put her head back on his shoulder so he wouldn't see.

"I had this damned fever, you see, and at that time I wasn't sure it wouldn't get worse instead of better."

She made a little sound and burrowed deeper against him.

"I appointed the finest man I know. I hope you won't mind. It's Danvers."

"How splendid."

It was his turn to pull away to look at her.

She sat up, smiling. "Lois has developed a tendre for him, you know. They'll make wonderful p-parents." She put her hands over her mouth to stop her lips from trembling.

"Don't cry. Please don't cry."

She took her hands away and smiled at him tremulously. "They aren't altogether sad tears." She tried to explain as he kissed them away. "They were only sad to think of what a wonderful father you've already been to the twins, teaching them manly things. And they were glad tears to know that you'd been so thoughtful about their future . . . and done it so well."

The room shook then, and she threw herself back into his arms. A rumble of ominous proportions drowned out his soothing murmur.

When it passed and she could hear him, he said, "Perhaps we should dress."

"Y-yes."

He took his time dressing her again. They kissed and touched and engraved forever on their memories the scent and texture of their bodies, building talismen to hold throughout eternity.

Both of them were solemn. No moment of these, their last together, was going to pass unremembered, unrejoiced.

Neither of them noticed the chill blast of air that entered the secret room from the solid wall behind them.

Jared came and saw them and smiled. Then he left them to their loving to return with the good news to her sons.

Passing again through the wall of the secret room, he saw how the mortar was cracking under the strain of the pushing rubble below. Slowly the room holding the lovers was being forced to break away, and for the first time in his existence, Jared St. Legere knew fear.

Jared wasted no time reporting back to the children and Bethany. He tore madly through the wall of the enchanted couple's prison, through the rubble and several other walls and floors and back up to his tower room.

He'd lingered in the secret chamber only an instant after he ascertained the couple should be left their privacy, but it had been long enough to see the document that Anne had found. With a glad cry he burst into the room. *"They live! Sir John has her safe in the secret chamber we sought!"*

"Thank God!" Bethany began to weep happily.

"We've no time to lose! That whole part of the castle may drop into the sea at any minute!"

"Jared! The children!"

"Blast and damn, madam! 'Tis the children must effect the rescue! Go, boys! Find Danvers. Tell him that the room has narrow windows just under the eaves of that last bit of roof still attached to the castle. The damned room's outside the walls of the castle. No wonder I never found it. And for God's sake, tell him to be careful. The whole thing could go at a touch!"

"Yessir! The twins cried in unison. Then they turned as one boy and dashed out of the tower room.

"I wish they wouldn't do that."

"But you told them to make all haste."

"No. I didn't mean their running. I meant their confounded habit of speaking in unison."

"Jared!"

He looked a little ashamed. *"Well, you have to admit it's disconcerting."*

Bethany laughed at him, a delicious gurgle of sound.

"Ah, how I've missed that." He swept her into his arms and hugged her tightly. An instant later, he thrust her away and demanded, *"How is that our Great-granddaughter wears your locket?"*

Bethany lit up with joy. *"He has given her my locket! Oh, Jared. That means that Sir John has found his Forever Love!"*

Chapter
Thirty-three

Lois stood on the battlement in the wind and crammed the back of her hand against her mouth. She wouldn't scream, she *mustn't* scream.

Watching Danvers work his way carefully to the edge of the dangerously sagging roof was almost more than her tortured nerves could bear. Full of fear for her dear Anne's safety, she clung to the twins, a boy on each side, and never took her eyes off Danvers.

Half the household stood behind her, sternly forbidden by Danvers to come closer and endanger their lives—or by their weight the lives of the two people below.

"We should be the ones to go." Brandon watched anxiously as another shower of stones plummeted seaward.

"Yes. We're much lighter," Brian agreed.

"No!" Lois clutched them all the tighter.

Just then, Higgins panted up with the long coil of rope

the Captain had left in the west tower, saw the precarious position Danvers was in, and gasped, "Why didn't you make him wait for this rope?"

Cook, hanging on to the jamb of the door at the top of the tower stairs behind him and fighting to catch her breath, said, "Ha! You don't . . . stop Mr. Danvers so easy . . . Mr. Higgins. That . . . you don't."

The ghosts floated just beside the tower, watching intently. Bethany was wringing her hands. *"Oh, Jared. Is it as dangerous as it looks? Will the secret room fall into the sea?"*

"They must be quick, my love." Jared looked as if he would willingly die again if he could help his great-granddaughter and the man she so obviously loved. *"Ah, God!"* The words were torn from him. *"If only I had corporeal strength. If only I could touch and hold!"*

Bethany clung to him, her eyes luminous with tears. She touched his face, and he turned and gently kissed her. Softly she told him, *"We can pray."*

Danvers reached the edge of the roof. Just under him was where the boys said that the ghost had told them Lady Anne and Captain Sir John were. Danvers didn't believe in ghosts, but for the first time in his life, he wished with all his heart that he did.

He sent up a prayer. Then, hoping against hope, he shouted, "Captain! Are you there, sir?"

The resulting wind-tattered answer set all their hearts soaring. Clearly those assembled on the battlement heard Sir John shout, "Danvers! Thank God! We're here!"

Anne threw herself into John's arms. "We're saved, John!"

Not certain that rescue would occur before they fell into

the sea with the wreckage of the room, John smiled tenderly down at her and lied. "Yes, dearest, we're saved."

Hanging out a window, he called, "Can you get a rope down to us?"

"Aye, Captain, we shall!"

While Sir John stood waiting with Anne clasped in his arms and the floor groaning under their feet, Danvers made his careful way back to the others. As he went, stones slithered down into the sea from the wall supporting the far corner of the roof.

Lois and Higgins froze. They stared with horrified eyes at the small avalanche.

Suddenly, Brandon squirmed out of Lois's horror-slackened grasp. Snatching the coil of rope from Higgins, he cried, "Bri. Hurry. There isn't much time." He ran the rope around a merlon in the battlement, tied it as he'd been taught, and tugged at it fiercely. Then he threw one end to his twin and tied the other around his own waist. "Come on!"

Lois screamed, "No!" and reached for them, but Higgins held her back. She was too late, the twins had already stepped out on the roof.

"No, Lois!" He held her tight. "Your weight added to theirs might send all three of you plunging down into the Channel!"

"Ah, dear God!" Lois stopped struggling and watched the twins with her heart in her throat.

Danvers, white as newly bleached linen, stood stock-still where he was at midpoint between the edge and the battlement, arms outstretched to block their way. "Here now, boys."

Brandon and Brian stopped short of his reach. The three of them stood in frozen tableau. Under their feet the slate roof undulated once and was still.

"Stand aside, Danvers," the young Marquess commanded. "We're their best chance!" His eyes were suddenly old. "You know we are!"

Danvers hesitated. The decision was beyond him.

Brandon saw his hesitation and knew he'd won. "Good man! See to our ropes, please."

Danvers closed his eyes against the pain of letting the boys go, then capitulated. The boys *were* the best chance they had of saving Lady Anne and Sir John. And maybe, just maybe, he thought grimly, the ropes would save the boys if the whole thing—God forbid—spilled down into the sea.

Brian saw the difficulty of his decision in Danvers's eyes and offered by way of consolation, "She is our mother, you know, Danvers."

Lois began to sob.

The Athelstains rushed up the tower stairs just then, their faces strained. Lord Robert hurried over and put an arm around Lois.

The twins started walking cautiously forward.

Higgins began to pray out loud.

Cook sent up a wailing that set all their teeth on edge.

"All right, men. To the edge. Carefully." His course decided, Danvers took command. "Stay ten feet apart. Remember, this isn't like the garden wall or tower."

He struggled hard to think of the boys as young Dragoons, not children he was sending to possible death. It was almost beyond him. "When you get to the edge, lie on your bellies and let yourselves over easy-like."

In spite of the cool breeze off the water, sweat stood out on Danvers's forehead. "You won't have a wall to put your feet on to walk down. You'll have to swing in under the eaves to where the Captain can grab you. We don't know for certain how far that is. Use your heads . . . and be careful."

In an agonized whisper he added, "For God's sake be careful."

The boys lay down on the edge of the slate roof. First Brandon and then Brian disappeared over the edge.

Cook threw her apron over her head and flopped down in a heap, keening.

Before his father realized what he was up to, George darted lightly forward. Just out of parental reach he announced, "I'll tend the ropes at the edge, Danvers!"

Luther, clinging hard to his mother, screeched, "Get back here, George. You'll be killed."

George threw him a scornful glance, moved closer to the edge, and sent a steady look to Danvers.

Danvers looked as if he were about to faint, but his voice was strong as he said, "Good lad." Tossing his coat aside, he removed his waistcoat and ripped it in half. "Here, try to pad the ropes where they rub on that sharp slate at the roof's edge. Do it just as soon as you see any slack in them." He threw the two pieces of fabric to George.

George caught the remnants of Danver's vest and moved carefully to the very edge.

Luther yelled, "Mama!" as Lady Becky fainted and lay in a graceful little heap on the stone walkway of the battlement.

Lord Robert removed his own coat to cover his wife and told his heir, "Be quiet, Luther." His attention never left the edge of the roof and his younger son.

Danvers watched the ropes.

After what seemed an eternity, a shout carried up to them from Brandon. "We see them, but it's too far to swing in! We shall have to go lower and climb back up, Danvers. Give us more rope!"

At the sound of Brandon's voice, Anne flew to the window beside Sir John. "Oh, dearest God! My boys!" She sagged weakly against John, her mother's heart frantic. "Tell them to go back, John. Oh, tell them to go back!"

His face grim, he told her, "They're our only chance, Anne. They know that. I could order them back until I was hoarse, and they'd still refuse to go." He turned to look at her. "You know your sons, Anne. You know they'll never turn back until they have you safe."

She fell apart then. Sobbing wildly she dropped to the floor at his feet.

He bent to lift her. "Stop this, Anne. You mustn't." His eyes were compassionate in his stern face. "Just now they're men. Don't dishonor them."

His words were like a dash of cold water. Stifling her sobs, Anne struggled to appear to watch her sons calmly as they slid past her to swing out and back onto the wall further down to begin their climb back up it to rescue her.

She had to press her hands over her mouth to keep from crying out to them to be careful, but she knew that John was right. She must encourage and approve.

Oh, dear God! How could she approve something so dangerous for her children? How could she sanction such hazardous behavior? Of what value was her life when compared to theirs?

John spoke quietly beside her. "Good girl. Good brave girl." Then he was hanging too far out the window, watching the boys put to use the skills he'd so recently taught them. Skills that had been merely an exercise with no more intention than to make the twins more manly. "Lord," he murmured, "what odd twists fate takes!"

The twins climbed well, and in a few moments they had reached the narrow windows. Their Captain hauled them in, hugging each one unashamedly before he put them down.

The minute their feet hit the floor, Anne gathered them into her arms, crying with relief. "Oh, my darlings! How could you do such a thing? How could you?"

Brian was elated. "It was easy. Captain Sir John and Danvers showed us how on the garden wall. Don't you remember, Mama? We told you." His eyes were shining with pleasure at his accomplishment.

She smoothed his curls. "Yes, dearest, I do remember." Tears coursed down her cheeks. "I do remember." She hugged them both close. "Now you must go back very carefully." She traced their features in turn. Her fingers trembled.

Brandon looked at her stubbornly. "We aren't going to go back without you and the Captain, Mama. That was the whole point in our coming down here." For the first time in his life, he realized that his mother was a mere woman.

"But . . . "

Sir John stepped forward. "No, Anne. The boys are right. You must go with them." He took the rope that was around Brandon's waist and secured it to Anne as well. Lifting her to the sill of one of the windows, he shouted up to those above, "Lady Anne's coming up. Steady her well, Danvers." With that, he pushed Anne and Brandon out from the wall.

He saw Anne close her eyes and clutch at the rope that held her. Then Brandon was shouting, "Pull us up!" and Anne was looking back to him, her eyes huge in her pale face.

"Come! Come now," she begged as she rose toward the roof above. The last glimpse she had of her beloved and her other son showed her Captain Sir John boosting Brian up onto the windowsill, ready to swing him out and begin him on his way up to safety.

"John!" She lost sight of them as George reached carefully over the edge of the roof to help her to climb up onto it.

With a grumbling mutter, the far end of the secret room fell into the sea. George flattened himself and kept a desperate grip on Anne's wrists. The roof shuddered ominously, but held.

Danvers, Higgins, and Lord Robert pulled with all their might to bring them safely over the edge of the roof. With the rope taut, Anne managed somehow to get over the edge.

Brandon scrambled up beside her. He put his arm around Anne and urged her toward the battlement.

Anne nearly sobbed aloud. John had been so right. Brandon was a man grown at this moment, and if she lived to be a hundred, she would never forget it.

From below, they heard Brian shriek, "No!"

If Danvers hadn't grabbed and held her arm firmly, Anne would have run back to the trembling edge of the roof. "Get back milady! Stay back!"

She looked at him, frantic. It was *her son* who had called out "no." It was her beloved John who was out of sight down there below her. She was so afraid she could hardly stand, but she knew that if Danvers would only let go of her, she could climb back down a rope to help her son . . . and her dearest love.

Danvers read her distress easily. Gently he told her, "Your weight on this roof endangers them, milady."

Without a word she turned then and let Brandon lead her quietly up the slope of the roof to the battlement where her friends waited to help her over the low parapet and take her in their arms. Once over the low wall, she clung wordlessly to a grim Lois.

Danvers and Higgins were hauling at the other rope. Anne's heart was in her throat, trying to suffocate her.

With a distress that threatened to kill her, she watched

the ease with which the two men pulled in the rope. There was no way they could be recovering it so quickly if it had had the combined weight of Brian and Sir John at the end of it. She sagged weakly against Lois whispering, "John!"

Danvers and Higgins came to her with Brian. "Your son's a brave lad, milady."

"I have to go back, Mama! Sir John pushed me out the window before he had time to tie on to my rope." His eyes begged her. "I have to take a rope back to him."

Anne felt tears slide down her cheeks. "No, darling. I don't think he meant you to."

She didn't know how she could speak so calmly. She wanted to sob and scream. John had given Brian the best chance he could by sending him up alone, and in doing so he had forfeited his own life . . . and their happiness.

Despair rose in her to match the wind that was rising around them. Far below they heard the grumble and mutter of the sea. The storm that had battered the castle for days had left a remnant to defeat them now.

"He gave me this to bring you!" He reached into his coat and removed a folded sheet of parchment.

Lord Jared shot forward, Bethany streaming out behind him like a banner.

"The letter! Brian! It's the letter, isn't it?" the ghost of his great-great-grandfather demanded of Brian.

"Yes, sir. I believe it is," the boy told the empty air.

Jared St. Legere glowed warm and golden. *"Thank God! We're free!"*

Brian smiled at a vacant spot on the roof and told it, "Yes. I suppose you'll be going now. We shall miss you, sir."

"And I shall miss you both, my brave lads." His broad smile was tinged by sadness. *"I'm proud to have known you!"*

Bethany, misty with tears, said, *"Oh, Jared, dearest. They are so precious, our descendants. Must we go just this minute?"*

Jared St. Legere looked over his shoulder to where several of God's bright Angels were hurtling down toward them. Even from a distance he could see the fierce determination on their faces. *"I don't think I shall argue that point with our escorts this time, my love."*

Bethany looked up toward the awe-inspiring beings coming for them. *"Tell the boys I'll be watching over them always!"*

There was a mighty whoosh of wings, and Jared called out to his young friends, *"Thank you! And goodbye. We'll be watching. Always. Remember! Live with honor!"*

"Goodbye!" The twins waved to a spot in the sky.

Everyone was straining to see to whom the boys waved. Before anyone could ask them what in the world was going on, Anne noticed a movement at the roof's edge.

George had picked up the discarded rope Brandon had used. Even as she watched, horrified, he twisted it around his waist and between his legs. Before she could cry out, the boy, the youngest of them all, had stepped back off the roof.

"George!" It was his father's agonized shout.

"I'll be all right, Papa!" The child's cry carried back up to them on the fitful wind.

Below, Sir John was just climbing out of the window and looking around for any hand- and footholds that he might use to take him across the wall to a more stable part of his castle. It didn't look good.

Honed by centuries of wind and spray from the sea, this side of the castle was almost as smooth as a sheet of glass. He marveled that the boys had been able to manage their short climb even with their small hands and feet.

"Sir!"

Sir John nearly fell off the window ledge. "George!"

George hung there eight feet out from the wall and met his gaze solemnly. "I'm here to rescue you, sir. And I hope you will let me. I have had quite enough of my brother's bullying, you see."

"Oh?" It wasn't much, but it was all he could think of to say just then.

"Yes. This is my only chance to win my father's approval and enlist him to help me against Luther."

Sir John grinned. "So that's the way you have it figured, is it?"

"Yessir."

"I'd be remiss if I didn't tell you that your father probably already loves you the best."

"Be that as it may, sir, Luther is still firstborn." Swinging comfortably at the end of his rope, he regarded the Captain stubbornly. "It's important that I give Papa an excuse to treat me more . . . more p-persferentily."

"Ah, yes." Sir John was grateful for the relative quiet here under the eaves. It enabled him to say distinctly, "So you wish to be treated more *preferentially,* do you?"

"If you will help me, sir."

"It will be my pleasure, George Athelstain." He sat astride the windowsill, swinging a booted leg out over eternity. Grabbing the window's edge, he leaned precariously out toward the boy. "If you can manage to swing in closer, we can shake hands on it!"

Chapter
Thirty-four

When Sir John and George appeared above the edge of the roof, a ragged cheer went up from the little crowd on the battlement. As they struggled to pull themselves over the edge to safety, Anne dissolved in merciful tears of relief.

When Sir John caught George by the seat of his pants to hoist him over the last bit, her tears turned to joyous laughter. She stretched her arms out for him as naturally as Lord Robert reached for his son. Long hours ago, Anne had decided she cared nothing for the proprieties where this man was concerned!

His face alight with his love for her, Sir John swung his rescuer to his shoulder and strode across the trembling roof. Haste was the order of the day, and he knew it. He could feel it in the treacherous sway of the roof under his boots.

"Higgins! Tea in the drawing room, please," Sir John ordered as he jumped over the low parapet. "And something special for our hero!"

Slipping an arm around Anne as he relinquished George to his grateful sire, he said, "I think it would be a good idea if we all got away from this section of the castle."

Cook said a hearty "Amen!" and began an immediate retreat.

Lord Robert scooped up his fainting wife, Danvers put a masterful arm around Lois, and the twins jostled George along in their wake. Luther tagged along behind them all.

Brandon was enthusiastic. "I say, George. That was absolutely smashing! You saved Sir John's life!"

Brian grinned at his friend. "And like the Captain said, you're a hero, George!"

George glowed but let his modesty keep his tongue still.

Luther glowered, but his heart wasn't in it. What if anyone found out that he'd caused the avalanche? He tried to quiet his conscience, but it kept hammering at him. His feet dragged as he walked down the steps after the others. He could have caused the death of Lady Anne, Sir John, and the twins. Most of all, he could have caused the death of his brother. It surprised him greatly, but he had to admit that he would have missed George awfully.

High above them, hidden by a drift of cloud, Bethany and Jared and their escorts hovered. When it became apparent to them that all down there on the battlements of Castle Caldon were safe, one of the huge, winged beings said, *"Enough,"* in a voice that sounded like thunder from a far horizon.

Lord Jared responded with a heartfelt *"Thank you."* Bethany gave them a timid, radiant smile, and they continued their upward progress, content.

Below them on the battlement, Sir John stopped in the tower doorway to look back. Anne lifted her head from his shoulder to look back, too. She was so terribly grateful he was safe.

Suddenly, even as they watched, the slate roof Sir John and George had just crossed buckled and screeched and jutted upward above the low rim of the parapet. Then, with a rumbling whoosh, the secret room under it broke free of the wall against which it had been built centuries ago. It plummeted in a shower of loose stones and debris down to the Channel far below. An instant later the roof tore free and followed it in a hail of screeching slate shingles.

"John!" Anne clutched at him fiercely, staggered by the awful realization of just how near he'd been to being in that avalanche. How nearly she had lost him! "Oh, John!"

He bent his head and claimed her lips. The tower in which they stood shook and trembled as he kissed her. He lifted his head and smiled down at her. "I think it's time we got out of here, my love. Your renovations are trying to do us in."

She was so relieved that he was alive, so happy to be granted a future, a future they would spend together, that she couldn't be afraid . . . nor annoyed by his accusation.

Smiling radiantly and crying, "Yes!" she grabbed his hand and together than ran lightly down the steps to a safer part of the castle.

Halfway to the drawing room, he pulled her to a halt.

"Anne." His voice was low and husky, his eyes earnest. "You do realize that you are mine?"

She watched his face and waited.

"You're my Forever Love. The locket you wear betokens that." He grinned. "Your Great-grandmother Bethany gave it to me to give to my true love. My Forever Love." His last words were a reverent whisper, then he said almost briskly, "And you are my wife, as well. We have only to satisfy some magisterial requirements to make it plain to the rest of the world, but you are my wife."

When she just continued to look up at him, he took her shoulders and gave her a little shake. "You do understand that you are irrevocably my wife, don't you?"

Anne felt all her bones begin to melt. Happiness flowed through her like sun-warmed honey. All her life she'd prayed that she would find a true love, but reality had given her just the opposite . . . until John. Tears of joy gathered on her lashes. When she spoke, however, it was to ask mildly, "John, are you always going to try to shake a response out of me?"

With an exasperated groan, John leaned down to kiss her. He hesitated as a horrible thought intruded itself into his mind. "Anne! Oh God, Anne, tell me you're not sorry!"

The agony on his face tore through her. "No! Oh, no, my *dearest* love. How can you think such a thing?"

She was reaching for him as he snatched her to him and crushed her there against him, his arms steel bands. With a frenzy she found very pleasant, he kissed her again and again.

Anne threw her arms around his neck and returned every kiss with all the longing and love that she had saved for him all her life.

Soon she was breathless from the fierceness of his embrace and her own joyous response to his kisses.

She pushed him away, gasping. "Dear . . . John . . . I must breathe."

He loosened his embrace and let her catch her breath, grinning down at her. "God, Anne. I've waited so long to find you."

"Ah, but you *have* found me." She ran trembling fingers over the sensual curve of his mouth. "And I am yours." She pulled lightly at his lower lip and tiptoed up to place a kiss there. "And you are mine." She experienced a delicious sense of triumph at the shudder her kiss sent through him. "And all the world is wonderful."

His smile was that of a very satisfied male, and it sent shivers down her spine. Then his eyes changed. "I think we may find a problem or two when we get to the drawing room."

Startled, she waited for him to explain.

Instead he took her hand and drew it through his arm. "Come and see."

Together they walked the rest of the way to join the others.

In the drawing room, they found Lord Robert standing with his hand on his wife's shoulder, a grim look on his usually amiable face. He spoke the instant his hostess appeared in the doorway. "My wife has something to tell you, Your Ladyship."

Anne was shocked by the grimness of his tone and his formality of address. Robert had always called her Anne, or at worst Lady Anne. Whatever could be wrong? She looked to Becky, seeking help to understand.

Becky, her face streaked with tears, looked up at her tragically. "Oh, Anne! If you'd been killed it would have been my fault!" She began sobbing. "If I hadn't burned the plans to the castle, we'd have all found the secret room together that night."

"Burned . . . " Anne was so shocked she couldn't marshal her thoughts.

"*My* Great-grandfather was one of the true traitors, Anne." She twisted in her chair to look back up at her husband. Lord Robert's face was implacable. She went on miserably. "I, as the oldest of my generation, was entrusted with the awful secret." She cringed back into her chair. "It was the reason I befriended you."

Anne stood stock-still, shocked to her very center. She felt Sir John's arm come around her and leaned back into his embrace, taking comfort from him. Becky had become her friend to be certain that she didn't find the letter that would clear her family of the stain of treason!

It was almost more than Anne could bear. All those visits to Kent Hall, Becky's allowing her sons to be the only playmates the twins had who were of their own class, had it all been false?

She'd loved Becky and her children. Yes, and Robert, too. She felt John's arm tighten, and it returned her to her senses. She *still* loved Becky and Robert and their children, and she didn't believe that Becky, with her generally forthright and certainly mercurial temperament could have sustained a lie for years. Becky was too lazy!

Her last thought surprised a startled laugh from her.

Sir John whispered, "Good girl. She *is* your friend."

Anne weighed all the happy hours Becky and her family had given her against Becky's reason for befriending her. In her heart she knew that the friendship had been genuine in the end if not at the beginning, and she treasured it.

She made her decision. She was not going to lose Becky now. She'd get over the hurt. She'd spent most of her life getting over hurts.

"Silly goose." Anne went to Becky. "With such a weight on your mind, it's no wonder you made such a stupid hasty decision to burn the plans."

"But . . ."

"No 'buts.' Of all the *ton,* you have been my only friend, Rebecca Athelstain. I don't intend to give you up."

Becky flew from her chair and cast herself into Anne's arms. "Oh, Anne, thank you, thank you. You *are* my dearest friend, and if you'd sent me away, I'd have been so miserable." Her eyes entreated Anne. "I'm so, so sorry. Can you ever forgive me?"

Anne's hug was all the answer they needed.

The others in the room smiled to watch. Lord Robert's grin was the widest of all.

Luther watched the way his mother clung to her friend and decided this wasn't the time to tell Lady Anne and Sir John that his spying on them had caused the cave-in. He straightened his shoulders and decided that it would be best for all concerned if he just told the twins later and let them pound him to sand if they wanted to.

It would be fair exchange for nearly killing their mother, after all. Besides, doing it that way would save added strain on the adults' friendships. Why, he'd even help the twins think up some good excuses for the bruises he knew he was going to get from them!

Satisfied with his solution, he settled back to watch the adults. Most of his attention was focused on the door however. He, if only he, had not forgotten the offer of a special tea.

Lord Robert visibly relaxed, and when John caught his eye, he knew that Lord Robert, too, had treasured Anne's friendship.

John stepped forward and told him, "I hope you will be the first to congratulate me, Lord Robert."

The other man understood at once and shook his hand heartily. "Indeed I shall." He clapped Sir John on the shoulder. "Anne is a splendid woman. You're a lucky man."

Becky was suddenly aglow. "Oh, Anne! How marvelous! May I be at your side in your wedding?"

Anne smiled to see Becky's instant change. "Whom else?"

Into the general joyous laughter, Higgins came carrying a huge silver tray full of all sorts of delicacies. A footman followed carrying the silver waiter with the tea service on it.

"A celebration!" Sir John announced. "I give you the heroes of the day!" He shepherded the twins and George Athelstain forward, their faces aglow with pride and embarrassment.

"Here, here!" Lord Robert's own face glowed as he watched his younger son take his place with the twins around the tray.

Leaving the others to celebrate, Sir John drew Anne away through the newly installed French doors out onto the half-finished terrace. Closing the door softly behind them, he turned her and took her into his arms. Their kiss left her breathless and longing for more.

Sir John held her tight another instant, then turned her so that they looked out toward the far end of the east wing. Seeing the jumble of stone that had almost been their tomb, he sighed.

Anne could feel the sigh as she stood leaning against him. She looked back up over her shoulder at him, her eyes inquiring.

"You know, our grandchildren will find it hard to believe that Castle Caldon was haunted."

She enjoyed the rumble of his words against her back. She rubbed her cheek against his chest. "I shall tell them the story so well, that they shall have no choice but to believe it."

"We were saved by the ghosts of your great-grandparents."

"We were, weren't we?" She snuggled closer against him as a breeze from the Channel touched them.

"Hmmmm." He kissed the top of her head, trying to ignore the way his pulse had quickened as her body moved against his.

"I suppose we will have to tell them how dreadfully Great-grandfather Jared frightened us that night in the passageway when I was trying to show you where I was going to put windows in your castle."

He pulled his head back to look at her sternly.

"Well, *I* was certainly dreadfully frightened." She was half-laughing.

"Deliciously."

Anne's face flamed, and she momentarily resented the laughter she could feel in him. He was remembering the shameless way she'd flung herself against him, she knew it!

For playful spite, she turned and did so again. There was no fear in her now. His body had become a familiar thing to her. She was no longer afraid of the maleness of him. She could relax and enjoy the havoc she knew her faint movements wrought on his senses.

John seized her chin. "That's a dangerous game you're playing, Lady Anne."

All the laughter had gone out of him now, and his eyes glinted down at her. Then his mouth claimed hers and the stars went spinning from the skies above them.

When he'd kissed her until neither of them could trust themselves, he said unsteadily, "I shall procure a special license tomorrow. Any wedding you may want to have, you had best prepare speedily."

"Yes," she answered simply, aching for him as badly as his body proclaimed he wanted her.

They stood long moments watching the last of the stars come out and letting their heartbeats slow. It had been a long and eventful day, but they were reluctant to see it pass.

"John?"

"Beloved?"

"*Must* we tell our children and grandchildren that the castle was haunted?"

He was still for a long moment. The only sound was the whisper of the night wind around them.

He bent his dark head and kissed her ear. Then, his lips still touching it, he asked, "What is it you'd rather tell them, my love?"

She shivered with the delicious sensations he was arousing in her. Then she looked back up at him from where, secure in his embrace, she rested against his chest. Her eyes were dark with desire and solemn with the words she was about to speak.

She turned to offer herself to his kisses as she told him, "I believe . . . that I should rather tell them that the castle was . . . *enchanted*."

**And now for a preview of the next
Haunting Hearts romance**

A Ghost of a Chance

Coming in August 1996 from Jove

"Dearly beloved . . ."

Daphne crossed her fingers in a plea for luck and hid them in the folds of her wedding gown. *Luck.* Dear heavens, she would need more than mere luck to survive this next hour. She would need an honest-to-God miracle. She glanced to the back of the altar where the morning sun shone through the stained-glass window. At least she was in the right place.

Pleated through the gown's shimmering white fabric, her gloved fingers shook with cold. The church felt as icy as a crypt, belying the droplets of sweat trickling down the vicar's jowls. *Poor Reverend Lenox.* Daphne experienced a twinge of pity for the cleric, wondering if he might not be even more nervous than she was. The vicar was one of the few people aware of the tempest that could explode at any moment in this remote country chapel. A red-headed tempest by the name of Isadora Harkwell.

Reverend Lenox swallowed hard as he turned the page of his prayer book and Daphne bit down on her lip. Now was the time for that miracle. And she did believe. She did believe in miracles.

Please God, don't let her say anything. Oh, please . . .

"Into this holy union, Daphne Eloise Harkwell and Iain Frances Edward Ashingford now come to be joined. If—" the reverend's voice cracked and he noisily cleared his throat—"if any of you can show just cause why they may not lawfully be married, speak now; or else forever hold your peace."

Daphne knew it wasn't so but, to her ears, it seemed as if all occupants of the church held their collective breath.

Then, from behind her, Daphne heard her mother sniff and her heart sank. Isadora's snorts and sniffles were more eloquent than the most lauded poet's verses. The wealth of meaning conveyed in that single sniff would have put both Byron and Blake to shame. It was a disdainful sniff, a preamble to the fiery denouncement that Daphne was certain would follow.

But just as she thought that all might be lost, the vicar proved himself to be truly of divine inspiration. He did not permit any expounding on that expressive sniff, nor did he even acknowledge Lady Harkwell with a glance in her direction, but launched into the service with a speed and loudness of voice that was awe-inspiring. If one could be said to bellow swiftly, Reverend Lenox did so, setting his jowls to swinging with his vigor.

Daphne breathed a silent sigh of relief, but did not uncross her twined fingers. She dared a sidelong peek at her groom to note his reaction to the vicar's bellows and abruptly felt that sigh catch in her throat.

The Marquess Lindley. It really is a good thing, Daphne thought, *that I'm sensible or else I might be feeling a bit weak in the knees.* She, Daphne Harkwell, a well-bred lady of modest fortune and even more modest beauty, was marrying the most elusive bachelor ever to be born to English soil. And although she'd had three weeks to prepare herself for this event, she still found it incredible that this day should actually come to pass. Her wedding day.

However, as her gaze slid over her soon-to-be husband's profile, she knew that she—like every other woman save her mother—was not proof against Ian Ashingford's striking good looks. From the moment she had first seen him, over four years earlier at a neighbor's summerhouse party, Daphne had been captivated.

Although she had outgrown gawky adolescence, she'd never quite abandoned her dreams of white knights on destriers. A romantic and an optimist, Daphne had clung to her dreams with a steadfastness worthy even of the tenacious Isadora.

Therefore, when her father had called her to his study a few weeks earlier to inform her of the betrothal, Daphne had, for the space of a heartbeat, believed her fantasies had come true. But she had allowed herself only that momentary delusion before logic had stepped in.

Despite her romantic tendencies, Daphne possessed a fair measure of common sense and, as her father had explained it, she could hardly have hoped for a better match. The wealthy and handsome Marquess Lindley was the catch of the *ton* and she had seen no reason to object to the marriage. Her mother, however . . .

"Ahem."

Reverend Lenox discreetly called Daphne back to the business at hand. With a wiggle of his bushy gray brow, he signaled for Daphne to offer her fingers to Lord Lindley. She did so, raising her gaze to her groom then hastily lowering it to hide her disappointment.

Honestly, she scolded herself, *'twas foolishness itself to expect more than a smiling politeness.* She should be glad that he spoke his vows easily with no hint of reluctance or uncertainty. His deep voice resonated with a confidence that bolstered her spirits and she reminded herself that it had been Lord Lindley who had approached her father with the offer of marriage. Iain Ashingford could have chosen any woman in the kingdom, and he had chosen her. Daphne was human enough to feel flattered, if honest enough to recognize that nothing so banal an emotion as love had prompted the proposal.

"In the name of God, I, Daphne . . . "

She spoke her vows softly in marked contrast to the booming cleric. When Lord Lindley slipped the diamond-and-gold band onto her finger, she did not meet his gaze again but only stared at the brass buttons on his coat.

Reverend Lenox then joined their hands and, with the ceremony nearing completion, Daphne sensed that the vicar grew bold with his success.

"Those whom God hath joined together let no man"—the reverend paused for effect before fixing a quelling look in the direction of Lady Harkwell—"or *woman* put asunder."

"Hhmph," Daphne heard her mother retort but, at this point, the indignant sound carried little weight. It was done.

"Amen," the witnesses echoed.

Daphne had wed the Marquess Lindley.

Strangely enough, as her new husband led her out of the church, Daphne could not identify any of the faces that blurred before her. She was simply too shocked. The wedding had taken place in spite of her mother's opposition.

As far back as she could remember, Daphne could not recall her mother ever not settling matters exactly as she pleased. If Isadora wanted the withdrawing room decorated in the Egyptian style while Percival Harkwell preferred the Greek, Egyptian it would be. If Daphne's mother desired veal for dinner while her father had a hankering for lamb, most assuredly veal would be presented at the evening table.

Thus it had been Daphne's entire life and she had never known her father's will to prevail over that of her mother. Once or twice in the past, her father had tried to overrule the headstrong Isadora. When her mother announced last year that she would not send Daphne to London for a season, both Daphne and her father had hotly protested the decision. But to no avail. Isadora Harkwell had adamantly refused to auction off her daughter "as if she were nothing more than a prize heifer." No amount of logic could sway Isadora, and Daphne was too proud to resort to tears. Tucked away as they were in the remote Cotswolds, Daphne had nearly resigned herself to spinsterhood until her father's startling announcement.

Stumbling on the single step leading away from the church, Daphne felt Lord Lindley's grip tighten on her arm. She looked up at him, then followed his gaze higher to where ominous, black thunderclouds threatened to let loose their stores. The wind gusted around them, pulling at Daphne's veil and flattening the dark curls on her husband's forehead.

Daphne frowned, remembering how clear the skies had been that morning.

"I wager Mother arranged this," she muttered beneath her breath.

"I beg your pardon?"

Daphne looked up to find her husband's face very near hers, and her pulse accelerated.

"Oh, nothing, my lord. I was thinking of the breakfast arrangements."

He smiled briefly into her eyes, then turned away to watch the wedding guests file from the church.

Shame on you, Daphne's conscience chided. It would only make matters worse if Lord Lindley was to learn of her mother's aversion to him. Then again, "aversion" might be too faint a term for her mother's sentiments, Daphne conceded as the Baroness came into view.

On the bright side, her mother had not worn black. And despite threats to the contrary, she had attended the ceremony even if that outlandish scarlet gown with dyed boa was raising a few eyebrows. But as always, she carried herself like a queen, her crown a feathered turban that looked as if it might topple with each windy gust.

Daphne smiled. The turban would not dare fall from Isadora Harkwell's head. She would never permit it. She stood there tall and proud and Daphne thought she did not look too cowed by her defeat. No, not at all. Not in the slightest. Apprehension caused Daphne's smile to grow stiff. *Oh dear, Mother was looking calm. Determined. And that glint in her eyes. Oh, no.*

A shiver raced through Daphne that the marquess must have attributed to the cold.

"Come, we should go," he said.

Daphne was just settling herself in the carriage when the first raindrops began to fall. The marquess took his place beside her and the coach set off with a bounce, jostling them together. Daphne realized that she was alone with the marquess for the first time.

"You handled yourself well."

Daphne started, squeezing her hands together. "Thank you, my lord. So did you."

A spark of amusement flashed in his generally sober gaze. "Yes. Considering how neither of us has been married before, we did quite well, I think." He leaned back, stretching out his legs as far as he could in the coach's narrow confines.

Daphne kept to her thoughts as the rain fell more heavily and soon they pulled up in front of Harkwell House.

In the entrance hall, Daphne paused and ran a hand over her mist-dampened curls. "If you'll excuse me, my lord, I need to refresh myself before we sit down for breakfast."

"Of course." He bowed over her hand, hesitated, then turned her fingers and pressed a kiss to her palm. The heat of his mouth seared right through the glove, causing Daphne to suppress a shudder of delight.

"Excuse me," she whispered again before pivoting away to hurry up the stairs.

"Daphne."

Father. Daphne peeked around the corner and saw the good Baron huffing as he reached the top of the long, winding staircase, his face ruddy with exertion.

"Here, Papa," she called.

"And how are you, my pet? Holding up?"

"Any regrets, is that what you're asking?"

"I suppose I am," he conceded with a nod of his head. Tight white curls clung to his pate like hardy snowflakes.

"No. No regrets. Should I have any?"

Her father's expression softened. "No, I think he's a good man, Daphne, or else I would never have accepted his suit. I believe he can make you happy."

She laid her hand on his arm. "I know, Papa."

"About your mother . . ." He clumsily patted her hand where it rested on his coat sleeve. "I suppose you've heard some of what's been said but I don't want you to worry. Your mother's a proud woman—too proud if you ask me—and she refuses to see Lindley for who he is."

Daphne waited for an explanation, but finally had to ask, "Why?"

A sigh rose and fell in his father's chest. "Many years back, a dispute arose between the Ashingfords and your mother's family, the Whitings. The feud has stood for decades and your mother will not put it aside. It's that cursed pride of hers, Daphne. It's truly a curse."

"A feud?" Daphne shook her head. "I cannot believe that Mother would take a family rift so personally."

"For her, it is personal, my dear. She has taken this alliance with the Ashingford name very badly and I doubt whether she'll ever forgive me for my part in it."

Daphne emitted a weak half-laugh. "Father, now you sound like Mother with your dramatic declarations."

"I suppose I do, but I fear 'tis so. She would have done anything to keep an Ashingford from marrying into the family. Absolutely anything."

Alarm weaved its way up Daphne's spine as her mother's determined expression outside the church resurfaced in her mind's eye.

Anything? She silently echoed.